O·V·E·R·T·H·R·O·W·N
THE GREAT DARK

Judd Vowell

© 2016 Judd Vowell. All rights reserved.

www.juddvowell.com

Cover photo by Connie Migliazzo, courtesy of Morguefile.com

This book or any portion thereof may not be reproduced or used in any manner whatsoever without the express written permission of the publisher except for the use of brief quotations in a book review.

This is a work of fiction. Names, characters, businesses, places, events, and incidents are either the products of the author's imagination or used in a fictitious manner. Any resemblance to actual persons, living or dead, or actual events is purely coincidental.

978-0692744338

For Charlie

TABLE OF CONTENTS

PART ONE: GETTING THERE…………...…………1

PART TWO: MOMENTUM……………...………..169

PART THREE: GETTING OUT…………...……….225

PART FOUR: CONTROL………………..…………293

PART FIVE: GETTING HOME…………...………..399

EPILOGUE: STILL ALIVE………...………………....447

PART ONE: GETTING THERE

1.

This may sound like the others at first. But it's not. Sure, there was death and destruction. Widespread riots and murder. But this story is different.

It was all too familiar to me, too. Post-apocalyptic wasteland where only the strong or evil survive. I saw the movies, read the books. Maybe it's in our nature to wonder what would happen when the whole thing comes crashing down. The only similarity I can attribute to the movie versions is that the whole thing came crashing down. It wasn't a nuclear war, or an asteroid, or some disease outbreak. Even though disease became a significant problem within that first year. No zombies, no vampires. Just the end of life as we had lived it for the past however-many years. ANTI- wanted a re-set. We re-set, alright…the birth of a new civilization. Hell, maybe we became more civilized after than we were before. Maybe that's what ANTI- was trying to show us all along.

2.

Traveling alone had become more and more difficult. Small packs began to seem like the better option. It was a lot like those nature channel shows we used to watch together. Herds, packs...they're all the same. Just hope you're not the weakest one with the slowest legs. The problem was finding a pack. Survival sure makes humans unbearable. At least they were to me. So there it was, halfway through the journey, decision at hand: pack animal or lone wolf?

Ok, so lone wolf is not exactly accurate. Three lone wolves. What do they call that? An oxymoron? However you label it, it's what we had become. It's what we had been forced to become.

Life devolved into "every man for himself" rather quickly. It's a complicated proposal when you make that a family man. We knew it was getting bad, but we never saw the end coming. Once the government structures collapsed, it was a matter of weeks. Banks, transportation, communication...each fell like dominoes. The global pyramid that we thought could never crumble. So where did we go from there?

The "we" in my little piece of the world was myself, Henry, and Jessica. The Triumphant Triumvirate. I gave us that name the Christmas day we put up the basketball goal in our driveway. I was always naming us things. But that one stuck, probably because it took me so long to explain what it meant. Kids and their never-ending questions. I loved watching their vocabulary grow, even if it meant I had to look up the definition of a word I had spoken with such confidence.

We shortened it to the Triumphs. Still a difficult word to pronounce for Henry, but easier. When he first said it that Christmas morning, it came out as "Tie-ups." He had outgrown his speech impediment not long after. But we still used the shorter version of our family nickname through the years. Probably more in those last weeks than ever before.

"We're still the Triumphs, right, Dad?"

"Always, son…forever the Triumphs."

3.

The name started appearing in the news more and more: ANTI-. Certainly not scary. Maybe a little foreboding. They wore masks and held rallies on Wall Street. I think everyone felt like it was just a bunch of rebellious kids lashing out at authority at first. Harmless, but just sensational enough to get on the nightly news. Occupy this, occupy that. I ultimately learned to never underestimate the power of a protest.

It was the hacking that really turned heads. Big, important heads. Multi-billion-dollar companies suffered the first strikes. CEOs emailed form-lettered apologies to credit card holders:

> "Dear Valued Customer, (Insert Global Corporation) has discovered that a file containing your email address may have been taken during the payment card breach we recently announced. Etc, Blah, Etc, Blah…"

No big deal to me. Cancel the credit card, get another one. And while we're at it, go ahead and extend my credit line another $5,000. I was starting to wonder how I was going to pay for that upcoming Disneyworld trip anyway. That should cover it.

And that's how it all started. The snowball at the top of the mountain. Only difference was, this snowball had a guidance system, controlled from within by ANTI-. Once the world's credit was maxed, they had us set up for the fall. Start with the money, and the rest will follow.

Greed had been very good for a very long time. Seemed to be the American way, disguised as capitalism. We even got a wake-up call with the Great Recession. A chance for a do-over. And we proceeded to do exactly nothing. Back to business as usual. Should've known it wouldn't last.

4.

They came into this world too early. Way too early. 14 weeks and 4 days too early to be exact. Jessica arrived about 15 minutes before Henry. She always brought that up when they were arguing. They didn't argue that much anymore. I kind of missed that.

Their strong wills, their conviction – that came from their mother. She had laid flat in a hospital bed for 37 days straight to get them here alive. Alive accomplished. Healthy was another story.

Jessica fared better than Henry. Apparently girls always do. Some issues with her lungs that never went away completely. Still, she was out of the hospital in half the time that Henry was. He refused to breathe on his own. Stubborn in the worst way. That never went away completely either.

Henry's lasting complication was his leg. Still bothered him just enough to slow us down. If he focused on it, he could run pretty well. The problem was staying focused. There was a lot to think about in this new life. Too much to think about for a 15-year-old.

The day I realized my kids had grown up, we were crossing one last clearing before setting up camp for the night. I had probably pushed us too far that afternoon, because darkness was setting in fast. Dusk can obscure things worse than midnight with a moon. He was only ten feet away by the time I even knew he was there.

5.

Turns out the corporate hacking was the warm-up. Just a little show-and-tell. It was ANTI-'s war on terrorism that demonstrated just how powerful they had become.

Terrorism was nothing new. Something terrible, but unfortunately nothing new. Been around throughout history, I suppose. But ever since that fall morning in 2001, it was ever-present. We found ourselves looking over shoulders in airports, analyzing every face in football stadiums. We were protecting our homeland, our future. Time had eased the anger, but the fear was ingrained.

That fear was fed a steady diet of small-scale attacks that led to weeks-long news stories. A bus blows up in England, a train derails in Spain. And then the crazed sympathizers here. A couple of pressure cooker bombs destroyed arms, legs, and families in Boston. Some New York cops brutalized by a hatchet-wielding lunatic. It got to where we expected a violent terrorist act every month, then every week. What was worse, retired intelligence officials started telling *60 Minutes* and CNN just how many terrorist plots were thwarted before they occurred. Part of me thought that made us all feel a little better. We felt like our governments had some control in this so-called war.

But the radicalized Muslims that formed organized armies to continue this war in the two years leading up to ANTI-'s retaliation were different. Sure, they used classic terrorist tactics. But they were also networked, plugged in. They used all forms of social media to espouse their evil propaganda. And Middle-eastern media was on the take, never hesitating to broadcast the beheading of children or public-square hangings. I swear it felt like we were living in the 1300s. This was medieval. But it was also just a few keystrokes away. That's what led to all the one- or two- or three-man attacks. Inspiration to destroy Westerners was anywhere and everywhere, on your TV and in your laptop. At least it was until *La Censure Vendus*.

The year ANTI- decided to fight back, homegrown terrorists had attacked in the streets of Paris. Cultural, historical, beautiful Paris.

La Censure Vendus, or *Censorship Sold,* was the most popular European underground rag. Circulated both in print and online, its following was massive. It was founded in 1967 by a group of college dropouts, seeking what they saw as truth in a world built on falsehoods. Typical '60s hippie shit, right? Perhaps more apropos in the end than when it began.

The paper's popularity rose and fell with the tides of political dissension. But it lasted through the years because of its bravery, or because of its salaciousness. Sometimes there was no difference between the two.

For a decade, *La Censure Vendus* had not once backed off from its vitriol against the terrorist flavor of the month. Viable threats were persistent, especially when an edition questioning the radicals' mutated interpretation of the Koran was released. One year, their downtown office was firebombed after business hours. But the editors never wavered. It was freedom of speech, by God...or by Allah, if you dare. No matter your spiritual affiliation, in the free world it was a basic human right.

So when news of the Paris incident broke, we all felt violated. It was an attack on our way of life. The two men used military-grade assault rifles and grenades to slaughter seventeen editors, journalists, and staffers. Four more Parisians were killed in the streets as the terrorists escaped. French police found and captured them three days later. Wounded and imprisoned, they claimed allegiance to the most powerful terror-based Islamic army of the day. That was all ANTI- needed to hear.

6.

He was big, but not the biggest we had seen on our journey. Wiry and stiffened, I could just make out his shape. Coyotes had forever been known for hunting neighborhood cats and farm chickens, but things had gotten desperate, even for the animals. They were willing to come after humans. And the smaller the human, the better.

I didn't panic though. We had a plan. Before we had set out on our expedition, I had gone through as many possible defense scenarios as I could imagine. And as soon as I realized what we were dealing with, I put the plan in motion.

"Ruuunnnn!" I yelled as I took off headfirst at the animal.

Jessica knew to run left. My left side was the one she always flanked. Henry had been instructed to run backwards. Always backwards. And of course to focus on his steps. "Focus!" I would encourage him in the days of soccer and baseball practices. This wasn't practice anymore.

My loud yelp and aggressive move toward the coyote was meant to startle the animal, and therefore give the kids a big head-start. If I had enough time to grab the gun at my hip, I would try and get a shot off, too. Worst-case, I had the machete. Hadn't had to use that one yet.

Just as I hoped, the coyote jumped back a few feet and froze. Bought me enough time to pull my pistol and fire a shot. If I hit him, I never knew it. My attention shifted to Henry as soon as I pulled the trigger, as soon as I saw the second coyote in my peripheral vision.

The sinewy beast was galloping full speed from my right. Closing in on Henry fast. The boy didn't stand a chance. I raised my gun, but the dusk was too much and the animal too fast. So I ran. If I could cut him off, I'd at least have a fight with my knife. My angle was good, but there was no way to know if it was good enough. Just had to try. Adrenalin is a strange thing, because you never know it's there until it's gone.

The moment I realized I wasn't going to make it, I heard the shot. A different sound than my pistol, but familiar. It came from behind me. I heard the bullet push the air past my right ear. The coyote fell without a whimper. I guess that's what they meant by dead in his tracks. I turned my head and saw Jessica, rifle in hands, as still as the night that was beginning to envelop her.

Henry was still running, bad leg and all. Focus. I yelled for him to stop, then rushed to Jessica. We had hunted together at the farm plenty of times in the past year. But this was different. I knew she would be emotional. But the emotions I expected weren't there. She was stoic, confident. Her concern was Henry...and me.

We gathered up, made for the woods ahead. We had to move quickly and get the fire built before complete darkness set in.

7.

The latest jihadi terrorist movement was gaining momentum faster than any that had come before. It was also the most evil that the world had seen. Their way or the highway. The metaphorical highway here being death. Not just death to the non-Muslim world, but death to anyone who didn't believe their version of Islamic ideology. Their exact version. There were the stories of mass village executions, even after the villagers had disavowed their generations-old beliefs and converted. And the children. So many children, either massacred or brainwashed or used as suicide bombers.

I think that was the big disconnect, especially for Americans. Our society, our culture, was based on our differences. Hell, the reason our country was founded was religious freedom. We were living in the most tolerant country in the most tolerant period in history. Funny how tolerance becomes apathy over time. When ANTI- attacked the terrorists, we didn't know apathy would be next.

The retaliation was direct, organized, effective. It was as if the terrorist armies vanished, at least from an online perspective. You couldn't discount the power of this type of strategy. After all, global movements inherently need worldwide visibility. And the latest and greatest terrorist regime was most definitely a global movement. But without visibility, how much more could they accomplish?

Instead of reports about the latest Westerner beheading with attached footage, news stories began describing the lack of communication coming out of the Middle East. Internet bomb-making instruction manuals? Gone. Sponsored links to jihadi training videos? Gone. The terrorist connection to the modern world was finished. Any momentum they had mounted ended the moment ANTI- wanted it to end.

Not only did the radical propaganda to which we had grown so accustomed encourage recruitment of western converts to the movement, but it also perpetuated the fear on which the terrorists' basic existence depended. Without it, we regained our confidence, our power in the world. And to whom did we owe thanks? To ANTI-, no doubt, who claimed victory over terrorism, victory over evil. Looking back, it was brilliant.

Intrigue and obsession soon followed. Who was this group of international vigilantes, so obviously formed to save our free society? The headlines wrote themselves.

The ANTI- leaders were intentionally mysterious. That just made them more appealing. They already had the masks, some sort of blank-faced everyman thing. Pale white, with two black sunken eyes and a black mouth agape in astonishment. Would've been scary as shit as part of a Halloween costume. But not these guys. These guys were superheroes.

Every media outlet started digging. Truth be told, every government intelligence agency started digging, too. But ANTI- was entrenched. Nobody knew where they were based or how big their network was. How many actual people were involved? What was their nationality? When did it all begin? Once the answers became clear, it was too late to stop them.

8.

Meg was the love of my life. No doubt about it. I knew it the moment I saw her. Hold on, I take that back. Not the moment I saw her. That was something else. It actually happened over our first conversation. Because that's what we had from the beginning. Conversation, talks, laughter. I'm pretty sure that's the stuff that matters in marriage. If you can really talk with each other, you can get through anything. We learned that. Because we went through anything and then some.

We met in our 30s, both having bounced around relationships that always met the inevitable dead end. She was so full of energy that it was infectious. You could hear her laugh from across a full room of cocktail partyers. And her passion for life flowed into everything we did together. We would stay up late, drinking vodka and listening to music. We would spend entire Sundays making love. I had never experienced anything like her.

Like the women in her family before her, she had that old-Hollywood, classic kind of beauty. Tall, blonde. She had been on the cross-country running team in high school and college, and she maintained that same level of athleticism for as long as she could. She also held on to the competitive pride. It made her a very bad loser. More than once she had thrown the Trivial Pursuit board across the room when I got an easy question for the win. Let's just call that passion for life, too.

Our courtship was frenetic, and we were engaged in a matter of months. We got married in the small chapel at her parents' farm, then honeymooned in Mexico. It was a goddam fairytale. But it didn't take long for the tragedy in our story to appear.

The Wednesday after we came home from our honeymoon, Meg's mother passed away. She had gotten out of bed at 7 that morning, eaten two eggs and a bagel, dressed for a workout, and died in one of her living room chairs. The coroner told us the massive heart attack likely caused no suffering. She never felt it coming.

Meg was devastated. It took her months to recover, if she ever really did. Her mother had been a guiding force in her life, raising her only daughter virtually on her own while Meg's father was on the road or in the sky most days of the year. The two of them were best friends, and I don't think Meg ever imagined a world without her mother in it. Maybe she was trying to fill that void, or maybe she was trying to prove something to herself in her competitive way. But when her passion for life finally returned, it was stronger than ever. Except it became a passion for creating life.

    Meg and I had worked on a baby for three years. The miscarriages were emotionally draining, for both of us. But we powered on, we talked, we kept trying. We went through all the motions that struggling parents-to-be go through. Ended up in a fertility expert's office hoping for an answer. But there wasn't one. We had no fertility problem. And Meg's body was built for reproduction - the doctor had a much more tactful way of explaining that part. But the truth of the matter was that we should've been parents by then.

    So when the next pregnancy test came up positive, there was no celebration. After all, getting pregnant was the easy part. It was time for patience and fortitude and all of the hardest things to be.

    Meg did everything the books told her. Take these vitamins, sleep in this position, chant this or that mantra at such and such time of day. It was exhausting to watch her want that baby so badly. Then we found out there were two. Double the exhaustion.

    Jessica and Henry are fraternal twins, meaning they were growing in two separate sacs in Meg's womb. The fragility of the matter was overwhelming. Not only did we have our unsuccessful pregnancy history, but now the stress of twins on Meg's body would be that much greater. We found ourselves talking more than we ever had.

As the days became weeks and the ultrasounds showed nothing but health and growth, our stress became excitement, hope, and happiness. We couldn't help ourselves. Meg was getting more and more tired as the pregnancy progressed, but that was to be expected. Especially with twins, right? It was on the day that she couldn't get out of bed that I began to worry.

The doctor had given us a short list of warning signs to watch for during the second trimester. Bleeding, early contractions, depression. None of it applied. Meg couldn't place it, but something wasn't right. Maternal instinct already kicking in, I suppose.

We arrived at the hospital at 7:33 that night, two days before Thanksgiving. I remember the time because later I calculated down to the minute how long Meg spent in a hospital bed without sitting up, without standing or stretching or walking. 37 days, 14 hours, 21 minutes. The will of a mother is remarkable.

The doctors diagnosed Meg as having an incompetent cervix. I thought it was such a ridiculous adjective for a body part, as if it had a mind of its own. What it meant was that Jessica had started descending into the birth canal with nothing to stop her. I don't think they ever knew what was really happening. As advanced as they may have thought they were, science could only take them so far. I had never seen educated guessing more at work. We all believed that Jessica would keep descending over the next few hours, but she stopped. No reason for it. She just decided, in her barely-developed 20-week-old brain, to stop. The conviction of her mother transferred through amniotic fluid. It was miraculous. She not only saved herself, but her brother, too. Another thing she never let Henry forget.

Getting through the first few days was agony. We talked, cried, grieved. Then, much like the early part of the pregnancy, days turned into weeks. And each week meant a better chance for Jessica and Henry. And in the end, that's all we could hope for - a chance.

Christmas morning that year was white and sublime. Big, puffy flakes. The contractions that had subsided for so many weeks resumed around nine o'clock. Meg knew it was time. We all did. And so we prepared ourselves to deal with the next act of this next tragedy. But it wasn't tragic at all. It was beautiful. Our children, too soon and so tiny, were beautiful.

9.

The weekly online videos that ANTI- created were meant to look raw, unproduced. But there was a lot of work that went into them. Film experts began breaking each one apart after the terrorist silencing. See the way it cuts here, look how they edited this together there. From a media standpoint, it became obvious that ANTI- had professionals involved. The viral videos were viewed by hundreds of millions.

And the grassroots part of the movement grew exponentially. Protests continued. Environmental, financial, civil rights issues. They called themselves "ANTs," a reference to both the ANTI- name and the way in which they operated throughout the world. On the ground, almost invisible, but always working. It was like they were pushing against everything that seemed to be moving in the wrong direction in society.

In Moscow, there was the desecration of the Russian constitution on the steps of the Kremlin by a small group of ANTs. According to the video released following the incident, ANTI- opposed the current political direction of the Russian government. It was true that Russia was returning to its Cold War mentality of isolationism, and recent reports had told of in-country atrocities against its own people. ANTI- was applauded by forward-thinkers throughout the world, and human rights groups demanded the release of the arrested ANTs involved.

The rally in Athens and ultimate Greek government shutdown that followed showed us that ANTI- was a larger group than anyone had imagined. Greece had been struggling for years financially, with its leaders demonstrating incompetence in every decision they made. The unemployment rate was double that of any other European country. And when the Greek president announced national restrictions on wage rates for hourly workers, ANTI- struck back. The number of individuals involved in the protest was estimated at more than 10,000. All in those blank-face masks and black-cloaked clothing. It was three days before the military was able to disperse the crowds and end the madness. And again, universal sympathy for the ANTs and their cause was reported throughout worldwide media outlets.

People even began to wonder about ANTI-'s involvement in significant changes from the recent past. Rumors about the last pope transition began swirling in the global ether. Typical conspiracy theory stuff. After all, there was no way a group like ANTI- could be involved. Or could it?

The Roman Catholic Church, as powerful an entity as the world had seen, rarely saw a pope leave his position before his death. In 2,000 years of papal supremacy, only a handful of popes had resigned. And none since the 1400s. The new pope assumed his position on a wave of religious excitement and vigor. He was humble, liberal, and Spanish-speaking. His universal appeal was greater than any of those who had come before him. And he affected change within the establishment immediately. Church bans against gay marriage, contraception, and divorce? No more. And the Vatican Bank? Disbanded. It was revolutionary. The ever-growing part of the population that supported the societal and cultural shift that ANTI- was promoting began to believe they were behind it all.

10.

After the coyote incident, our traveling dynamic changed. I knew that Jessica could handle more responsibility. And she had created another layer of protection. But it still wasn't enough.

I had determined early on in the expedition that I would include the kids in all decisions regarding our group. I needed them as much as they needed me. If, for any reason, just to keep ourselves sane. If any of us started thinking too much about our situation, we might not be able to continue.

The morning after Jessica saved Henry, we were all a little groggy. I'm not sure any of us slept very much that night. As soon as we had some breakfast in our bellies, I called for a family meeting.

"All right, guys, first things first. Where's everybody's head at?" I always liked to talk like a coach in these situations. Try and keep us motivated.

Henry spoke first. "I guess I'm okay. Tired, but okay."

"Jessica, how about you?" I asked. She was the one I was most worried about.

"Dad, I'm fine as long as you are. But I gotta ask, don't you think it would be better if we found some other people to travel with?"

Wow. She was on the same page already. I was proud, but also a little sad. Growing up too fast, but maybe that was for the best.

"I agree," I said. "Henry, what do you think?"

He mulled over his response for a while before he spoke. "I think we'll have trouble finding people we can trust." Then he hesitated. "And I don't want to be left behind if something happens."

He was on the same page, too. But I didn't want to tell him that his concerns were exactly the same as mine. More than anything, I wanted to reassure them. Besides, Henry didn't acknowledge the problem with his leg that much, so I knew that he was worried. Probably more worried than he let on.

Jessica spoke before I could think of what to say. She turned to Henry, took his hands in hers, and looked him in the eye. "Henry, I will never let anything happen to you. And I will never leave you behind. Triumphs forever." Then she turned to me. "Right, dad?"

It took me a few seconds to overcome the lump in my throat. "Of course, Jess," I tried to say with confidence. "Here's what we'll do. We head out today with a new temporary mission: find a group of people moving in the same direction. A group that can help us. Then we get back on track." I put my arms around both of them. "We're gonna make it through this thing, guys. Triumphs forever."

And so it was decided. We packed our things and cleared the campsite. We would need to start moving toward a highway or interstate. There certainly weren't any vehicles left, but people still tended to use roadways. If we were going to find ourselves a pack to join, it would be there.

I pulled out my map from so many years ago. Meg always made fun of me for keeping one in the glove compartment in the days of GPS and iPhones. "I told you so, Meggy," I whispered to myself. The closest road was 19 miles northeast. A long highway that cut a path across the southern part of the country. It would take us the better part of two days to get there. So we walked.

11.

The general public believed that ANTI-'s motive was simple: revolution. Global revolution. But that was impossible. Sure, they could disrupt a city government for a few days, or cause a corporation some financial embarrassment. But to flip the world as we knew it on its axis, to destroy the system that we had unconsciously become so dependent on, that was so much bigger. Not too big for ANTI- as it turned out, even with the world's powers trying to stop them.

Once ANTI- neutralized the terrorist influence, the governments of countries across the globe woke up. Yes, it was something to celebrate. But here was the thing about superpowers: if they weren't the ones in control, they rather preferred the status quo. Even if the status quo meant war, genocide, and human suffering. Developed countries were insulated from that stuff in the 21st century anyway, right? So we thought.

The concerns about ANTI- were so elevated that the United States' CIA and Europe's Interpol formed a joint task force to investigate the whos, whats, and wheres. Some committee in some back room came up with the name. The International Security Agency, or ISA as everyone came to know them. Very creative. They spent months interrogating imprisoned ANTs.

They raided all kinds of neighborhoods, barrios, and villages. Spain, South Africa, Sri Lanka. The media reported what they knew, but that wasn't much.

When ANTI- had their ISA mole leak the tactics of the organization, documented with memos, emails, and approvals from the heads of governments, the uproar was deafening. ISA was tapping everyone. You, me, everyone. And the small details in conversations that led to home or business invasions didn't even make any sense. Just a mention of "hacking" or "code-breaking" could get someone arrested and held for questioning. Once in custody, the interrogation techniques were downright frightening. Sleep deprivation, water-boarding, electric shock. Real torturous kind of stuff. The stuff we as a civilized society would never do.

Universal reaction to the leaked information was dramatic and, at times, violent. Support for the ANTI- movement reached an all-time high. Tens of millions took to the Internet to express their disgust with the current state of our governments. Either they felt that their seemingly anonymous usernames could hide them from retribution, or they just didn't care. The world had come to a virtual breaking point, but no one thought it would truly break. No one but ANTI-.

12.

Meg and I didn't treat the twins any different than we would have had they been completely healthy. To be honest, we didn't know what the hell we were doing anyway. Any first-time parent will tell you: it's trial by fire. But we did make the conscious decision before their first birthday that they wouldn't have any limitations in life. Long, late-night talk on that one. In the end, we decided - we could never predict how success and failure would affect our children. We would let experience guide them, as it should.

Jessica was athletic from the beginning. In the female genes, I guess. She was walking months before Henry. And there wasn't a tree she wouldn't climb. We enrolled her in year-round soccer at age 5 just to get some of her energy out. She had the proverbial on/off switch, and just get out of the way when it was on. But it wasn't just spirit and skill. Jessica also possessed that innate characteristic of trailblazers, motivators, and influencers. From the ball field to the classroom, she was a natural leader.

We were warned by doctors early that our kids may be smaller than other children their age. And it took some time, but eventually Jessica started showing more signs of her mother's genealogy. Tall and lean, with a long blonde mass of hair. She was pushing 4 feet by age six, then 5 feet by age ten. She had been defying the odds since before she was born.

Henry's growth was different. First of all, there was his leg. Often with premature infants, there is a lack of oxygen to the brain, resulting in a level of cerebral palsy. Some kids are so debilitated that they can't control a single muscle. We were thankful every day that it was just Henry's left calf. But it did prevent him from being as involved in sports as his sister was, even though he pacified us by trying every one. Soccer, baseball, basketball. He put his time in with them all. He was never very good, but he never complained. One thing about Henry, you couldn't rattle him, couldn't make him feel insecure. He carried the same confidence as his sister, just quieter.

And what he lacked physically, he made up for with his intellect. He had learned the alphabet by the time he was two. He was reading full sentences when he was four. And so that became his escape from the long summer days. Instead of swimming and running and biking for hours on end like the other neighborhood kids, he would spend most of his time buried in books. He would find novels on the den shelf that Meg and I had barely cracked, and he would devour them. His appetite for reading was insatiable.

The other issue Henry struggled with as he slowly grew was his speech. Yet another common preemie problem. He knew the words, so many words. But his mouth and tongue fought against his brain to form them. He had been social and outgoing in those first few years, but his speech impediment pushed him further into the fantasy world that books provided. I would often find him still awake late at night, deep inside some author's imagined universe. I would rub my hand through his dark shock of hair and kiss his forehead.

"This brain of yours is going to explode, Henry," I would joke.

"The mind will journey as far as one is willing to carry it, Dad."

I told you he was smart.

13.

The first governments to collapse were in the Middle East. The region was ripe for rebellion. Many of the Arabian regimes were dictatorial and corrupt. And when ANTI- took the terrorists' power away, the people grabbed the chance for change. Egypt, then Libya. Syria and Iran soon followed. The problem was the power vacuum left behind. There wasn't a domineering force strong enough to take control of these countries, which led to brutal in-fighting between rival insurgent groups. In retrospect, it couldn't have been set up for ANTI- any better.

The revolutions of the Middle East were certainly newsworthy, but not surprising by any means. That region had seen uprising after uprising throughout its centuries-long history. But when the Spanish government fell, the world took notice. The revolt there was decisive and startling. It occurred with such ease that it must have taken months of planning. Never underestimate the element of surprise, especially in a large-scale attack. Spain's government had no response and was in shambles within 48 hours.

Spain had been suffering the same problems as other countries in the European Union since the financial collapse a few years earlier. High unemployment, especially at entry-level positions of companies. Well-educated young Spaniards couldn't find jobs, and the Spanish tiered occupation system led to massive attrition of the lower-paid workforce. Add that to the decreasing value of the euro, and government approval ratings in the country were at their lowest ever. Maybe they should've seen it coming. But even if they could have predicted an uprising of sorts, the details of what actually happened revealed how elaborate the operation truly was. The whole thing was disturbing.

Most reports soon told of the "inside" story. The organizers of the revolt, as yet to be named, had multiple conspirators inside both the government and military. High-level elected officials overtook their counterparts and allowed the revolutionaries access to government buildings. Thousands of members of the military turned and fought against their generals. The number of people involved was staggering. It became apparent rather quickly that perhaps this attack had not been planned for mere months. This level of destruction had taken years to design.

14.

Traversing through woods and underbrush was difficult for all three of us, especially Henry. But it provided a sense of invisibility. The world had become hopeless, and that made other humans unpredictable. Part of me was looking forward to walking on a flat surface with no rocks or vines or thorns to contend, but I was also wary. I knew, like Henry forewarned, that we needed to find people we could trust. I also knew how hard that was going to be.

We arrived at the highway just after lunch the next day. Excellent time, considering. Coming out of the woods just thirty feet away from the road, I noticed its vastness. And its emptiness. I instructed the kids to stay at the edge of the tree-line while I did some surveillance. I crept to the edge of road, crouching the entire way. The absence of maintenance had allowed the grass to grow to four feet or more over time, and I was able to use it as cover.

The surface of the roadway was sun-cracked and pot-holed, and any painted lines that may have once been there were completely faded. Nothing but a dull gray streaking across the landscape, with clumps of brown grass and green clover speckled throughout. The few cars and trucks I could see had been left behind long ago.

I had packed a pair of binoculars that I found in my father-in-law's hallway closet before we left. Probably hadn't been used since some bygone sporting event, before high-definition big screens had changed the way we watched football and baseball from the upper deck. I reached into the side pocket of my backpack for them. Just wanted to confirm the emptiness I had assumed. I looked west, then east. As far as I could see, no one. Only pavement and tall grass splitting a 200-foot wide gash through deep forest, dotted randomly with abandoned vehicles.

I eased back to the kids, described what I had seen. "Nothing up there, guys. Just us and the road. You ready?"

"Ready," Jessica said in her classic go-get-'em style.

"Yep, ready," Henry said. "But let's stay aware of our surroundings, make sure nobody sneaks up on us. Right?"

I knew they had heard the stories. Henry had stayed abreast of everything that had been happening. Certainly more than I could imagine for a kid his age. He had been able to tune us in to the underground broadcasts very early. Information had been spotty in the first weeks, but there was enough coming through to keep all of us on edge.

"Right, Henry," I confirmed. "Same formation as always. But remember, if we do see someone, they may be harmless. And they may be able to help us. After all, that's why we're here. So, defense only, guys. Got it?"

They nodded. I couldn't believe the pressure I was putting on children.

"We travel east." Coach-speak time again. "Keep your head on a swivel."

15.

(Partial video clip from speech filmed at underground ANTI- rally. Posted by user @progressispainfull on Twitter one week before the global shutdown. Speaker presumed to be Salvador Sebastian.)

"...the time has come for a natural purge and a new beginning. Our leaders have lost their way, and most of the people of the world are following them down an inevitable path. A path that can only lead to self-destruction. We aim to bring that self-destruction now, on our time-table. If we control the destruction, we control the reformation.

"You have been patient. For that, I thank you. Change on this scale takes time. It takes years, sometimes decades. For your patience, you are soon to be rewarded."

16.

Jessica and Henry's diverging lifestyles made our house feel a bit schizophrenic at times. But it also made it feel like home. I always found it amazing how unalike the members of a family could be, and yet still remain family. We were no different. Especially the kids. They had a connection so obviously formed in the womb, like so many twins do. Sometimes Meg and I would laugh that they had their own clique, and we were most definitely not cool enough to be asked to join. When they were toddlers, we would wake just enough to hear them scamper through the hallway before dawn, off to build some architectural disaster or dress themselves as characters from their favorite cartoons. There were even times we listened in on their secret language, trying to decipher the strange words and sentences. To no avail, of course.

They both excelled in school, much more than we could have ever hoped. Meg and I were smart, each in our own way. She was resourceful and headstrong, whereas I considered and conserved. We, like all parents, assumed our children would inherit the sum of our parts. And they did. But they also became something greater.

They called a family meeting the summer after their third grade year in school. Pretty sure that was the first one they had ever called. First of many. It was obvious that there had been some private conversations between them before they approached the two of us. They had a presentation.

Meg and I were blown away. I looked at her when they finished, she at me. Neither of us knew what to say. So we "took it under advisement." That sounded parental. The kids had asked to transfer to a specialized school system. They weren't pleased with the education they were getting at our local public elementary. And to be honest, we weren't either. But what kind of kid asks to go to a tougher school, desires a more difficult life?

We did take it under advisement. We wanted Jessica and Henry to be challenged, too. And more than anything else, we wanted them to be happy. But there wasn't enough time left in the summer to consider enrollment in a different school for the upcoming year. That would buy us a few extra months to weigh our options. We spent countless hours re-budgeting our lives to make private school work, but we couldn't find a way. The middle class squeeze seemed to be affecting us more than it ever had in the past.

The other option was the magnet schools, which focused on educating kids at a higher level than the norm. There were a few available to us, with each one specializing in a specific type of learning. If a child excelled in math, there was the School for Engineering and Analytics. For creative kids, it was the School for Art, Music, and Theater, and so on. After some intense research, we discovered it was a well-planned and well-executed program.

As we discussed the schools over the fall of that year, the four of us began to get excited. Meg and I were the proud parents, having conceived such superior beings - parents always take too much credit. More importantly, Jessica and Henry would be able to give their brains and souls the exposure and workout they so desperately craved. And we wouldn't have to move from our district as long as the kids qualified for the programs. But there was that one thing, the apprehension that we all felt but didn't express. The twins would most likely qualify for different schools, and that would mean that they would be separated.

The separation anxiety that we all feared was unfounded. The kids were stable, strong, confident. We had raised them to be all of those things, and we knew they were. But the fear still hung in the house air.

After all, they were so young. And to us, so dependent on each other.

We had planned on a final family meeting in the winter to discuss the possible separation and finalize the applications. We needed to have them turned in by March 1 of that year. But it was February 14th when everything changed. Valentine's Day. The last morning that we didn't know about the cancer that was eating Meg alive.

17.

The first day and a half hiking the highway was uneventful. We passed three sets of fellow journeymen, all walking west. The first group was older, borderline elderly. Two couples who looked to be in their seventies, but easily could've been 10 years younger. With the low supply of available medications and limited access to food and water for the masses, the collective aging process had grown faster by the month. They walked slowly and carried little. I felt a bit of sadness when I saw them.

The second group was a family, not unlike our own. A father and two children. But they also had their wife and mother, the missing link for us. I gave a slight nod to the man, feeling a kindred spirit passing. There was the sadness again. A different kind though. God, I missed Meg.

It was the final group of travelers that scared me. We encountered their smell before we could see them. The smell of uncleanliness, sickness, death. Then we were able to make out their size as they came into view. I told the twins to hide in the tall grass just off the road. I laid down on the asphalt and pulled out the binoculars.

They were a large crew, comprised of mostly men and a few women, who lingered behind. They moved slowly and haphazardly, as if they were a group of drunk college kids finding their way home from a late-night bar binge. But I knew better. This was the reason I had wanted to avoid the open road from the beginning.

Once I realized what we were facing, I rolled myself into the grass next to Jessica and Henry. I filled them in quickly and succinctly.

"Nine men, three women. Hunters." I stared at them deeply to make sure they understood. "No sounds, no movements."

As the group got closer to our position, the smell became almost unbearable. *"Don't cough,"* I told myself. I shot the kids a look to convey the same message to them. They were loud, like I imagined a band of pirates may have been centuries ago. Their speech was base, their laughter guttural. I put my hand on my pistol, just in case.

Like the travelers before them, they weren't carrying much. Two of the men had homemade backpacks, loaded with who knows what. People like this needed very little to survive, if you considered it survival. All of the men had weapons, most of them shotguns. A couple had rifles. And I assumed plenty of small arms. They were known to hunt for their sustenance. Deer, rabbit, squirrel. But the animals had been getting scarce, and smarter. There were stories of cannibalism on the roads and at the rural homesteads. Desperation had turned the worst of us into something even less: sub-humans.

I watched closely as they passed, making sure to move only my eyes. I remembered clearly one of my father's early lessons. *"The best fight is no fight at all, son."*

Once they were a hundred yards or more past us, I raised to one knee and pulled the binoculars to my eyes. They showed no sign of recognition. I was pretty sure we were safe. I turned to the kids to give a thumbs-up. They had done well, but this was no time for back-slapping. There was a slight decline in the direction we were heading. Once we made it there, we would be out of the hunters' hindsight. I leaned over.

"We stay in the grass and low," I whispered. "No matter what, do not let your heads rise above the tops of the grass blades, understand?"

They both gave me one nod, like soldiers.

"If you hear anything behind you, anything at all, you stop and drop. We stay invisible, ok?"

Again, one nod each. I led the way, crouched as low as my 6-foot-3-inch frame would allow. I kept my ears alert and my hand on my gun.

Even as our distance between each other grew, we could still hear the raucous group. If they were hunting, they sure didn't care about scaring off any animals, which frightened me even more. We had almost reached the out-of-sight point in the road when we heard one of the men yell above the din.

"Shut up!" Not everyone listened, as the talk and laughter continued. "I said, shut the fuck up, dickheads!" Then silence.

The kids did exactly as I had instructed. Straight to the ground. I did the same. After a minute of nothing, I raised my head enough to barely see through the foliage. With the binoculars, I could make out the group looking around, sniffing the air. They reminded me of a pack of hounds searching for the scent of a fox or raccoon. Then the fear that had become relief as we neared our escape came rushing back as the men turned and looked directly at me.

18.

The Sleeping Giant, a London-based progressive blog, was the first to report an exposé on the leader of the ANTI- movement. Apparently, he had reached out to them, looking to extinguish the bevy of rumors that had been circulating about him. It was released as a serial piece. It read like a goddam Steinbeck novel. What the world learned from the report made Salvador Sebastian more popular than ever:

ANTI-Authority - Leader of the New Unknown

Part One: The Soil of Cuba

The story of Salvador Sebastian began 100 years before his birth, in the rural farmlands of western Cuba's countryside, where Salvador's great-great-grandfather Juan found himself abandoned and alone at age 13. Many orphans like Juan made their way for Havana, for the city streets to beg and steal. But most of them never made it, swallowed up by the land around them. Young Juan thought better of himself. He saw the land as something to conquer, to tame. He found work at a local farm. There he learned the fragile process of growing the world's best tobacco. He also saved enough of his earnings to buy his own plot of rural Cuba. And at 16, Juan dug trenches into his purchased piece of earth and planted enough tobacco to sell and survive on his own. The next growing season, the heavens opened and the soil was rich. His tobacco crop quadrupled.

Juan's hometown of Vinales was located in the heart of Cuba's most fertile ground. By his 21st birthday, the enterprising young man had acquired 20 hectares of land for growing his perfect plant and had farmers working for him. By age 25, he was cultivating all three types of tobacco used in making the cigars for which his country was known. Growing the wrapper, the filler, and the binder allowed Juan to maintain control over the quality of all parts of his product. And the Sebastian product was gradually becoming one of the most renowned in the country.

Juan married and had two sons, and each of them was raised in the family business. In the small town where Juan had started his family, schooling was secondary. But he made certain that his boys would become well-rounded men. Ernesto and Rolando spent nine months of each childhood year in the fields, learning soil and leaf and harvest. Each year's three months of tobacco offseason were spent in a home classroom, built and run by Juan. He taught them economics and history, the subjects that he had spent teaching himself at night as a teenager. They grew smart and experienced, and soon had ideas of their own concerning the cigar company that their father had founded.

Ernesto and Ronaldo enjoyed great success over time, taking advantage of the high standards that their father had instilled in the farmhands and cigar-makers who worked for him. They purchased adjoining tobacco farms aggressively, understanding the importance of investment. Years were lean as money was spent. But as each season yielded bigger harvests, the Sebastian empire began to take hold. By the turn of the 20th century, the Sebastian Tobacco Company was one of the top five Cuban cigar manufacturers.

The second Juan Sebastian in the family line was born in 1907. He was the last son of Ronaldo Sebastian, the last grandchild of the great Juan who had started it all. He was born two months before his namesake's death into a newly famous and wealthy family. His father and his uncle Ernesto had built the Sebastian Tobacco Company into the largest cigar exporter in Cuba. Nearly half of all of the cigars they produced were shipped to the United States.

Juan had two brothers and four sisters, plus five more cousins from his uncle. Ernesto and Ronaldo gave their children more than they ever had, and this proved to be their undoing. Juan's generation of

Sebastians grew up with servants and waiters, imported clothing, and monthly trips to Havana. Their fathers tried to teach them tobacco, but it was in vain. They never had respect for the business, the employees, or the money.

American companies had begun to move into Cuba in the first years of the 20th century, taking advantage of the country's ripe industrial landscape and cheap labor force. And high American tariffs were making it more and more difficult for Cuban businesses to export their goods and turn a profit. Add the Sebastian grandchildren's mismanagement, and it was a recipe for disaster. By the mid-1920s, the Sebastian Tobacco Company was barreling toward collapse.

As his siblings and cousins bickered over control and direction of the fledgling empire, Juan contemplated and thought. He had always been a thinker. He studied hard in school and rejected the passive lifestyle created by his surroundings. He was his grandfather's grandson, at a time when the Sebastian name needed him most.

19-year-old Juan acted on his own when he negotiated the merger with the Americans. If he had gone to his family for permission, it would have never been approved. But when he brought the deal to his fellow Sebastians, no one resisted. It was the only way forward.

Juan was named President of Cuban Operations for the newly-formed Sebastian and Cole Cigars, and he retained 51% ownership for his family. He gave positions to a few of his family members, but most took a payout and quietly retired to the Cuban countryside. The company rose to cigar prominence again, a second coming of sorts. Tens of thousands of acres of Cuban farmland were developed, and tens of millions of cigars were exported. But Juan's only son saw a bigger future for the family – a future across the Straits of Florida, in the greatest land of opportunity that the world had ever seen.

19.

The tumor wrapped around Meg's spine was inoperable. More accurately, there wasn't a doctor willing to operate on it. Too risky, they all said. Better to let a woman die a slow death than possibly paralyze her, I guess. We were bitter, we were angry, we were sad. But after weeks of tests and biopsies and MRIs, we became determined. There had to be something out there besides surgery. And after a little digging, we found the man that would change our lives. The man that would save Meg's.

Dr. Raj Khurana was conducting his cancer experiments just a few hours from where we lived. His funding came from private donors, as his work was considered too experimental for federal grants or university studies. But based on the information we could collect from the Internet, he was making progress in cancer treatment. Especially those cancers for which there was no operable solution. Testimonials from former patients were resounding with praise for Dr. Khurana's healing powers. Hope on a computer screen. Meg and I both wept the night we found him.

He scheduled an appointment for Meg immediately. We would come to find out that he insisted on attacking the cancer cells quickly and aggressively. The first meeting lasted a day. The morning consisted of filling out paperwork. Past surgeries, family medical histories. There was even a psychological questionnaire. When we finally met the great doctor just before lunch, he greeted us with happiness and glee. It seemed as though part of the healing process for him included treating the patient's spirit. Eastern philosophy meets Western medicine. Brilliant concept. He insisted on us calling him "Dr. Raj." Sounded more like some Indian sports superstar than a cancer specialist. Meg and I would later relish in the sense of calm and serenity that Dr. Raj brought with him into the room that day.

He wanted to discuss Meg's previous hospital stay while pregnant with the twins at length. As he detailed to us after we related our story, his patients needed to be strong in mind and spirit. The procedures and medications that he prescribed were not for the weak. Hence, the psychological test. We were learning rather quickly that Dr. Raj was qualifying *us* for *his* program rather than the other way around.

Meg was then put through a battery of physical tests throughout the rest of the day. Her running dedication had not slowed, even with the mysterious pain in her back she had felt for a year or more. So, her body was ready, confirmed by the results of these tests. Dr. Raj called us two days later to congratulate Meg on being accepted into his experiment. He even had a positive spin there, too.

Treatments began within the week. Heavy doses of high-grade medications, combined with doctor's office visits every other day. Meg's father had helped to alleviate the travel expenses, while the private funding covered what our insurance didn't. Jessica and Henry promised support and not distraction. All we needed to focus on was getting Mom better. And better she got.

The drugs tore into the tumor in Meg's body, breaking it into smaller pieces that her own immune system could better fight. Cancer cells were removed from her spine, replicated in Dr. Raj's lab as healthy versions of themselves, then re-introduced in order to multiply and overtake their deadly cousins. It all sounded like some dark battle of the future, playing itself out inside my wife's diseased body. And the good guys were winning.

Meg kept on a strong face, but the fight took its toll. Her once toned, muscular limbs became flaccid and soft. And her infectious energy was intermittent at best. But part of Dr. Raj's treatment included spiritual guidance. That's one reason he wanted her in the office so often. He believed that constant attention to the mind during a trial like that was essential to victory and complete recovery. Meg loved this aspect of her battle. She dedicated herself to the mission of mind and spirit over body. It was inspirational to watch.

After 472 days, Dr. Raj declared Meg tumor-free. The experiment had worked. Now we were a testimonial on a computer screen, giving the next helpless victim hope. Meg and I declared our transformation that day, to live life differently, to appreciate the little things. I think it may have given us more strength than anything ever could have. And we were going to need strength above all else for the days that lay ahead.

20.

Jessica had proven she was an excellent shot with the coyote just two days earlier, but I couldn't put her through using that skill on another human. Not yet. I had to come up with something quickly. The hunters had sniffed us out. I didn't know how they had developed that skill in such a short time. Perhaps it was the lack of industrial pollution that had filled our air for so long. Or maybe it was just a primal hunger that reappeared in those who were desperate enough. None of that mattered in that moment. What mattered was protecting my kids.

There was still a great distance between us and the group of savages. If we could make it the fifty or so feet to the woods at the side of the road, we may have a chance to conceal ourselves. But we had to make it. Henry had to make it. I turned to the kids and described what I thought we should do.

"Alright, guys, no games here. We need to hightail it to those woods and separate. I'll go west, and you guys continue heading east." I knew this would give us a better chance, while also putting myself in more danger. But I was willing to take the chance that the men would come after me instead.

"No way, Dad," Henry said. "That means you'll be heading right back into them. No way."

"No time to argue on this one, Henry. We act or none of us makes it." And with that I stood and ran. I knew they would follow, banking on that childlike belief that your Dad can do no wrong. And Jessica did just that. But when I looked back as I neared the edge of the woods, Henry wasn't there. He hadn't moved a muscle.

I stopped just inside the tree-line and started to feel panic course through my body. I looked at Jessica, but all she could offer was a shrug. As well as she may have been connected to Henry, she had no idea what he was doing either. I peered through the binoculars to see what the hunters were doing. Seven of them had begun running in our direction. They left the two men with the knapsacks behind to stand guard over the women. They were led by a large man, taller than me and brutish. Their mangy beards couldn't hide their delighted, snarly smiles as they approached their prey. Some of them whistled and whooped. Only one thing I saw eased my mind: they were all coming after Jessica and me. They didn't know Henry was still hiding in the grass.

I told Jessica to find a tree nearby that she could climb quickly. Not too high, just enough to give her a good view of the approaching men. And then I said to her what I had been dreading since she killed the coyote.

"Jessica, you're going to need to use that rifle again. This time, on those men." No time to let her absorb the gravity of what I had just said. Just had to power through the reality of it all. "I'm going to run deeper into the woods so that they follow me. Just shoot as many of them as you can. Don't worry about me."

She didn't flinch. "We'll come find you, Dad." And she was off.

I took one last moment to survey how far they'd come and make sure Henry was still invisible to them. They had closed on us fast. Only a hundred yards away or so, but they were still just focused on Jessica and me. I turned and ran deeper into the woods.

It wasn't long before I heard the first shot. Its sound echoed through the limbs and branches above me. Then another. The men's crazed whooping ceased.

"What the hell?!?!" I heard one of them yell.

"Where'd it come from?" asked another.

Then that rifle sound again. And again. I had stopped running. I needed to get my bearings, see if they were still following me. They weren't. Instead, I heard one of them say, "They killed Big Nick." And then, "Let's get the fuck outta here!"

My heart was racing, and then I was, too. I had to fight through thick brush and low-hanging limbs to get back to Jessica's hiding place in the trees. I didn't know exactly what tree she had climbed, but I knew it couldn't be far from where we left each other.

I was running so hard that I didn't notice the lifeless body until I had tripped over it. I thought it was a fallen tree trunk at first. Must've been Big Nick. I recognized him as the leader of the group from what was left of his face. She had shot him through the back of his head. I was sure he had died before he hit the ground.

I saw two of the other hunters nearby, both still. They lay face down in the leaves and dirt, shot through their backs. I didn't see the result of that fourth shot I had heard.

Jessica jumped down from a tree twenty feet to my left. She looked so much older. She ran to me and shook my shoulder. "Come on, Dad!" she screamed. I woke from the stupor that had overtaken me, realized where I was, remembered Henry.

As I took off toward the highway, my ears were assaulted by an abrupt noise. Loud and metallic. I saw black smoke through the remaining trees in front of me. My lungs and gut started pushing the yell from my mouth instinctually. "Heeeenryyyyy!!!!!"

21.

ANTI-Authority - Leader of the New Unknown (continued)

Part Two: To America

    Salvador Sebastian's father Alejandro was 12 when his sister Isabella died, leaving him an only child to Juan and a solitary heir to the family's cigar empire. It was a short but deadly bout of smallpox that overtook her before her 10th birthday. As he watched his father's grief take him deeper and deeper into depression, Alejandro vowed to carry Sebastian and Cole Cigars into the second half of the 20th century on his own. And in the moments of Juan Sebastian's greatest despair, his son promised to make the company bigger than he could imagine. That seemed to be the only thing that would bring a smile to his father's face in those dark days.

    Six years after his sister's death, Alejandro walked into his father's long-empty office and declared his leadership to the Cuban employees of Sebastian and Cole. The morning was filled with phone calls to partners in the U.S. and lawyers in various places. A company memo was written and issued by day's end:

It is with great regret that we announce the resignation of our respected President, Mr. Juan Sebastian. He led our company through tumultuous times and made the organization what it is today. Let us never forget his importance.

His son, Alejandro Sebastian, will assume his father's position effective immediately.

For the first few months, Alejandro did all he could to keep the cigar company at a break-even point. The accounting department had slowly fallen apart in his father's absence. There were outstanding bills to be paid, and debts were owed from as far back as two years. The American partners were kept ignorant of the situation by Juan's loyal office managers, who felt as if they were protecting the boss they loved. Alejandro was forced to come clean, but he did so with confidence. He assured his partners that the company would return to profitability within the year – it was making money again in eight months.

The opportunity to move certain parts of Sebastian and Cole Cigars to Florida had come up before. In fact, many Cuban cigar companies had transferred distribution to Tampa, known then as "Cigar City," years before. But because Sebastian and

Cole was running such an efficient operation in Cuba, the American partners were resistant to any move at all. Alejandro saw it differently. It may have cost more to warehouse the finished product in Florida, but it would eventually save a tremendous amount on distribution, since over 50% of their cigars were being sold in the United States already. Alejandro's enthusiasm about the change convinced the partners to support him. He moved his new bride to Tampa in 1951, where he oversaw the transfer and start-up, and where he hoped to raise a new Sebastian family in America.

Lola Sebastian loved Alejandro enough to follow him to America, even though her instincts told her otherwise. She tried to make a life for herself in Tampa. There was a large Cuban population, and at times it felt like home. And Alejandro had plenty of money to take care of her. On the rare nights when he would be home before 11, he would take her out for elaborate dinners. And if he had enough rum with his meal, they would go out dancing. But for most of those first seven years, Lola was lonely.

They tried to start a family, as they both wanted a houseful of children. But whether it was the stress of Alejandro's job, or Lola's growing hatred of her new life, pregnancy eluded them. Finally, in the spring of

1958, Lola knew. And the baby growing inside her brought her the happiness she had sought for years. It filled her days with planning and preparing and purpose.

On January 1, 1959, Salvador Juan Sebastian was born, the same day that Che Guevara's rebels won at Santa Clara and Castro took over Cuba. It was the greatest day of Alejandro and Lola's life together, as they would not receive news of the revolution until the next morning. The news that would fracture the Sebastian family tree forever.

22.

There was nothing routine about life after Meg's victory over cancer. The sun shone brighter, the wine tasted sweeter, and we loved each other deeper. Near-death will put everything in perspective. Meg and I were more passionate than we had ever been. And happier.

The twins were accepted into their respective magnet schools. The time we had delayed on enrollment to deal with Meg's disease helped. They were ready to become independent of each other.

Jessica attended the School for Language and History. She had become obsessed with her family history the year before. Then, the history of it all. There's a part of that in everyone, but Jessica went much further down the rabbit-hole. She studied wars and battles and coups. She researched generals and presidents and czars. Meg and I thought it was odd that our little girl was so enthralled by military history, but we never slowed her down. And she was such a good writer. She could produce a paper on Patton or write a review on *Robinson Crusoe* without breaking a sweat. When she was 11.

Her new school reinforced her spirit for athletics, too. She played basketball in the fall and ran track in the spring. She was a natural runner, like her mother. The mile was her favorite, but she could leap hurdles with the best in the city.

Henry could've been enrolled in any of the schools that were available. English, art, math. He was a true academic. He chose the School for Science and Exploration. His compulsive reading had become more focused leading up to attending the magnet school. Chemistry, physics, even anatomy. We didn't have a clue where his interest in science came from. Certainly not from Meg or myself. Hell, I couldn't even give blood without lying down.

He embraced the school's rigorous study schedule. There were days when Meg had to canvas the school's science labs to find him when she went to pick him up. And our garage was soon transformed into his at-home experimental research center. Frog dissections, chemical reactions, animated robotics. I couldn't believe he didn't burn the house down.

The four of us were in such a good place. That's the way life would get you back then. Flip you upside-down when you were least expecting it. If anybody should've known that, it was us.

23.

The smell of a homemade bomb is strange, acrid. The smell of four is overwhelming. When I broke through the edge of the woods, I thought, *"This must be what a battlefield smells like."* I squinted through the smoke. *"And looks like."*

The retreating hunters all lay on the ground, two of them silent, the other two writhing and screaming in pain. There were stumps and blood. And death.

As I regained my senses and began to understand the carnage around me, I noticed the movement down the highway. The two men who had stayed back to guard the hunters' women were running toward us, their guns drawn. I aimed my pistol without thought and shot twice in succession. They fell at the same time and laid motionless on the road. I breathed again.

Henry eased out of the trees. He came to me, grabbed me with both arms. Then Jessica did the same. Family hugs had been rare on our journey. It was just what I needed in that moment, watching my children transform into warriors. There are conversations and experiences and feelings in our lives that stay with us no matter how much time passes. I never forgot the love I felt from my kids right then.

Henry had told me he was bringing some improvised explosive devices with him the day before we were planning to leave. I had no idea what to say. My initial thoughts went to the danger of carrying these "devices" with us. But Henry assured me they were safe. He would insulate them in a separate pack, then keep them at the bottom of his hiking backpack. I was hesitant.

But it was hard not to trust him. He had become a wizard with wiring and electronics. He took our old cell phones, broke them apart, studied their inner workings for hours. Then he'd put them back together, and they'd be as good as new. One winter, he spent a month tearing apart our lawnmower's engine. I swore I'd take away his garage privileges if he didn't have it running again by spring. "No problem, Dad." Apparently so. The grass got cut just fine that year.

It was also hard not to stock up on protective gear. Weapons. Guns and knives. But I hadn't been so sure about bombs. I had a little experience with pistols and shotguns, but none with explosives. And what would we need a bomb for anyway? After all, we weren't preparing for a war. Just a mission. A journey there and back.

But Henry had been relentless about taking them. "What if we need to take down a tree for shelter?" "What if we get trapped in a cave one night?" He was always good at thinking up every scenario for any situation. I gave in, and the bombs came with us.

While Jessica and I had been making our dash for the woods when the hunters spotted us, Henry had been coming up with his own plan. So much for following the infallible father, I guess. He told us that he knew he might not make it to the woods with his undisciplined left leg. It didn't take long for the lightbulb to go off. It never did with Henry.

He had predicted my idea, having Jessica fire on the men as they chased me into the woods. And he had predicted the hunters' response, to turn and run from the gunfire. But he also had to time and place his bombs perfectly for them to register their full effect.

He had army-crawled his way through the tall wheat-like grass, just behind the hunters' rushing onslaught. He had spaced out four of the explosives in a diamond pattern, right in the path that the assaulting men had just taken. He had then made the rest of his way to the cover of the trees and waited. His bombs had electronic timers taken from digital clocks he had collected. Calculating the time it would take for me to draw the hunters in, for Jessica to shoot at them, and for them to react and retreat, Henry had set the timers for 1 minute and 15 seconds each.

As the hunters came bolting from the woods, Henry knew his time calculations had been perfect. The savages reached the explosives just as they detonated, with fire and shrapnel coming at them from all directions. Two died instantly. The other two were mortally wounded.

Thank God for Henry's bombs.

24.

ANTI-Authority - Leader of the New Unknown (continued)

Part Three: Growing Up

On New Year's Day, 1959, Fidel Castro's six-year revolution was realized as rebels took the cities of Santa Clara and then Havana. The newly established Communist party transformed Cuba from vibrant to banal with a wave of government regulations and sanctions. Under the National Institute of Agrarian Reform, traditional family-operated tobacco farms were confiscated and re-distributed into collectives of common farmers. The Sebastian and Cole Cigar Company suffered dramatically.

Alejandro flew home from Tampa three days after the birth of his son Salvador. He was misguidedly confident that he could maintain his company, his tradition, and his family. It took months for the drastic changes to take hold, but Alejandro could see the writing on the wall early. He shored up his assets. He pulled money from his accounts. He assured his employees that the company was stable. But his friends in the government were gone, ousted by the new regime. And his partners in America were worried. The day Alejandro received notice of the annexation of the Sebastian farm, he went to his patio and wept. The work of four proud generations was no longer his. He cursed the land, and he chose to challenge his new country.

Before he sat to write his wife and infant son, Alejandro lit a cigar from his great-grandfather's humidor, which was consistently stocked with the freshest product from the family farm. He poured himself a rum and inhaled the tobacco that had created an empire. Once he had loosened his thoughts enough to put truth onto paper, he described the desperation he now felt for himself and the hatred he felt for his Cuba. He told of his love for Lola, but even more for his baby Salvador. The son he may never know, but who he would always hold in his heart. He wrote of his plans, to flee to the Escambray Mountains, where he had heard rumor of a counterrevolution taking shape. He had decided that his only remaining path in life was to fight for what his country once was.

Alejandro then packaged his letter with the money he collected from his bank accounts before the new government was able to seize it. Along with his savings in the United States, it would be enough to take care of Lola and Salvador for many years. He entrusted the package with one of his most loyal office workers, a man who planned to escape to Florida by boat in a few days. Alejandro then walked the long drive leading from the Sebastian farm for the last time. He turned at the end of it and blew a kiss to his family's former lifeblood. Then he went to join the ranks of the resistance.

Alejandro's courier arrived at Lola's door three weeks later. He delivered the letter, but there was no money. Between boat captains and border agents, Alejandro's Cuban nest-egg had been spent. Lola was a mess, left husbandless in a place where she had never wanted to be. Her only solace was Salvador.

1960s Tampa became a desolate place for its Cuban population. As the cigar manufacturing of the city vanished with the decreasing tobacco exports out of the home country, so did the biggest source of income for its immigrants. It wasn't long until Lola's American savings account was depleted. She was forced to take work where she could find it. First as a hotel maid, then as a waitress. Salvador spent his days in a makeshift daycare, run by an older Cuban immigrant woman they called Miss Maria who had lived in Tampa for most of her life. By all accounts, he was a quiet and happy baby, unaffected by his difficult surroundings. In the beginning, Lola lived only for him.

Lola tried for a couple of years. At least that's what Salvador told himself later in life. But it was too much desperation and despair for her. She dropped him off at Miss Maria's on a humid August morning and never came back.

Maria de la Coba took care of Salvador as if he was her own child. Her heart was soft for children, even though she had none of her own. She had come to Tampa just before America's Great Depression, when the cigar business was booming. She had seen one giant stroke of hardship consume her community before, and she had seen that community recover. She never understood Lola's choice, but she never questioned her role in Lola's absence. Salvador was fortunate to have her in his life, and this he never forgot.

Miss Maria taught young Salvador how to read and write, both Spanish and English. He was very bright, and showed a great hunger for knowledge early. She enrolled him in school. She helped him with homework. He excelled, and his teachers fostered his advance. As he neared high school age, his guidance counselor began discussions with him about private school. The school had a scholarship program for under-privileged, over-achieving students from local minority groups. Salvador's counselor was confident that he would qualify. The school was miles across town, but the scholarship included boarding for students with transportation issues. With Miss Maria's blessing, Salvador applied and was promptly accepted.

He thrived in his new environment, surrounded by higher-class teenagers. Salvador had always exuded a natural charm that made him popular in any group. He fit in with the rich kids just fine. And he was his teachers' favorite, with a sharp mind and a clever sense of humor. By his junior year, he was considered a shoe-in at any college he may want to attend. Life for Salvador was about to take him further than he could imagine, when news of Miss Maria's death shook him to his core.

25.

We were visiting Meg's father at the farm when her back pain returned. The same pain she had felt in the early stages of her conquered cancer. Dr. Raj had forewarned us that the chance of a recurrence was possible. He had said it with that gentle, healing voice - "Not probable…" *wink* "But possible." I could tell by the look on Meg's face when she told me that she was scared.

Things had been getting strange that winter. More protests and sit-ins. Organized attacks on police precincts in the larger cities. Weekly marches on state capitols. It felt dangerous. So we decided to take a couple of weeks off and drive the kids over to Meg's farm to see their granddad. Business had gotten slow anyway. And we didn't know when we'd get another chance to visit. Meg's father was still travelling overseas for business, even more than before her mother died.

The impromptu vacation had been idyllic for the first ten days. The farm was expansive, but not wild. We could let the kids spend the days on their own, exploring and adventuring, without worry. And Meg's father let me be, for the most part. He had always been distant. I had always liked that. I got to relax and forget about work for a few days, and Meg got to rejuvenate her body and mind. She needed that every now and again since her cancer battle. The spiritual side of Dr. Raj's treatment had never left her.

But there was no rejuvenation and revitalization for Meg on that trip. I had sensed the distraction before she brought it up that Wednesday morning.

"Sit down, Gordon," she said. Shit. Being asked to sit down was like someone telling you about a sucker punch before they sucker-punched you. I braced myself. "It's back."

So matter-of-fact. Her competitive nature always came out when we discussed the serious stuff. What's-the-problem-and-how-do-we-solve-it attitude. I knew what she was talking about, what was "back." But I played the inevitable conversation game that Meg hated so much. "What are you talking about?"

"The tumor, Gordon. I can feel it, grabbing my spine with its tentacles again. There's no other feeling like it in the world."

"How long?" I asked desperately.

"There was some pain a few weeks ago that never went away. But now I can feel...*it*."

We sat silently for a long period of time. Maybe ten minutes, maybe twenty. We had already been through so much pain and heartache and struggle. It started to seem like it may never end. Finally, I summoned the strength to get up and go to her.

"I know, Meggy. Here we go again," I comforted. "But listen. We go home, we go see Dr. Raj, and we win. Just like before. It's the only way. Right?"

"I suppose," she answered resignedly. "I'm just ready for our life to be calm and peaceful. For us to be happy and healthy. Everyone else is. Why not us?"

I wished I could answer. I wanted to answer. But I didn't have it in me. I couldn't find it. I had searched for it many sleepless nights, wondering why we were suffering when so many others weren't. But we didn't know true suffering. If we were being honest with ourselves, we still had it so much better than so many in the world. But that was all about to change.

26.

The two remaining hunters who had survived Henry's surprise bombing were silent within minutes. The massive bleeding from their multiple wounds didn't take long. Unconscious and soon to be dead, we put them out of our minds and made for the edge of the woods.

I was mildly concerned for the safety of the women down the road. They posed no threat, as they were most likely heavily sedated with homegrown drugs. Women on those types of expeditions were used for nightly entertainment, and the drugs ensured their vulnerability. Rural farms were known to grow various opiate hybrids just for this purpose. The expeditions could last days or weeks. Even if they understood where they were once they awoke from their narcotic haze, they wouldn't survive the new wilderness. I couldn't think about that then. Compassion had become a thing of the past, even for us nice guys.

I thought it was best to travel the rest of the day just inside the trees alongside the highway. After all, Henry's bombs could have been heard by anyone walking the road close by. The hiking would be tougher, but we needed to stay out of sight for a few miles.

We didn't speak much the rest of that day. I had no idea what to say, but I knew I had to say something. Being a parent had changed me. For the better, I hoped. I never cared for confrontation or hard discussions. But you can't avoid them as a parent. Unless you want to seriously screw up your kids. So I used the rest of the day's journey to think of what I'd say that night. I didn't think there was any right or wrong way to say it, but we had to talk.

We veered deeper into the woods before sunset to make camp, just as we did every night. Henry and I set up the tent while Jessica scoured the area for firewood. I had told her not too much that evening. I didn't want to attract any extra attention considering that afternoon's incident, so we would keep the fire small. We prepared our dinner from the few canned goods we were carrying, and we sat around the fire to eat. Dinnertime had always been the time for quiet, for family conversation. It seemed like a good enough time to broach the subject.

"We had quite a day, guys," I began. "I want to talk about it."

They didn't look up from their meals. Still teenagers in so many ways.

"Ok, listen, I know you guys are going through some crazy emotions right now. I guess I just want to make sure you know you can talk about them. To me, to each other. But I don't think it's best to not talk about it at all."

More silence.

"Well, here goes," I tried. "I'm going to tell you how I feel about everything, and you guys can just listen." There was no way in hell I was going to let them off without discussing what had happened. It was one thing to kill an animal, but these kids, *my kids*, had taken the lives of men. I had to know that they were going to be ok. "I think what the both of you did today was incredibly brave. It may feel like it wasn't right now, like you've done the lowest thing a human being can do. But what you did took courage." I thought. "I'm proud of you guys. And I want to say thank you for saving my life."

Jessica spoke first. "I feel like I should feel worse about it, but I don't. Those men were trying to kill us."

"That's right, Jess," I said. "You had no choice but to defend yourself. We had no choice. And if we're put in that situation again, we'll do the same thing." Henry still didn't have anything to say, always the introvert. I wanted to get something out of him. "Henry, I hope you know that what you did back there was amazingly clever. It was smarter than anything I could have ever thought up. Because of you, we don't have to look over our shoulders the rest of the trip."

"Yeah, Dad, I guess so. But I never intended to use those explosives that way. I just knew I had to do something."

"Well, you did good, son. Very good." I had to admit that I felt a sense of pride, even though I wasn't so sure of what I was proud. "I realized today that each of you has very special talents that you can use to survive in this new world. Our society has become survival of the fittest in its most natural sense." I paused, wanting to deliver this next line with emphasis. "You guys are going to be the fittest, as long as you keep your heads about you. Understand?"

They both nodded, and I could see tears in their eyes through the flickering firelight.

"Now listen," I continued. "You're going to have to grow up fast out here. Faster than I ever thought. But after today, I know you can do it. I know how strong you two are. Let's stay focused on the mission." Time to get them back on track mentally. "Let's not forget about Mom. She's the only reason we're out here."

With that, I stood and went to them. I sat in between them and put my arms around their shoulders. "Triumphs forever, guys," I whispered as I gave them each a squeeze.

They answered the call at the same time, with the same heart. "Triumphs forever, Dad."

27.

(Excerpt from *Brave New Nothing: A Sociological Study of a Non-Social World*, by Salvador Sebastian, copyright ANTI-Knowledge Publications. Recovered from Jacob Marsh's last-known address, Baltimore, Maryland. The book was disseminated and analyzed once Sebastian became a household name.)

"...and with the rapid advance of technology negatively affecting our daily interactions, we have seen the human mind and society as a whole suffer. The relationships that fueled past generations' productivity have become non-existent. The value and pride of a life's work have disappeared. We have become completely dependent on computers, processors, and calculators. With that, we are losing the basic sets of skills that made us superior in the first place. We are, in fact, losing our humanity."

28.

Meg called Dr. Raj's office the first week of March. Six weeks before everything came crashing down. He scheduled an appointment for three days later. He wanted to see her right away. She was able to skip the better portion of the testing she had done two years earlier. Dr. Raj soon confirmed the recurring tumor and planned for surgery. Same gameplan as before. Remove cells, mutate them, return them to the battle. Then a regimen of high-powered medication and spiritual re-conditioning. The quicker the better.

We called a family meeting. Again. This one was tough. Life isn't fair, kids. Best to learn it early on. Jessica and Henry would have to manage their time better this go-round. Their schoolwork was double what it used to be. And Mom would be gone for treatments every week. We were all going to have to carry a bigger load.

Surgery went well. Meg's body had bounced back from the last cancer fight to prime condition. She was running almost as much as she had in her twenties, and she had adopted a daily adherence to yoga. Physically, she was as strong as she'd ever been. My concern was her mind. Fighting for your life can take your thoughts to dark places. Doing it twice in three years would take all of our energy to keep those thoughts at bay.

As I sat with her in the recovery room, waiting for her to wake, I listened to her mumbling her way through some desperate dreamscape. Later, she described to me the vague memory of the realm of subconscious she had explored that day. She said she saw herself in a big black cast-iron bed with stark white sheets and pillows. She was blind with pain and sweat, and she called out for me. But there was no response. She knew I was gone, that I had to be gone. I had told her I would return, but she wasn't sure in that moment of agony that I would. And if I didn't, she would surely die. That was all she could remember.

I reassured her that I was there for her, no matter what. We brushed it off. During her first battle with cancer, Meg had become fascinated with dream meaning, a side effect of her spiritual study, I assumed. There were the typical dreams that we all experience every now and then. Late for a college exam, free-falling through midair. They had their interpretations, easily explained. But this one confounded Meg. She kept saying that it had felt too real to be a dream. I chalked it up to the surgery, the anesthesia. I told myself that I would never leave Meg to fight her battle alone. But she had seen a glimpse of our real future in her dream that day. And it's the unthinkable things that we never see coming.

29.

Henry startled me from my sleep with an urgent whisper. "Dad, dad...wake up. There's somebody outside the tent."

I sat up quickly, but quietly. And listened. I could tell by the crack of light at the bottom of the tent's zipper that it was past daybreak. The footsteps were loud, but I knew the woods carried echoes far, especially in the early morning. I counted what I thought was five people walking, give or take a couple. And they were moving slowly, deliberately. I turned to Jessica and Henry and put my forefinger to my pursed lips. "Shhh."

We had been sleeping in our clothes on the journey. Had to be ready to move at a moment's notice. I slipped out of my sleeping bag and calmly unzipped the tent. Before I poked my head out, I listened again. Still the crackling of leaves and twigs under feet, maybe just a little closer. Or maybe the open air made it seem that way. No matter. The sooner I surveyed the situation, the sooner I would know how to handle it. I eased back the flaps and peered into last night's campsite. No one in sight, but the sound of footsteps continued. I gently crawled out of the tent, staying on my elbows and stomach and knees. Without the enclosed space of our nightly quarters tricking my ears, I was able to locate the direction of the walkers. South of us, but moving north. Moving toward us. They were still far enough away for me to strategize.

    I went back into the tent, gathered up my handgun and binoculars, and told the kids to stay put. "Remember, guys. Not everybody out here is like those men from yesterday. Start breaking down the tent and packing up, but be quiet about it. I won't be gone long." And with that, I slipped back out and set off southward.

30.

ANTI-Authority - Leader of the New Unknown (continued)

Part Four: The Benefactor

The one true mentor that guided Salvador through childhood had also been an heiress to a real estate fortune. Miss Maria de la Coba had moved to the United States with her father in 1919 at the age of five. Her mother had died before Maria had developed any lasting memory of her, and her father made their new home in Tampa primarily to leave his dead wife in the past. He had been a successful real estate developer in Havana, taking advantage of the tourism boom of the early 20th century. Hotels were his specialty.

Once he was able to liquidate his holdings in Cuba, Maria's father started over again in Tampa. Apartment buildings were his plan. The growing Cuban immigrant population in Florida made him an even wealthier man. Wealthy enough to survive the Great Depression. Real estate recovered as the country did, and Maria's father accumulated a small fortune. At the time of his death in 1948, he was worth over four million dollars.

Maria had no interest in real estate. She was too easily distracted to have interest in anything as a young woman. Her father spoiled her with gifts, parties, and money. As she drifted through her youth as an immigrant socialite, she never put much thought into what she may be giving up. And she wasn't prepared for her father's death when it came unexpectedly. His advisors told her to sell off his properties and invest the money under their guidance. She took the former advice, but thought better of the latter.

As she travelled the world on her inheritance, Maria tried to forget about the life she may have wasted. For 10 years she dined in the finest restaurants, drank the best champagne, and danced with the richest men. But she never found the happiness she so desperately sought. When the restlessness of her spirit finally subsided, Maria was too old for a family. Too old for the thing she had never had, and the thing that would have brought her peace. So she settled in the Cuban neighborhood in Tampa and surrounded herself with other people's children.

The principal pulled Salvador out of his fifth period calculus class to tell him. Miss Maria had suffered a stroke and was in the hospital. There wasn't much hope for her survival. He was allowed to leave school to attend to her, as he was the only family listed in her will.

Maria had adopted Salvador when he applied for the private high school. He needed a legal guardian for the application. She had then met with her longtime lawyer once he left for his freshman year. She knew her health was declining, and she wanted to make sure what remained of her savings went to Salvador. What remained was substantial.

Salvador arrived at Miss Maria's bedside in time to say "goodbye" and "thank you." She was paralyzed from the stroke, but he saw the acknowledgement in the twinkle of her eyes. He thought of that moment often. Once funeral arrangements had been planned, Maria's lawyer sat down with 17-year-old Salvador to review her will. The estate would be his in its entirety. There were very few physical assets, but the money left was six and a half million dollars. Miss Maria had invested the little she had left from her ramblings wisely. The money would be held in a trust until Salvador's 18th birthday.

Salvador finished his studies at the private school, but his teachers saw his enthusiasm disappear after Maria's death. He lost interest in applying for colleges, and when graduation day came, he had no plans to continue his formal education. He graciously accepted his diploma, called for a taxi, and asked for a ride to the airport. He had emptied his trust fund six months earlier in anticipation of that day. First to Miami, then to Cuba.

31.

Dr. Raj must have known things were about to turn. I thought about it many times, and that was the only conclusion that came to me. Maybe some sort of Indian intuition.

Meg's surgery had gone as well as possible, and it allowed for her medication regimen to begin immediately. Dr. Raj still wanted to see her twice a week to check her cancer cell levels, administer the correct dosages of medicine, and monitor her chakras. Healing of the body *and* spirit, remember? For four weeks, Meg and the rest of us got back into the familiar routine from a couple of years earlier. But at the end of that fourth week, Dr. Raj told us he wanted to make a change.

"Meg, you are strong in mind," he said during that last office visit. The last time we would ever see him. "Your spirit is powerful. Your energy points need no further monitoring by me."

We were confused. What was he telling us? Were we finished with her treatments?

"What exactly are you saying, Dr. Raj?" Meg asked.

"I am saying that you are your own guide now on this journey. I do not need for you to come see me twice a week. I will continue to medicate your body, but your spirit is intact."

He took a long pause, which was not unusual for him. He was slow and deliberate when explaining things, unlike most doctors we knew.

"I will want to see you monthly to keep your medications updated," he continued. "I will supply you at each visit, hopefully decreasing the dosage each time." Another pause, then he rolled his chair close to Meg. He took her hands in his. "You will beat this disease, Meg. If you never hear me say anything again, know that. You are one of the strongest patients I have ever had. Stay focused, repeat your mantras." He squeezed her hands. "Win."

The nurse came into our room not long after Dr. Raj finished his pep talk to Meg. She had four small boxes that held Meg's life-saving pills. Dr. Raj signed off on a check-marked sheet of paper and took the boxes from her. Then he described the daily procedure. Two pills with a large breakfast, one with lunch, and one more with a light dinner. Easy enough. And no more driving half-a-day twice a week. Our family life might actually get back to normal. We couldn't conceal our excitement.

"Ok, you guys are done for now," Dr. Raj announced. "But one more thing before you go."

He pulled out a local medical center map. Dr. Raj's office was adjacent to a large hospital complex that took up more than eight city blocks. His trial medications were stored in a building two blocks over. He pointed it out to us. He then took out a red marker and circled the building twice. It seemed insignificant to know that information at the time, but it would become immensely important before long. For the record, I don't think the good doctor was a fortune-teller. But I did get the feeling that he knew something that we didn't. Somehow, he knew we may never see each other again.

32.

I tried my hardest to move softly across the damp forest floor. The last thing I needed to do was make the unknown travelers aware of my existence. *Our* existence. I chose to move southeast to flank them, get a look at them, and then get back to camp to devise a plan. I stopped every few yards to listen for their footsteps. Trot, listen, trot, listen.

When I got close enough for a good look, I found an oak with a trunk wider than my body. Using the binoculars, I peered around the tree and focused on the group of hikers. Five of them. Damn, my ears had gotten good. Two women and three men. Younger than me, but all adults. They were spread out from each other, as if to better defend themselves in case of an ambush. And they were walking slowly, just as I had thought I heard. They had packs and guns, but that wasn't abnormal, considering. I didn't feel intimidated or fearful of them. I had always been a gut guy, and my gut told me they were harmless. And maybe helpful.

I hoofed it back to our campsite as quickly and silently as I could. The kids had dutifully packed up the tent and sleeping bags. We were ready to move if we chose, but I wasn't so sure.

"Alright, guys, decision time," I started. Then I described the group of hikers to Jessica and Henry. "I really believe these people are like us. No way to know it. But I believe it. What do you think?"

"Your call, Dad. I trust you," Jessica said.

"Ok, Dad," Henry began, "but let's be smart about this. If we want to approach them, we need to be careful about it."

"True, Henry," I said. "How about we hike out to the road and wait there. I'm sure that's where they're heading anyway. Open air, they can see us, we can see them." They both nodded in agreement.

Then Henry came up with an added protection. "And let's put Jessica in a tree out of sight. Sniper-like. If they aren't who you think they are, at least she can give us a chance."

"Not a bad idea, Henry," I agreed. "You alright with that, Jess?"

"Of course, boys." She winked at us. "I got your back."

After we found a tree for Jessica to climb, Henry and I walked out to the empty highway. I was nervous, but I didn't want to betray that to Henry. It wasn't long before we heard the group coming through the woods. I saw the first of them get to the edge of the trees and stop. He held up his fisted hand like some platoon leader directing his soldiers to hold where they stood. I didn't delay our introduction.

"Hello," I spoke in a loud but restrained voice. "We mean no harm." I raised my arms in the air. Henry did too, just as I had instructed.

The only member of the group that I could see crept out from the trees, his hand now on his holstered pistol. "Your names and your intentions. Now," he said with authority.

"I'm Gordon, this is my son Henry. We are traveling the road, looking for companions."

The man took three more steps forward, then looked left and right. "Where are you going?"

"East," I replied. "About 100 miles. To the university hospital complex." We kept our arms raised toward the sky.

I knew the rest of his crew had their weapons pointed at us as he approached, even though I couldn't see any of them. He looked us up and down as he got closer. He stood tall right in front of us for a few seconds, turning a resolution over in his mind. Then he extended his hand to me. "Jeff," he said. Maybe he had that same gut feeling about us that I did about him.

"Hi, Jeff. Good to meet you." I shook his hand.

He introduced himself to Henry, then called the others out of the woods. They slowly revealed themselves and walked up to us on the road. First was

Paul, then Anthony. The women were Beth and Madeline. They were all about the same age, in their early twenties I guessed. I liked them immediately.

"So, where are you guys heading?" I asked.

Jeff spoke. He was the obvious leader of the group. "Same direction as you. We figured it would be easier walking on the highway." He paused and looked at the others, then back at me. "We could join you two if you wanted?"

You *two*. Shit. I had to explain Jessica. "That would be great," I said with a smile. "One thing though...we've got a third wheel around here somewhere. My daughter." Then I acted as best I could, looking around for Jessica as if I didn't know where she was. I put my hands around my mouth and yelled out, "Jessica!!! Come on back, honey!"

Right on cue, Jessica came rustling through the woods behind our new friends. "Hey, Dad," she said. "Sorry, I got turned around after I got done." Perfect. The good old pee-break excuse. Jessica's wit and charm always shone through to strangers. I saw the two young women smile at each other.

"Jessica, get up here," I told her. "We've met some people. Some nice people. They're going to join us on our journey." I couldn't help but smile as I said it.

33.

ANTI-Authority - Leader of the New Unknown (continued)

Part Five: Discovery

    The innate desire to explore the land that gave him his name had been with Salvador for years. He would drift into sleep as a child with Miss Maria's tales of Cuba, its people, its beauty. In school, he would find himself lost in Cuban history books during study hours. And then there were the parents who he never knew. He longed for their story, even as he hated them for their absence.

    In the summer of 1977, Salvador slipped secretly into Cuba under cover of darkness and clouds. He made his way to Havana, where he arranged transportation to Vinales, the town where the first Juan Sebastian had started what became a cigar empire. Salvador was determined to live as his oldest-known ancestor had. To perform manual labor. To get his hands dirty. He applied for a job as a farmhand, and soon found peace in the sweat and toil of field work.

    The work weeks were long, but Salvador rose early every Sunday to investigate his family's history. He attended church services and community gatherings. He spoke with city leaders and common townspeople. His natural charisma gained him access to anyone and everyone who might know information about the Sebastian family tree. Soon enough, he had developed a timeline, up to his father's disappearance into the Escambray Mountains in 1959.

After eighteen months of tobacco farming and ancestor research, Salvador's restless nature led him from Vinales east. To uncover what happened to the father he never knew, he would have to follow the man's path from so many years before. Salvador hitchhiked his way to the Escambrays, where he found locals who would describe to him what was known as the War Against the Bandits. He learned of the guerrillas who fought against Castro's overpowering military numbers. He heard the stories of extermination forces walking elbow-to-elbow clearing the region of anti-communist rebels. Finally, he found a man who had known Alejandro Sebastian, and who knew of his death. Alejandro had died as he had lived, with courage and resolve. He had been smart enough to know the futile outcome of his war, but he had fought it anyway. Salvador wept as the man described the last days of his father.

Once Salvador had learned as much as there was to know of his family in Cuba, he left the country far behind. He traveled for the next fourteen years, from Brazil to Bangladesh and from China to Czechoslovakia. His craving for world culture was insatiable. He was fascinated with the people of the world and what made them different. But perhaps more importantly, what made them the same.

When he returned to the United States in 1993, the dawn of the Internet was breaking. His fascination with the connection of people across countries and cultures had a new avenue of discovery. Salvador made his way to the tech valleys of California, and he came up with a plan to unite the world.

34.

The night after our final trip to Dr. Raj's office, I sat down at the kitchen table to organize Meg's medication. I opened the boxes that he had given us and started separating out the pills.

"That's funny," I said to Meg.

"What's *funny*?" She was always accusing me of over-exaggerating things.

"No, seriously. This isn't right. I'm counting six-months-worth of medication here. He told us we'd have to come back monthly, right?"

Meg thought back. "Yeah, every month. Definitely."

"Well, that just doesn't make sense."

"I'm sure they just made a mistake, Gordon," Meg said. "I'll call and find out tomorrow."

I couldn't sleep that night. The good doctor had me thinking too much.

35.

I let Jeff lead the way. He struck me as the classic alpha-male. I always let people be who they naturally were whenever I was faced with a group dynamic. My former consulting job, a job that mattered no more, had provided me plenty of experience in dealing with differing personalities. And no challenges to the dominant ones usually meant no problems. Usually. I guess I could've been considered a good mediator. And besides, for this group there was only one direction to go and one road to follow. No need to make any waves.

Jeff instructed us to walk in a pattern. He would be out front, then we would trail behind in two lines of three with the last of us anchoring the rear. The kids would be in the middle of each line. I didn't let him know that Jessica and Henry could hold their own at that point. Because I didn't mind the extra protection for them. Beth, Jessica, and Madeline in the first line. Me, Henry, and Paul in the second. Anthony would lag behind us as rear defense.

I knew Jeff wasn't military. His directions weren't that structured. They were more like something he had seen in a movie. But everyone seemed to feel safer following his lead. And safety was exactly what we had been seeking.

There wasn't much conversation as we walked. Everyone was concentrating on their surroundings. I checked with Henry every few hundred yards to make sure his leg wasn't bothering him. We hadn't let the others know about that just yet. Always the trooper, he never complained. But he did seem to be walking better. Maybe that was just wishful thinking on my part.

Jeff stopped us for lunch before noon. So far, we had been eating light midday meals on our journey. Big breakfast in the morning, big dinner at night, light lunch in the middle. If we were hunting for food, early morning or evening were the times to do it. Lunch was most importantly for rest. This particular lunch was also our first get-to-know-you conference. Felt like one of my old seminars.

We found an area near the woods so we would have some shade, and some cover in case any uninvited visitors appeared. We settled in. I was the first to speak. "So, everybody. What's your story?"

Jeff, accordingly, spoke up first. "I guess the easiest place to start is college. The five of us were students when it all went down." He glanced at Jessica and Henry.

"Don't worry," I assured him. "They know everything."

Paul stepped in and continued, "Jeff's my older brother. He and Beth were in graduate school together. Me, Anthony, and Madeline were undergrad."

"Anyway, we waited it out at school for a couple of months," Jeff continued. "Never thought it would last. Then when it did, we made our way home." He paused and looked around at each of them. "We're all from the same town."

"Yeah, I don't think anyone thought it would last, Jeff," I said. "What brings you guys back out after all this time?"

"The *gathering*," Paul blurted out. I saw a bit of fire in his eyes.

"Gathering?" I asked.

"Oh, you haven't heard?" Paul responded. "Go ahead, Jeff. Tell them."

Jeff put down his can of food and wiped his hands clean on one another. He cleared his throat, obviously preparing to speak of something important to him. "There is a gathering taking place. A convergence of like-minded and strong-willed souls who are ready to fight back." He waited. He was a very good speaker. Inspirational, in fact. "This world, but more importantly this country, came crashing down thirteen months ago in a matter of days. You remember." I nodded. "It takes a long time to recover from the magnitude of something like that. To come out of the shock of it all. To organize a resistance."

I looked around at the faces of our new-found friends. They were lit with excitement. I hadn't heard about any kind of resistance forming, but it was apparent that something big had invigorated these young people. It brought me a sense of joy that had been missing from life for quite some time. But there was also a sense of dread that accompanied it. The protective parent in me, I suppose.

Jeff continued. "We first got word about it two months ago. There's a state prison where they've set up headquarters. Anyone who wants to fight has been instructed to be there no later than Memorial Day." A half-smile crept onto his face. "Seems like a fitting day to start over."

I had to admit that it was exhilarating to hear, even as unrealistic as it may have seemed at the time. But I couldn't get caught up in anything besides our family's singular mission. If there was to be a war against ANTI-, it was one for the younger generation. To my consternation, nothing confirmed that more than the look I saw on Jessica and Henry's faces that day. The unmistakable look of defiance.

36.

ANTI-Authority - Leader of the New Unknown (concluded)

Part Six: Connecting the Human Dots

Salvador Sebastian founded Faultline Technologies with his remaining inheritance after years of exploring the world. His entrepreneurial spirit was natural. His computer skills were not. But he immersed himself in the burgeoning science of code and software and algorithm. Like so many Sebastians before him, he was a quick study. He was also an excellent judge of people's abilities, and his staff at Faultline was second-to-none.

The company focused on Internet capability, as Salvador foresaw very early the power of its connectivity across the world. Faultline developed some of the Internet's first large-scale websites. Soon, they were bidding on and winning government contracts for web development. By the turn of the century, they were a top ten company within the U.S. tech landscape.

With the exponential growth that Faultline was experiencing, Salvador took advantage of the opportunity to introduce technology into countries and cultures across the globe. He invested large portions of his profits into developing electronic infrastructure in places that couldn't afford to do it themselves. He built schools and donated computers. He created international scholarships for gifted children in poverty-stricken regions. He helped to make the world accessible to people who had no chance, no hope for something bigger.

Then, on September 12, 2001, Faultline Technologies became something else. The company was under contract by the National Security Administration when the 9/11 attacks took place. Mainly being utilized to assist in development of government website protection, the people at Faultline knew little of what their company was actually securing. Once the country's focus turned to Osama bin Laden, the contract became much clearer. Faultline was tasked with searching out and monitoring all Internet activity of known and suspected bin Laden associates. Salvador was not immune to the new-found patriotism that permeated through the American people in those months after 9/11, and he believed in the work that his company was doing. Until March 7, 2003.

Salvador knew that the information his company was gathering would lead to death. He was not naïve about government operations. But the United States' blatant inconsideration for innocent human life that was displayed on Faultline's internal system that early March morning changed Salvador forever. The target's location was identified by Faultline's advanced global positioning arm. He was in a village of two hundred people, nearly half of which were children. These details were known, but ignored. The village was fire-bombed as its people slept. The target was eliminated, along with everyone else.

Salvador's attempts to cancel Faultline's government contract were futile. He sold his stake in the company in December of 2003. And he thought. For two years, he questioned everything that he had done in life. He wondered if the technology that he once believed would connect the greatest of us was a sham. If, in the hands of the wrong people, it would only bring about more pain and suffering and evil. And out of this introspective desperation was conceived the way around it all: ANTI-.

With years of recruitment and growth, ANTI- has become just what Salvador envisioned it to be. Without the influence of government or money or corruption of both, he has still been able to connect the people of the world and affect change from within. To date, the number of ANTI- followers is unknown. Mr.

Sebastian does not claim to know how many people subscribe to his philosophy, and he refuses to answer how many the ANTI- organization employs. But his resolve would lead this interviewer to believe that the number is large in both instances. ANTI- is no doubt affecting change across continents. The only question that remains: where will this change take us?

37.

The first thing I did on a typical morning before the Great Dark began was find the remote and turn on the news. I was never at my best in the first moments of a day. Meg had learned early in our relationship to avoid speaking to me when I was just waking up. News, shower, coffee. Then, maybe, we could talk.

I was especially groggy the morning that everything changed. I had tossed all night trying to get Dr. Raj's hidden meanings out of my head. I clicked the bedroom television to life with my eyes still closed. The news was reporting some sort of electronic disruption in the government systems of countries in North and South America. The United States and Canada had been the first to acknowledge an outside interference with their internal servers, sometime early that morning. But it was unclear what that meant in my half-awake state. I decided to get up and shower away some of the cobwebs. It was probably typical media hype anyway.

Meg startled me just as I was turning on the hot water. "Hey." I almost jumped. Sometimes I thought she did it for a laugh. Not that day. "I think this is pretty serious. On the news. They're saying it's affecting satellite communications, that government security systems are completely down."

"Yeah?" I asked. I could sense her concern. I shut the shower off. "Let me get dressed. Pour me a cup?" She nodded.

The only way I can describe the next two hours is by comparison. Comparison to a decade-plus earlier when our country was under violent, large-scale attack. Comparison to the stunned shock I experienced with then-girlfriend Meg as we watched the day unfold on September 11, 2001. Yes, this was different. No death, no explosions, no sobbing bystanders. But the feeling I had was undeniably the same.

38.

"...and so, you see, we have to get to that pharmaceutical building as quickly as possible. And back." I was wrapping up our introduction to the others, our new fellow journeymen. I had tried to give them the short version of our story, but I wasn't so sure there was one. That was the first time I had told it start to finish. Ever. For the last year and a month, we had just been living it. Without thinking too much about it. I longed for Meg more than usual when I finished. Everyone sat in silence for a few minutes.

"I can shoot really, really good," Jessica announced, breaking the somberness. Everybody stared at her. "Seriously." She was smiling.

"Really?" Jeff asked. "Exactly *how* good?"

Jessica jumped into the story about the coyotes we encountered a few nights earlier. Then she started into our battle with the group of hunters without missing a beat. I didn't stop her. I was trusting Jeff's crew more with each minute that passed. They were good people. And they needed to know as much about us as they were willing to hear. Friends are much more protective than strangers.

When Jessica got to the part about Henry's explosives, I saw Anthony lean over and whisper something to him. Henry's mouth broke into a big grimace. He was proud. The others were enthralled in Jessica's storytelling. Jeff looked at me with question in his eyes. I winked and nodded at him, confirmation that the tales were true. I was glad to see the kids connecting with the group. We needed them to like us. But part of me was scared. Scared that my children were adapting to this new way of life too easily.

After a bit more levity, Jeff stood up. "Time to get moving, everybody. We can keep up the bullshitting once we make camp tonight." He walked up to Jessica and Henry. "Glad to know I've got two more soldiers in my platoon," he said to them. "Henry, you let me know if you need a break."

We walked through the afternoon without slowing. The section of highway we hiked was level, nearly flat. I had looked at my map during our lunch break, and I knew that the next day was going to be tougher travel as we neared the foothills. I suggested we look for a good spot to set up camp for the night. Jeff and the others agreed.

Our new friends were impressively efficient. In the time the kids and I had taken to put up our tent, they had staked their own shelters and started a fire. Paul and Anthony had already moved on to preparation for an evening hunt, checking their compound bows. Paul turned to us. "Hey, Jessica, you wanna see the *hard* way to kill an animal?"

"Sure!" She looked up at me. "Dad, can I?"

I saw no harm in it. "I guess so."

"How about you, Henry?" Anthony asked. "No work necessary. Just gotta be quiet."

"Yeah, ok." And they were off. *"Be careful, guys,"* I thought to myself.

I walked over to where Jeff had set up a low table, about a foot square. He had placed an old radio with antennae on it, from which I could faintly hear a steady voice crackling through light static. He had a notebook resting on the table in front of the radio. Every few seconds, he would jot down words or numbers in it. After a few minutes of watching him do this, the voice disappeared. Jeff closed his notebook.

"What was that all about?" I ventured.

Jeff stared at me for a moment. He hadn't known I was listening. Then he decided to tell me. "The voice you could hear? That was Lefty." I must have looked puzzled. He explained, "Ok, there's a communication system in place for the resistance. Antiquated, but it works. If you can find an old one-way or two-way radio, you can pick up their signal. They send out messages almost every evening at sunset."

"'They' being who exactly?"

"That's complicated. Like I said before, we've only known about it for a couple of months. A group came into our town and started talk of a meeting. It was very much a grassroots thing. Word spread from house to house through conversation. I would say curiosity brought most people out. We met at the local high school gym, hundreds of us. They told us that a movement was developing, an underground war against ANTI-. Across the country, there were bands of people gathering at base camps run by the new resistance. They call themselves the American Liberation Effort. 'Lefty' for short."

"Wow, it's that organized?" I halfway asked. "We've been so isolated from people that I hadn't heard of a thing. What's their plan?"

"Won't know until we get to the base camp. There were only a few of us who even decided to go. Seems like hopelessness is a hard thing to overcome." Jeff thought deeply. "For those of us that do show up, there will be a plan. I know it. And we'll fight for everyone else."

The hunting expedition returned soon with a good-sized doe. Anthony and Paul cleaned the deer. We cooked the meat of the animal over the open fire, and we tried our best to eat it all. I slept peacefully later, the first restful night I had experienced on our journey. I suppose I felt comfort in Jeff and the others' company. But there was something else. There was also a sense of comfort in knowing that there was a battle afoot, a battle for what once was good and right in the world. And that people like Jeff would be fighting it for me.

39.

(Internal ANTI- email intercepted and decrypted by ISA. Released to American and European media outlets three hours before complete blackout.)

> Salvador,
>
> Systems for all countries on the American continents are scheduled to go offline at 5 AM this Friday. Chinese reaction should be delayed based on time zone difference. The European Union will follow as planned, ensuring that they remain defenseless. The Japanese concerns have been eliminated; they may last a few hours longer than the others, but their systems will fail eventually. The global electronic infrastructure should be under our control by the day's end.
>
> The security team is recommending you stay in the bunker for 36 hours after we initiate. We do not expect any immediate response, but we cannot afford the risk. I will send you regular progress reports throughout.
>
> FtSoH
> Jacob

40.

We kept the kids out of school that day. It was more out of history than fear. I wasn't afraid that morning. That would come later. But Meg and I both knew that what we were witnessing was significant. One of those "where were you when so-and-so happened" moments. The four of us watched intently as reports rolled in from countries whose systems were falling offline just as America's had. England, France, Saudi Arabia, Turkey, Russia. It was an electronic tsunami traveling from west to east.

Once recognition of human involvement was realized, there was a global decision to ground all air travel and lock down border crossings. It was assumed that the next attack angle would be in the form of violence. A dirty bomb in a metropolitan area. An airplane used as a fuel-filled missile, like before. But this was going to be a new type of terrorism. Something I had never imagined.

We lost power that evening as the sun was setting. We had gone out for dinner. Had to get away from the TV for a little while. The waitress had just dropped food off at our table. Then, darkness. We ate anyway. But as the minutes ticked by and the lights didn't flicker back on, worry began to creep into my head. And by the look on Meg's face, hers too. I left cash for the food, and we took Jessica and Henry home.

The first few days were relatively calm. We had lanterns and candles and batteries. We salvaged what food we could out of the refrigerator. We talked with neighbors about what they may have heard, what the new conspiracy theory may have been.

By the fifth morning, there was fear in the air. Everyone was disconnected. No phones, no computers, no television. And as far as anyone knew, it was that way throughout the country. One of our friends had driven a couple hundred miles and back, the distance his car's tank of gas would carry him. He confirmed the blackout as far as he had been. More fear.

Now, in general, I was never one to wait around for the other shoe to drop. I always had a good sense about what might be coming in life. And I could predict what was going to happen if the power didn't come back. There was too much evil in the world to deny it. It was time to get my family away from the general population. I had to insulate us from...*people*.

Family meeting time. We rounded up the basics: food, clothes, anything that was important. "Everybody, we may not be coming back. Whatever we can fit in the truck, grab it." I could hear Meg crying as she loaded our suitcases.

The plan was simple. We would gather as much of our belongings as possible and head for Grandad's farm. Meg's father was always stocking away food for that once-in-a-lifetime snowstorm that never came. Plus he had guns, unlike me. I had always jokingly told him it would be a perfect place to wait out the apocalypse. Joke was on me, I guess.

The interstate was littered with abandoned cars and trucks and tractor-trailers that had run out of fuel. The gas stations we passed were overrun with vehicles, seemingly stacked on top of each other in mechanical desperation to fill up their starving tanks. The glass that acted as the front walls of these stores was gone, shattered by thieves and looters. I was fortunate to have a half tank in our SUV. Just enough to get us to the farm.

Despite the number of vehicles, there was a disturbing absence of people. We drove without speaking. I weaved my way through the dysfunctional traffic jam, silently praying that I would get us to our destination before the sun set. I pulled off of the interstate with thirty miles to go. The side roads were completely different. No empty cars and trucks. The houses that began to crop up outside our windows showed some life, with residents on their porches or front lawns. Most of them looked at us as we passed in disbelief, stunned to see and hear a working automobile, I suppose. I was anxious to get to my father-in-law's.

We arrived at the farm at dusk. The gate protecting the mile-long driveway was closed and padlocked. Meg and I got out, and she rolled the lock combination into place. We pulled back the gate doors. I told Meg to get in the driver's seat and drive through, that I would close and secure the gate behind her. I looked down the road both ways to make sure no one had seen us pulling in as I clicked the padlock back into place. There was nobody in sight. I climbed back in on the passenger side and we drove up the driveway.

From a distance, the house looked dark. And as we got nearer, I could tell that it was empty. *Hoped* that it was empty. If something had happened to Meg's father in the last week, there was no way we could've known. There was no way anyone could've known. We parked the SUV, and Meg went straight to the side door. She used her key and ran inside. I held my breath, waiting for Meg's scream. The scream that would come if she discovered her dead dad.

41.

The prison that Lefty had transformed into their southeastern base was located just twelve miles outside the closest city's limits. The same city where we had journeyed so many times to see Dr. Raj. The same city that now held Meg's only salvation.

Jeff and I had discussed it early one morning before everyone else had woken up. Based on the path we were traveling, our group would reach the prison base first, with the city still another half-day's hike away. Jeff said we would stop at the base for a night, and then he and Paul would escort the kids and me into the city. I wasn't about to turn down the extra protection, so I gladly accepted his offer. As long as we didn't encounter any obstacles, getting to the hospital, into the pharmacy building, and back to the base shouldn't take more than a day, especially with Jeff and Paul helping us. And then the twins and I could get back to Meg. It sounded too easy, but I didn't let that get to me.

It was visible from the highway. One of those landmarks you notice the first time you see it, but then block out of your vision in subsequent passes. It occupied two and a half square miles of land, having once contained working crop and cattle farms. Most prisons, including this one, had been overtaken by the inmates within weeks of the Great Dark's beginning. It had been abandoned since, left to stand as some colossal reminder of what our former society deemed as power and control. We didn't know true power until everything was out of control.

The Lefty leaders were clever. They saw the advantages that a prison's design could provide for their strategy. The intent of every American prison was two-fold. First, they were built to house a shit-ton of people. Second, they were intensely secure. Of course, the object of security was originally meant to keep people inside the walls. All that Lefty did was reverse the idea and use the walls and barb wire and watchtowers as defense from the outside. What this prison then inherently gave them was plenty of vacant, secure room to accommodate the new rebel force they hoped to form. Lodging, training grounds, fortification. It was a perfect military base.

Part of Jeff's radio journal transcriptions had been instructions on gaining access to the base once we got there. He guided us to the south entrance, where there was no chain-link fence. Instead the south wall was made entirely of mortared stone, twenty feet high. There was a large opening in the middle of the wall, wide and high enough to fit two tractor-trailers side by side, protected by a giant steel door. Jeff stopped us. "We wait here," he said. "Someone will come for us."

After a few minutes, a group of four men appeared around the southeast corner of the wall. They approached with confidence. And with assault rifles held at their chests. Unlike Jeff, these guys were obviously real soldiers.

"What do you want?" one of them asked, harshly.

Jeff spoke up. "Retaliation."

"What do you want?" the same man asked again.

"Redemption."

"What do you want?" one last time.

Jeff looked hard into the man's eyes. "Resurrection."

The lead soldier stepped over to Jeff. He spoke to him in a more conversational tone. "Where have you come from?"

Jeff recited off coordinates. Then, "Lefty sent for us."

The soldier nodded and smiled. "Welcome to Overlord."

42.

Meg had tried calling her father at the farm the day it all started. But there was no answer. No surprise there. He rarely told Meg when he was travelling, or for how long. She could always reach him by cell phone if she needed him. But that had gone straight to voicemail, too. And then all communications went down.

So we convinced ourselves before we left that if the house appeared empty then that's precisely what it was. Empty. That Meg's father had been away on business when the Great Dark hit. But there was the possibility that we hadn't discussed. The chance that he was dead inside the house. That's why Meg went running for the door when we got there.

She reappeared in the doorway within a couple of minutes. "Not here," she said, as she held up a piece of paper with a handwritten note on it.

"What's that?" I asked.

"It's from him." She was having a hard time talking. "I don't know."

I took the paper from her and squinted to read it in the fading outdoor light. It was strange. Almost cryptic.

Meg,

I cannot express my joy if you are reading this, for that means that you made it to the farm. I hope you have Gordon and the twins with you. And above everything that may happen now, please know that I love you all. Even Gordon.

I know that I was always a difficult man. In all honesty, I have always had a hard time living with myself. But I have found a way to make sense of this life. You may never understand, but that is the risk I choose to take.

I always tried to teach you how to be independent and self-sufficient. You will need those qualities now more than ever before.

The garden has been planted. The pantry is stocked. Remember me for the good things I've done.

Love,
Dad

"Ok, so this is...weird," I said after reading it twice. I looked up and saw that Meg had tears welling up in her eyes. "Listen, honey, we'll figure this out.

Let's get unpacked, get some food in our bellies, and we'll figure it out." She nodded her head in a quick motion and wiped her eyes.

In the five days of darkness, I had not felt as safe as I did in that house on the farm. Meg's father had prepared for us in hopes that we would make it there. The morning after we arrived, I took the key that he had left on the kitchen counter next to a note that read "BASEMENT - SUPPLIES" in big block letters. For all the time that I had spent there, I had never been below the first floor.

The door leading to the basement was underneath the second-story stairway. It was a substantial metal door, which had deterred me from ever asking about it. I guess I always had the feeling that dear old dad-in-law didn't want me down there.

I eased the key into the deadbolt and turned it. Behind the door was a long staircase made of unfinished wood. Daylight bled into the open doorway and the vast space below came to life. I descended into the underground area, amazed at the size of it and at the amount of supplies it held. Hanging from a nail on the first wooden support at the bottom of the stairs was a clipboard with a list attached.

Propane Generators - 2

Propane Tanks (40 lbs each) - 28
High-Beam Flashlights - 10
Bolt-Action Rifles - 2
Automatic Rifles - 2
Pump Shotguns - 3
Automatic Shotguns - 2
9mm Handguns - 5
Ammunition Boxes (Various) - 200
Insulated Jackets (Adult) - 4
Insulated Jackets (Children) - 4
Outdoor Clothing (Various - Adult and Children)
4-Person Tents - 2
Canned Food
Bottled Water

The food and water took up most of the shelving that lined the basement. The generators and propane tanks occupied the area next to the far wall. The clothing and tents were stacked along the wall nearest the bottom of the stairs. I noticed a large metal cabinet alongside the hanging jackets. Must've been the firearms. A sense of calm came over me. I could feed, house, and protect my family here. For a long, long time. I looked out the lone basement window and said aloud to my missing father-in-law, "Quinn, you sonofabitch. Thank you...wherever you are."

43.

The Overlord complex was teeming with activity. There was an organized hustle and bustle as we walked through sections of the former prison. Cells were being cleaned and renovated into living quarters. Boxes of food and water were being loaded into the enormous kitchen. Holding and visitation areas were being overhauled into classrooms. One thing that was glaringly obvious, in more ways than one, was the electricity. Lights. Motorized tools. A constant hum of current that had been missing from my ears for so long. Lefty had power.

Our group was led through a labyrinth of long hallways until we reached a vast round chamber that I assumed was the center of the facility. Waiting for us there were three individuals who reminded me of our traveling companions. Maybe a little older, but still youthful. Two men and a woman. Although they weren't in uniform, they were sharply dressed in a military style.

The man standing in the center spoke first. "Good afternoon. My name is Daniel. And this," he said as he spread his arms, "is Camp Overlord. We're glad you have joined us. As you've seen, there are many like you here. Preparing. As you will." He looked to the man standing at his left. "Greg will show you to your rooms. There will be an orientation meeting in one hour, here." A warm smile appeared on his face. "Welcome, to all of you. And thank you."

I decided it was best then to let Daniel know that I wasn't there for the war they were getting ready to wage. "Excuse me, Daniel? A quick word?" He nodded and motioned me over to the side. "With all due respect, my children and I are not here to fight. We just need a night's rest, maybe two. We've got a wife and mother back home, and we need to get back to her."

"Of course," Daniel responded. "Of course. You look like you could use a shower and a night in a bed, at the very least. Come to the orientation, and afterwards you can tell me exactly why you're out here. After all, it's a dangerous world these days. I'd be interested in hearing why you're out in the thick of it."

We attended the orientation that evening with twenty-eight other people who had arrived at Camp Overlord in the past two days. The meetings were held three times a week to accommodate what had become a daily flow of recruits into the camp. Daniel was there, but the forum was directed by the woman who had been at our introduction earlier. Her name was Anna, she said, and her job was information. Collecting it, analyzing it, and using it. Each Lefty camp had an information specialist. She was Overlord's.

Anna was business-like and went about her lecture as a college history professor would have. "So, today you learn the basic story of ANTI-. Who they are and what they control. As you train, there will be classes on their formation, their systems of power, and, of course, our plans to dismantle them. But that's later. Let's talk now about exactly what we're facing.

"ANTI- consists of approximately 62 million people across the globe, with roughly 18 million of those here in the United States. The ANTs are fiercely loyal to their movement. They are also disciplined and patient. The organization is structured much like an army would be. Layers of command with decisions distributed downward. A pyramid of power, with one man at the top.

"That man is Salvador Sebastian. You may have heard of him. The mainstream had become aware of his existence just before the Great Dark began. In fact, the media made him seem quite likable. There is no doubt that he is highly intelligent. And highly influential. His intentions when he formed ANTI- were to take the world, the human race, back to zero. To take away human controls: government, money, technology, and so on. He did just that. But by taking the controls away, he left a power vacuum that only he could fill. We now believe that was his plan all along.

"Sebastian and ANTI- are headquartered in the United States. Our intelligence tells us somewhere in the northeast corridor, but we are still awaiting confirmation on that. We do know that close proximity to metropolitan centers are essential to their operations. And we know that Sebastian is heavily involved in the day-to-day activities and decisions of ANTI-. But he also has a tight-knit circle of directors on which he relies.

"His right-hand man is Jacob Marsh, an expert in computers who went by the name MARSaHacks in the former tech world. We've learned that Marsh was the mastermind behind the global computer crash that brought about the Great Dark. We also know that Marsh created an internal ANTI- network for Salvador that was up and running as the rest of us fell into chaos." She hesitated, and then acknowledged our astonishment. "Yes, they are still connected."

Anna stopped to drink from her glass of water. She was also using the break to let us absorb the information she had given us. One young man sitting near the front of the room took the opportunity to ask a question. "How do you know all of this stuff about them?" His query had a tone of disbelief.

"Stuff?" Anna responded. "We know this *stuff* because we've been working. And digging. Because for the past eight months we've been recruiting analysts and interrogators and hackers of our own." The question had inspired a fiery reaction, but she calmed herself enough to explain. "ANTI- used years and years of underground tactics to build a revolution. There are tens of millions of ANTs in the world. And they are well-organized. And they are well-trained." She was pacing now. "But we are forming our own army. And *we* are organizing, and *we* are training." She stopped in front of the recruit who had regretfully asked the question. "This *stuff*, as you put so eloquently, just might save your life."

Daniel stepped in to save the young man from any more humiliation. "Anna, everyone!" he announced as he clapped his hands together. "Thank you, Anna," he said to her, and she moved to the side of the room. Daniel continued, "And that's what we know. Over sixty-million people worldwide. A dynamic leader. A brilliant programmer. A perfect storm." He was working the room like a motivational speaker. "And then there's the rest of us. In the dark and out of touch. Left to tear each other apart in the name of survival. Well, we've said no. And you have, too, by joining us." By then, Daniel was standing at the center of the room. He crossed his arms and took a deep breath. "Salvador Sebastian stole our world from us. We're here to steal it back."

44.

Meg was depressed for a while after we settled in at the farm. Truth be told, we all were. But Meg especially. And her cancer drug's side-effects weren't helping. The first two months of medication wreaked havoc on her organs while her body adjusted to its changing chemical balances. It had been the same as the treatments before, except this time we had added pressure. Her father's strange disappearance, the tumor steadily wrapping itself around her spine, and the Great Dark. It was almost too much for her.

I tried to distract the kids the best I could, and we fell into a routine of sorts. Very quickly, we focused on endurance. What it was going to take for us to make it in our new world. Without acknowledging it, the three of us knew we had to adapt. We didn't ever talk about the alternative.

Basic survival comes down to three things, really: shelter, water, and food. The first two were thankfully under control. We had the house, a solid brick structure built in the 1950s. Quinn had always paid a staff well to maintain it throughout the years, so I felt confident that it was in good condition. And there was the spring at the back of the property, about a half-mile behind the house. With it and the supply of bottled water that Quinn had stocked, hydration wasn't a concern.

Food, on the other hand, was always on my mind. As the days became weeks without any change to our situation, I began to realize how important it was going to be to provide for ourselves. Sure, we had canned goods in the basement, but that wouldn't last forever. We had to become farmers. And hunters.

Quinn's garden was large, and he had planted it with an array of vegetables. He had also built a chicken coop and housed it with ten hens and a rooster. And the farm itself occupied a significant amount of land, containing all kinds of animal life. Now understand, I was never a hobby gardener or a hunter for sport. But necessity will force the learning curve straight every time.

The kids and I attended to the food growing underneath and out of the ground, harvesting when we guessed the time was right. And we taught ourselves to use the shotguns and rifles that Quinn had left for us. First, with targets of bottles and cans. Then, with the smaller animal life we could track. Rabbits and turkeys. Fortunately, Henry had read somewhere in his independent studies about cleaning animals for cooking. And after a few kills, we became fairly skilled at preparing meat. Soon enough, we were hunting boar and deer, and living off the land.

45.

The kids and I met with Daniel after the orientation meeting. I asked if Jeff could join us, as I planned that he would be involved in our excursion to the hospital complex the next day. I had also grown to like Jeff a lot, and I thought it might give him a chance to impress Camp Overlord's leader. I could foresee Jeff becoming an integral piece of the liberation effort.

I related our journey and the reason for it in detail to Daniel. Meg's cancer, its creeping death, the desperation to get more life-saving medication. He listened with intent and concern. Some people have a natural compassion for others. I sensed that Daniel honestly cared for our situation.

"But I can't let you go," he said when I finished.

I was confused at first. "Excuse me?"

"I can't let you go to the hospital."

"I'm not sure that you understand, Daniel," I responded hastily. "I'm not asking for permission here. We've got our own agenda, and it has nothing to do with all of this…"

He broke in, speaking calmly. "Hang on, Gordon. I'm just trying to protect you. And your kids. The city is under ANTI-'s control. And you can bet they've got the hospital on lockdown. What you're proposing is just too dangerous. I can't let you do it."

I didn't know what to say. I was feeling the beginnings of anger brewing inside me. I wished I had never agreed to stay the night at the camp. We had been on our own for months now. I should've known better. I was about to stand and direct the kids to get ready to leave when Jeff spoke up.

"Daniel, you're not gonna be able to stop this man." He said it boldly, matter-of-factly. "We've been traveling together for a while now, and I think I know him well enough to say that there's no stopping him. But hear me out, because I've got an idea."

Daniel was shaking his head before Jeff got the last word out of his mouth. "No way, not happening. Too risky, guys."

"No, Daniel, listen. I can get us into the complex, without a fight." Jeff looked around, and then he leaned in as if to tell us all a secret. "You see, it's my brother. Paul. He's one of them. He's an ANT."

46.

Henry found the old stereo receiver our first week at the farm. It was at the bottom of a closet in his grandfather's office. He took it apart and reassembled it as he had with so many other electronics in our garage before. Using metal coat hangers for antennas, he transformed the receiver into a low-frequency tuner that could pick up signals from great distances. It became our only contact with the outside world.

The broadcasts were steady at first, with television and radio stations in the larger cities using the generator power they had prepared for disasters, natural or otherwise. After those resources were depleted, reports became irregular. Sometimes we went days without hearing anything. I developed a new respect for the journalists that were brave enough to keep us informed during that bleak time. What we learned was disheartening. Eventually it turned horrific.

ANTI-'s hold on the country, and the world, was centralized to the largest metropolitan areas. In the United States, that equated to around twenty-five cities. There were certain power grids in those cities that ANTI- kept online. These grids were cleared so that only ANTs had access, and they were heavily guarded. Selective electricity is an unbelievably powerful system of control.

Reports of skirmishes on the edges of the ANTI-strongholds began to surface. People by themselves, then small disorganized groups, tried to break through. But ANTI-'s defenses were strong. Heavy equipment seized from militarized police departments protected each grid's borders. The ANTs were merciless, killing anyone who approached. One reporter described a group of teenage boys who rushed the ANTI- line in Chicago with just baseball bats and golf clubs. The ANTs ripped them apart with .50-caliber machine guns. Their bodies lay in the street all night, their families afraid to get close enough to retrieve them.

We waited for the day when a broadcast would come through announcing ANTI-'s defeat at the hands of our government, our soldiers. Instead, we heard stories of mass military infiltration. For years, ANTs had joined the Army, Air Force, Navy, and Marines in the United States, as well as military organizations in countries all over the world. It was part of the grand plan, to be ingrained with enough soldiers to overtake the leadership once the Great Dark began. The colonels and generals of the world had never prepared for such a coup. I think we all had a blind dependence on our governments to protect us, even in their incompetence and lethargy. ANTI- exploited both and left us all helpless.

47.

Jeff's brother Paul was recruited into the ANTI- organization as a teenager. His story was compelling. It became the foundation of our strategy to save Meg.

Paul had first been introduced to ANTI- as a freshman in high school. Jeff, the classic over-achieving older brother, had left for college on a basketball scholarship that year after graduating with honors. Paul, on the other hand, struggled with his studies and had no interest in sports. He fought to find an identity outside of Jeff's very long shadow.

He had always been good with computers. Always won at video games against his friends, then against the broad online community. It was during a late-night gaming session when he met Gustav, an older gamer from across an ocean. They hit it off immediately and started gaming together often. Gustav was smart, and cool, and accomplished at the game to which they were both addicted.

After a few weeks, Gustav began to talk about a different online group. Not a gaming group, but something bigger. He made it sound exclusive and exciting. He said he could maybe get Paul inside, if they'd even consider him. Paul was intrigued.

His meeting with ANTI- was set up inside a private chat room. Paul, Gustav, and two other older guys. Paul was young, but smart enough to know that they were profiling him. Questions about his parents and siblings, about school and friends. They were interrogating him, but he didn't mind. He liked it. He liked the idea of it all. A secret online society, with an exclusive worldwide membership.

Paul was soon invited to join the anonymous group, agreeing to the oath that was presented to him as part of his initiation. Something about commitment to the cause, affecting wholesale change to the way humans exist. He found it all a bit overdramatic, but he appreciated the general philosophy. If he could be part of something big enough to flip the human race on its head, he was in.

He and Gustav remained close over the next three years. As Paul neared high school graduation and began considering college, he confided to Gustav that he was thinking of leaving ANTI- behind. After all, he needed to be focusing on his own life, his own path. ANTI- had been a fun distraction from the banality of high school, but where was it all leading? Gustav was flabbergasted at first, but eventually expressed understanding for Paul's hesitations to continue in the organization. Then, Gustav's tone turned foreboding. He warned Paul that ANTI-'s grand plan was soon to be set in motion, maybe within the year. He didn't think it was a good idea for Paul to leave, especially at that time.

Whether it was curiosity or fear or a combination of both, Paul decided to remain with the group. He would keep a low profile, which wouldn't be hard. He had never progressed farther than entry-level status in the organization anyway. Whenever a protest was planned, he was the last to find out. After all, the information stream was a vital component to ANTI-'s surprise tactics. An attack that may have been months or years in design wouldn't be revealed to lower-level ANTs sometimes until a few hours before it was to be executed. With his basic position in the organization, Paul would be able to live his life outside ANTI- for the next year or so while still maintaining his membership. Under the radar. That way he could verify what Gustav was telling him.

It was close to the end of his first college year when Paul had his last conversation with Gustav. It was the longest one they had ever had. Gustav informed Paul of all he knew. Of the planned shutdown and subsequent takeover. Of the role he would play in Berlin's electrical re-sourcing. Gustav was ecstatic and nervous. Paul acted the same, but knew his days with ANTI- were done. He wished Gustav luck and said he would see him on the other side of the revolution. Three days later, the Great Dark was underway.

Paul never reported to his final assignment. His orders came through an encrypted email less than 24 hours before the first shutdowns started. He imagined that a lot of ANTs got lost in the shuffling confusion of that day and never showed up to participate. He wasn't concerned that they missed him, and he felt confident he could still get inside their circle. He remembered all of the passwords to access his ANTI-email account. But he needed some sort of connection to ANTI-'s internal server.

"I think we can handle that," Anna said from over Daniel's shoulder. She had joined the group to hear Paul's story. Probably to verify its authenticity, too. She stood over all of us with her arms crossed. "We've hacked our way into their system. At this point, all we do is watch, look, spy. But we can send an email." She pointed at Paul. "You just need to make sure it conveys the right message."

"I know what to say," Paul retorted. "As long as they haven't changed their email protocols, then I know what to say."

"Well, there's a good chance that they have," Daniel said, thinking. "But it's the best shot we've got." He turned to look at me. "Gordon, maybe we can make this mission work for both of us. Let my guys come up with a good plan, and you've got my support. Give me a day?"

I had calmed myself while Paul told his story. I had also come to my senses about what we were facing. We were going to need all the help we could get. "Ok," I said. "And I'm sorry. Just help me save my wife."

"I will. I promise," Daniel said with confidence. He stood from his seat and announced to the group, "We've got 36 hours to make this work. Get on it."

48.

After three months of darkness, we tried to ration the cancer medication to make it last as long as possible. Dr. Raj had given us enough to make it six months. Once we were halfway through what he had allotted, we decided it was best to adjust. There was less and less news coming through Henry's homemade tuner, and none of it was good. It seemed like we were living the new normal. Like the Great Dark was here to stay, at least for longer than we could have ever imagined.

The only gauge we had for Meg's battle occurring within was how she felt. She had fought it once before, so we relied on her memories and her level of pain. She remembered the progression of her first disease and the way her body reacted and felt as she began to defeat it. After three months of daily medication, she was better, stronger. We cut the dosage in half to give her body another six months. She kept feeling better. And stronger. But time started to move against her quickly.

As the number of pills dwindled to just a few, we talked options. As if there were any. I guess it was more like we talked preparation. Meg said she felt almost as good as the day she was declared cancer-free the first time. But her manner betrayed how she was truly feeling. I knew the tumor was still there. All we had done was diminish it. But it was still there. The looming questions formed: would it come back once the medicine left her bloodstream? And if it did, how long would it take?

It wasn't two weeks before Meg started to weaken. Once the tumor came back, it came back with a vengeance. Almost as if it knew Meg was completely defenseless. She wasn't going to survive without medical help. That became painfully obvious.

I came up with the plan over a sleepless two nights. It was really the only plan there was. But I had to make sure I wasn't overlooking something. Something easier, less dangerous. But there wasn't anything else to do. More medicine was her only chance.

Meg and I discussed it over a long breakfast on a quiet, beautiful morning. She was relatively pain-free when she woke up that day. She resisted my idea at first. But the reality of the situation soon took over. I told her we weren't a family without her in it. I told her the kids still needed their mother, maybe now more than ever. I told her that she was the love of my life. And that, ultimately, I would rather die trying to save her than give up and give in.

We cried and we sat in silence for a long time. Then I told her how I planned to save her.

49.

Camp Overlord's strategic planners had the mission drawn up by noon the day after Paul's revelations about ANTI-. Daniel called a meeting to review it with everyone who was to be involved: the kids and me, Paul, Jeff, Anna, and six other Lefty soldiers who would provide reconnaissance and support. While the plan was simple and direct, it was going to require seamless execution to work.

Daniel informed us at the beginning of the meeting that things had already been set in motion earlier that day. Paul had sent an encrypted email through ANTI-'s darknet system using the network connection that Lefty had established at Overlord. His message, while brief, described a sophisticated yet fictional cover story:

ID: 2-370-552
SECTOR: NA-3
ACCESS CODE: 909487

April 30

At receipt of this email, please acknowledge. I have been traveling for weeks after recovering from injuries sustained in the initial revolt. I have companions with me, sympathetic to the cause, as I still am. They are my cousin, a female, and her two adolescent children. They are trustworthy.

I am within 10 miles of Sector 3's home base. I intend to seek refuge and admittance for myself and my companions into the base's active power grid. We will be approaching tomorrow from the east highway. Please instruct.

I hijacked power and network access from an unknown source to send this message, so I will encrypt per ANTI- protocol that was in place prior to the revolution. I will check for acknowledgement and instructions before sunset.

FtSoH

It was a brilliant communication, giving a valid reason for his long absence and setting up an "in" for Anna and the kids. And whoever validated his credentials within the ANTI- organization would know that he was computer savvy enough to be able to send a message with little resources. What made it all the more brilliant was that it worked.

"We received a return transmission two hours after Paul's was sent," Anna told us. "It includes instructions for the four of us - Paul, Henry, Jessica, and myself - to meet an ANTI- unit at the northwestern corner of the grid tomorrow morning. That corner is three blocks from the pharmaceutical building that holds your wife's medicine." She glanced at me as she said this with a half-smile on her face, then tried to reassure me about utilizing my children but not me for the infiltration. "Gordon, we think your kids will help defuse the ANTs' suspicion of our group. And any easing of tensions that we can use to our advantage, we'll take."

She continued to the rest of the group. "The purpose of this mission is two-fold. First, we will attempt to get inside the pharmaceutical facility and gather the necessary medicine. Henry and Jessica, make sure you know exactly what you need. I doubt we will have a lot of time inside. Second, I will be collecting as much information as possible about ANTI-'s operations inside that base.

"We fully expect an interrogation after we arrive, and they will most likely separate us to do that. The four of us will use the rest of today reviewing our cover stories and learning the layout of that medical complex. Gordon and Jeff - you, Daniel, and six of our people will set up overnight in groups of three along the eastern perimeter of the grid. You will have equipment to watch as we approach. You will have weapons, but only as a last resort. If this turns into a gunfight, we won't win. Remember that."

Daniel stepped in. "This operation should take less than 24 hours to complete. We believe that the majority of ANTI-'s security forces will be positioned along the outside of the grid, especially after nightfall. That means that the pharmaceutical building, *inside* the grid, should be accessible overnight. Once the group has the necessary medicine, it will be time to escape. We will handle the aftermath, although we do not expect any retaliation. We believe that their knowledge of us is limited, and we predict that they will pass Anna and the others off as a rogue crew looking for some free drugs."

I had listened patiently and silently as Anna and Daniel presented the mission. I knew deep down that it was the most logical way to get inside, and I also realized that there was no stopping what had already begun. But my paternal instincts were kicking in. I couldn't put this much responsibility on Jessica and Henry alone. I should be with them. "Daniel, isn't there some way for me to go inside, too?" I pleaded. "I can't let them do this on their own."

He walked over to me and knelt down to my eye level. "The wheel is already turning, Gordon," he said. "There's no reversing it now."

"I know, I know..." I said in desperation. Then I felt a hand on my shoulder, and I turned to see Jessica and Henry standing behind me, their maturity beginning to betray their young age.

"Don't worry, Dad," Jessica said. "We got this. For Mom."

"Yeah, Dad," Henry followed up. "Triumphs for Mom. Triumphs forever."

50.

The most difficult part of leaving Meg was leaving Meg alone. On her own to fight her cancer, and to fight off the silent, dark world closing in around her.

The kids had to come with me. Meg wasn't able enough to protect them, and they weren't old enough to protect themselves. At least, that's what I had thought at the time. We decided that if someone came to the house while we were gone, Meg would just play dead. Let them take what they wanted. And once they came to the bedroom, they certainly wouldn't bother with a dead Meg. We had a good laugh that it wouldn't take much of an acting job on her part. Cancer jokes. Sometimes they were all we had to get through the sadness.

Henry and I moved five crates of food and water from the basement up to the master bedroom that would become Meg's sanctuary after we left. We surrounded the bed with books and old magazines. I also had Henry relocate the radio tuner to her bedside table so that Meg could listen to any of the random broadcasts that might come through, if she wanted.

It was the best we could do. But without knowing how long the journey there and back would take, none of us knew if it would be good enough.

51.

I sat in with Jessica and Henry for most of the afternoon as they memorized their new identities and learned the layout of the hospital facilities. They would be using their same given names to reduce confusion, but their made-up back-stories were fairly elaborate to prepare for the possibility of a lengthy interrogation. My biggest concern was their safety. But as the day progressed and the plans were fleshed out, I felt better. As long as the four of them could earn the ANTs' trust, it should be a simple job. The only unknown variable was the building that held the medicine. They wouldn't know how it was secured until they were inside the grid. If it was guarded, access would be impossible.

When the afternoon transitioned into evening, Anna reviewed the mission with the group one last time. Then we broke to get a few hours of rest. She instructed us to rendezvous at 11 PM in the central prison hall. That would give us enough time to hike to the grid and stake out observation posts for the three surveillance teams before dawn. The kids and I went to our living quarters.

As we closed our eyes to try and sleep an impossible sleep considering what lay before us, I asked Jessica and Henry a simple question. "Are you guys ready?"

"I think so," Jessica said.

Then Henry said something introspective and prescient. "I'm pretty sure we could never be ready for something like this, because we don't really know what we face. We can prepare all we want, but the only thing we should truly be ready for is the unexpected."

Some may have viewed the number in our party as unlucky: 13. I even had a fleeting moment of superstitious fear myself. Fleeting because I had confidence in the people that Daniel had assembled. Anna was a picture of conviction and stoicism. Clichés and grammar be damned, she was a force to be reckoned with. And then there were the six Lefty soldiers that would provide support. Disciplined yet good-natured and friendly. They were able to keep the kids somewhat relaxed on the journey to the grid.

Daniel and Anna had codenamed the mission *Triumphant Return*, taking a cue from our family nickname. I had told them the story of the Triumphs after Henry mentioned it earlier in the day. They appreciated the sentiment, just as they had grown to appreciate our dire situation. Still, I knew we were both a reason to go inside and a justification. I just didn't know how much the justification would outweigh the reason if the mission started to fall apart.

We made good time traveling overnight. Within a few miles of Camp Overlord, the trees and brush started to dissipate as peripheral gas stations and strip malls began to appear. The road was empty, as were the buildings that we passed. An eerie quiet filled the vacant streets. I had been insulated from society for so long that the tall buildings and city blocks seemed alien to me as we trekked briskly toward our destination.

The glow from ANTI-'s powered grid had been visible from the edge of the city. But as we got closer, we could actually feel it. Man-made heat and buzz. The uneasiness about the mission that I had worked so hard to quell throughout the night was becoming harder to deny.

Two blocks from the grid's border, Daniel stopped us. He guided us up the steps and under the canopy of a towering office building, maybe thirty stories high. It was black dark, but a clear night. The moon provided enough light for us to see each other in close proximity. He directed two of his soldiers to move toward the grid and locate good vantage points in the block next to it. The rest of us would wait.

Anna took the opportunity to go over the plan with Paul, Jessica, and Henry for the final time. She asked each one of them to tell their fictional history. Not as a list of facts, but as a tale you might tell a new friend or a first date. The kids weren't nervous, which made me feel a little less apprehensive. Even so, I didn't know how I was going to calm myself once they disappeared into the ANTI--controlled area later that morning. I knew it was going to be the longest 24 hours of my life, but I could never have predicted just how endlessly grim that day was going to be.

52.

Jessica, Henry, and I used the morning on the day before we left the farm to pack. Tent, sleeping bags, extra sets of socks and pants and shirts, jackets, flashlights, two pairs of binoculars, and as much canned food as we could manage. We also cleaned and prepared the guns, planning to take all of them except for one pistol. I placed it in the top drawer of Meg's bedroom nightstand. Just in case her acting wasn't so good after all.

That afternoon, I prepared the meat from two rabbits that the kids had hunted earlier at dawn. I gathered and chopped some carrots and potatoes, along with a selection of herbs from our garden. After building a fire in one of Quinn's old barbeque pits, I added the ingredients into a mixture of flour, water, and oil. To finish it off, a half a bottle of red wine from Quinn's vast collection, something I had happily discovered the second week of our stay there. My own version of rabbit stew, which had become a specialty of mine.

Meg summoned enough energy to join us downstairs for a final family meal before our expedition. She ate as much as she could, and complimented my cooking. But her appetite was fading. That wasn't a good sign, and made the urgency of our trip that much more intense.

She and I held each other as we slept that night, both of us wondering if that would be our last together. I was up and dressed before daybreak. I woke the kids, then went outside to start a fire and cook some eggs. We ate breakfast in silence, knowing the inevitable departure was minutes away. When we finished, I told Jessica and Henry to go tell their mother good-bye. Then I did the same.

I held on to the image of Meg in her bed that morning. I willed my brain to recall it every night before I fell asleep. It was a very specific reminder of why we were on the journey. And as the sun rose on that empty city the day I let my children go into the hands of unknown danger, I closed my eyes and imagined Meg again. Except this time she was healthy and strong and happy. And in all my worry and trepidation, I had a brief moment of relief. And I knew that we were going to save her life.

53.

We split up at 5 AM. The nine of us that were in support roles needed to use the cover of remaining darkness to establish our positions. Although the group of four that were set to infiltrate the ANTI-stronghold wouldn't be making contact for another two hours, it was time to separate.

I gave Jessica and Henry each a deep hug, and they both squeezed back. I huddled them up with me and did all I knew to do: I gave them a pep talk, the old coach in me coming out again. "Alright, guys, go-time. You've only got each other on this one. Grow eyes in the back of your heads, and for the love of God watch out for one another. And if you get yourself in a fix, run. Don't think, just run. Understand?"

They both nodded. I saw tears beginning to form in the corners of Jessica's eyes. "No time for tears, Jess," I directed, as hard as that was to do. "Focus on the mission. This is for Mom. This is for us." I kneeled down so that I could see their faces from underneath their bowed heads. "I'll be right above you, guys. Don't forget that. Triumphs forever."

Daniel came over and interrupted us. "Gotta go, Gordon." I nodded once in recognition. Then he said to the kids, "Listen, guys, you're doing a brave thing today. You should feel proud. And don't worry. We'll have eyes on the grid at all times."

We said our "I love yous" and hugged one more time. And then, with reluctance, I was off.

Daniel stationed us in three different venues, varying in height along the northern half of the western border of ANTI-'s territory. I was at a point closest to the planned meeting site, on the fifth floor of a former office building, with Daniel and another soldier. The other two teams were positioned south of us, each with a different sight line. Each group had three sets of high-powered binoculars plus an observation telescope and tripod.

The sunrise was beautiful that morning. Its gradual brightening revealed to us the number of ANTs stationed along the border that we were facing. There were a dozen of them at each intersection, which they had blocked with military-style all-terrain vehicles. These were all black in color with .50-caliber machine guns mounted to the top of them. They appeared to be former police vehicles, with many city departments having purchased this type of equipment from government surplus in the years before the Great Dark. The ANTs themselves were dressed in urban camouflage, the gray- and black- and white-pixeled sort. They carried assault rifles at their chests, and their faces were hidden behind black goggles and masks.

At the northwestern corner, where they had directed Paul and the others to meet them, there was a gathering of twenty ANTs and two large cargo vans. It was as if they were preparing for an ambush. But I thought to myself after seeing their defenses that you'd have to be a fool to attack them. I was feeling that uneasiness again.

We didn't have a good visual of Paul and Anna and the kids until they were across the street from the grid. They approached the opposite corner with their hands raised and walked slowly, deliberately. They stopped on the double yellow line in the middle of the street and lowered themselves to their knees, obviously instructed to do so by the ANTs, even though we couldn't hear what they were saying. I tried to see if Jessica and Henry were trembling through my binoculars, but they seemed calm. That was all about to change.

Four of the ANTs walked toward them until they were a few feet away. The ANT standing in front of Paul drew a pistol from his side and moved closer. He put the end of the barrel against Paul's forehead and started speaking, aggressively. I wished that I could hear what was being said. My uneasiness was transforming into fear.

Paul seemed to be responding to questions that were being asked, one after another. This lasted for maybe two minutes, but it felt like a lifetime. Finally, the questioning appeared to stop. The ANT holding the gun against Paul's head glanced to the others and said something. And it was in the next few moments that I understood the reality of true terror. As Daniel held me back from jumping out of a five-story window to get to my children. As Paul was shot at point blank range, the back of his head flying away from the rest of his body. And as Anna and Jessica and Henry were hooded, shackled, and dragged to the awaiting vans, to be transported into a hell that I had commissioned.

PART TWO: MOMENTUM

1.

It was a blue room, small with no windows, sixteen feet by twenty. There was a single light bulb hanging from a cord that disappeared into a hole in the center of the ceiling. It was bigger than normal-sized bulbs, and it emitted a large amount of light that was soft and natural. It illuminated every corner of the room, and brightened the shade of ocean blue that covered the four walls. The room was empty except for two chairs, comfortable yet sturdy. Jacob Marsh had been sitting in one of them for twenty-three minutes when Salvador Sebastian entered through the solitary doorway.

2.

Simone Vincent was stunning. Jacob could see that from across the coffee-house - angular and lean with long jet-black hair and lightly-olive skin. She possessed that rare mix of beauty, confidence, style, and allure that few women could wrangle together and keep subtle enough to maintain intrigue. But there was also a streak of bitterness that ran through her core, invisible to others. It was born out of childhood tragedy, and fostered by contempt of corrupt authority. She kept it tamped underneath the rest, but it was always there.

She had first contacted Jacob online. It was virtually the only way he communicated then, keeping himself hidden from the outside world by choice. She wanted to meet him in person to discuss a business opportunity. She had seen his work, and she was impressed. Anyone who knew anything about computer-hacking at that time was impressed with the work Jacob Marsh was doing.

He agreed to meet her over a cup of coffee just around the corner from his apartment in one of the hundreds of coffee-houses that had seemingly appeared overnight in his Seattle neighborhood. He didn't mind the caffeinated entrepreneurial uprising that had been occurring around him. Coffee was lifeblood for him then, as he spent days-long hack benders creating viruses and unleashing them on the unsuspecting infantile Internet. When Simone contacted him, Jacob didn't know what to think. He didn't even know how she found out who or where he was. In the end, that's what enticed him to meet her in person.

"Simone, I assume?" he asked sheepishly as he walked up to her table. His go-to tactic with women was to approach them with a self-effacing demeanor. It made things much easier if they had dropped their guard. Jacob did very well with women, regardless of his occupational stereotype. He was the rare basement-dwelling computer guru with charm and charisma. Often in life, there are two sides to every coin.

"Yes," she answered, as she looked up from the newspaper she had been pretending to read. She revealed her astonishment in his appearance through a brightening in her eyes. He was boyishly attractive, with shaggy hair and strong cheekbones. "Jacob?" Her questioning nature revealed her astonishment even more.

"That's right," he said, as he sat down across from her.

She collected herself. "Forgive me. Mr. Marsh, I should say. Thank you for joining me."

He leaned his back into the top of the chair and slid down until he was comfortable. "No problem. But after all, it was you who made the trip all the way up here. Maybe I should be thanking you. Or maybe I should wait and see what this is all about first."

She folded up her newspaper. "Well, Mr. Marsh, I'm not one to beat around the bush," she said directly. She never understood the need for small talk. Neither did he. "My employer has been watching your online activities for quite some time now. And he likes what he sees."

"What exactly do you mean by 'online activities,' Miss Vincent?"

"Let's not play any games here, Mr. Marsh." She was regaining her conversational footing, shaking off her initial surprise and attraction to Jacob's appearance. He knew that she was accustomed to being the intimidating woman in a situation like this. She couldn't hide it from him. He didn't want her to.

"Ok, so let's say you know what it is that I do. How exactly do you know that?" He was not typically apprehensive, but this had become downright mysterious.

"My employer is deeply involved in your sort of business. He is constantly searching for new talent to recruit. You are talented. Very talented." She had begun charming him. "If you have an interest in taking your skills to another level - in getting out of the basement, so to speak - he would like to meet with you." She was clever. She could compliment and insult in the same breath.

"I need verification that this isn't a setup," he said. "There's plenty of talk going around about the FBI taking interest in our 'sort of business,' as you say." He leaned in and asked with a wink, "You FBI, honey?"

She smiled, then reached down into her handbag. She slid a letter-sized envelope across the table to him. "I have a feeling that you'll be able to answer that on your own soon enough, Mr. Marsh." She stood up and gathered her things. "Please contact us as soon as possible. Our project is moving forward rather swiftly."

And with that, she turned and made her way to the coffee-house's exit. He watched her walk until she was out of sight.

3.

Jacob Marsh taught himself code. That and everything else that comes with being a super-hacker: software, programming, and so on. He was, in a word, a natural.

His high school was the first in his city to install a computer lab and create a course teaching computer science. Mr. Sutcliff, fresh out of college with a mathematics degree and duly assigned to instruct the class, knew almost nothing about the new technology. He tried to learn just as the small handful of students who signed up for the extra-curricular program did. They would stay an hour after the last bell every day and experiment with the primitive machines. It was barely enough time to even get them up and running.

But before long, good fortune turned Jacob's way. For it was that school year's would-have-been scandal that he and his best friend Bobby agreed to conceal that truly opened the computer world up to him.

It all started quite innocently, just the two friends leaving their gym class early one day to talk with Mr. Sutcliff about getting some extra time in the lab. But when they arrived at his classroom, an opportunity presented itself. The door was barely open, enough to see and hear what was happening inside. And what they witnessed became an early lesson in the harsh reality of the world that Jacob was just beginning to understand.

The beautiful Brooke Landers, senior cheerleader and queen of the school's drastically broad social spectrum, was failing Mr. Sutcliff's Algebra 2 course. Jacob and Bobby could hear the conversation clearly. But she couldn't afford to fail, she said. She had to graduate, she pleaded. She would do anything, she promised. It was a subtle offer that Mr. Sutcliff would accept. And Jacob knew it.

Bobby distracted Mr. Sutcliff the next afternoon during lab while Jacob placed the two miniature video cameras on either side of the classroom, both facing the teacher's desk. He had picked them up a year or so earlier at a local spy shop. The images they were set to record would be grainy, but they'd be good enough for the boys' purposes.

They recorded the sexual favors Brooke gave Mr. Sutcliff in return for better math grades for two weeks. It was more than enough evidence – the trysts occurred almost daily. When they presented the teacher with the tapes, he was frozen in shock. They could've gotten him to do anything. But all Jacob wanted was a key. To the school. And to the computer lab.

4.

Jacob left the coffee-house quietly and rushed to get home and open the envelope. In it was a detailed but glossy description of Faultline Technologies, a company based in California. The company bio hit all the standard talking points, utilizing the buzzwords that every tech marketing department was using at the time. They had become the "benchmark" in "cyber-" and "micro-" and "e-" business, with a unique brand of "thinking outside the box." Jacob wasn't impressed until he dug deeper, delving into the numerical abyss of the Internet for answers, just as Salvador Sebastian had wanted.

Faultline had begun like so many dot-com startups in the 1990s, with one exception: a single investor. With solitary control, Sebastian was able to command the early destiny of his new company, keeping it small and focused. He hired two middle-of-the-class computer science students during their final year of graduate school, to teach him the basics of programming and develop the foundations upon which Faultline would be built. He gave them the freedom to explore the new world of electronic information, and they proved to be dynamic and creative programmers. Sebastian was perceptive – he had seen something in them besides their modest grade point average.

The small company grew rapidly, out-performing many of its competitors with limitless and aggressive web development. Within eighteen months, Sebastian had built a staff of fifteen developers, engineers, and programmers at Faultline. Within another year, that number was pushing one hundred. The more Jacob researched, the more impressed he became.

Faultline continued to gain momentum in America's growing technology sector throughout the last decade of the 20th century. Sebastian commissioned projects and contracts with both private corporations and government agencies. The company continuously re-invested its profits, while making Sebastian one of the wealthiest men in the country at the same time. He spent large amounts of his income on his own brand of philanthropy, developing technical institutes and computer science programs for less-than-privileged areas in America and beyond. His influence throughout the world was broad. Until 9/11 changed Faultline's direction and ultimately spurred Sebastian's exit.

Under contract with the NSA when mass-scale terrorism made its way across American borders, Faultline Technologies' government division transitioned from web security to enemy surveillance after 2001. The hastily-passed Patriot Act enabled the United States to gather information on suspected terrorists both inside the country and out after 9/11 - and Faultline became one of its most valuable tools. But as Jacob knew from personal experience, the definition of suspicion in the new millennium took on an entirely different meaning. Sebastian had found that out the hard way.

On paper, Sebastian sold his interest in Faultline Technologies in 2003. He had fought the NSA for over a year, doing all that he could to relieve the company from its contractual obligations, but they wouldn't relent. Faultline had become the means to both violent and unwarranted ends for so many. It was certainly enough reason for Sebastian to leave it all behind. But as Jacob continued investigating, he couldn't help but think there was something else to Sebastian's resignation. Something that he needed to conceal from the upgraded government scrutiny. He didn't completely disappear after he left Faultline, but any connection he had to the company was seemingly severed. Publicly, he retired to his California hillside home, selling his stock to a half-French, half-Algerian investor. Her name was Simone Vincent.

5.

Once Jacob and Bobby extorted after-hours access to the school from Mr. Sutcliff, they began a nightly ritual. They would sneak out of their houses and meet outside the school at nine o'clock, every weeknight and sometimes even on weekends. Jacob came and went as he pleased in those formative years. His father had abandoned him long before, and his mother was barely there herself. She was typically passed out by sundown every day after a happy-hour mix of vodka and Vicodin. Jacob was happier away from home, so he avoided it as much as he could.

Using Mr. Sutcliff's collection of keys, they had the run of the place. They would start their nights under the stars in the school's quad, smoking marijuana and drinking cheap beer. Occasionally, if they really wanted to see what the primitive processors could do, they would drop acid. But Jacob ultimately found LSD more distracting than mind-opening.

The two of them spent countless hours on the machines. They would stay in the computer lab almost all night, catch a couple of hours sleep before school, then power their way through the day's schedule of classes. High school-level curriculum was simple for Jacob. He never needed to study for taught classes. His real education came from overnight hours in an empty school. That is, until he and Bobby dropped one extra tab of acid that fateful spring night - and turned the place inside out.

It was Bobby's idea to vandalize the school, and even though Jacob still possessed the logic to know that it was wrong, he just didn't care. The large amount of LSD coursing through his body caused that non-reaction, the indifference. He never let himself forget about that side-effect.

The school's principal was obsessive about maintaining building decorum. So much so that even teachers found it distracting. Jacob always thought he was a man that valued appearance over substance. And he thought him weak because of it. The two friends began their destruction by dumping trash cans and ripping down homecoming and student election signs. Then Bobby found the paint supply in the second-floor maintenance closet. They didn't stop until the paint cans were empty. They streaked and coated the walls, floors, and ceilings. Abstract art in school-colored paint was everywhere.

Two months from graduation, authorities understandably expelled the boys. In order to avoid criminal charges, they were required by the judge to clean up the school, on weekends and under strict supervision. But the principal took things a step further. He recommended a three-month anger management course completion in order for them to receive their diplomas, and the school board supported him. In Jacob's mind, anger had nothing to do with it.

It took nine weekends for Jacob and Bobby to get the school back to normal. By then, the academic year had ended and graduation ceremonies had been performed. Bobby signed up for his anger management course and dutifully attended it. But Jacob refused. He didn't think the principal's extra punishment fit the crime. He had performed the proper reparations and suffered the equitable consequences. But he learned through the experience that life lessons sometimes come with a price. And that authority isn't always fair.

So he packed up the little that he needed to make it on his own and left. A metaphorical middle finger to the principal, the school board, and the society that was becoming so obtuse and illogical. Besides, having some paper saying that he had done this or that to whoever's satisfaction didn't matter to him. Not where he was heading.

6.

When Jacob learned that the woman he had met in his local coffee-house that morning was in actuality the head of Faultline Technologies, his intrigue grew exponentially. He had to know more about her.

Simone Vincent's story began on another continent, where she suffered immeasurable loss that shaped the road that would lead her to Salvador Sebastian. She was born in France to an Algerian mother. From what Jacob could find, her father was French military and most likely involved in covert operations. He was killed by a suicide bomber during a joint French-American support mission in Beirut in 1983. One truck bomb destroyed the U.S. barracks, another destroyed the French. Whatever may have been left of his body was never recovered.

The factual circumstances of her father's occupation, his assignment within the Beirut operation, and his untimely death were kept secret from Simone's mother. After he died, he was given neither acknowledgement nor commendation for his service, as the nature of his true business remained concealed deep in government files. Simone was born not long after, his only child. Out of frustration and anger, her mother moved her across the Atlantic to

Montreal, where they had Algerian relatives. To Simone's mother, it was the only place to start over for an immigrant widow whose country had no respect left for her dead husband.

Simone never knew anyplace as a child except for Quebec. She excelled in both school and society there. She attained full-ride scholarships to various Canadian universities, ultimately selecting Concordia in Montreal. She focused on political science and language studies, eventually speaking fluent Arabic along with her native French and adopted English. Deep down, she never let go of the father she only knew from pictures and romantic stories her mother would tell. She took a year after college to find him, and to uncover what happened to him in Beirut. She moved to Lebanon and hunted for answers, but was only left with more questions than before. The man and his mission would remain a mystery, and something that she would struggle with forever.

She left the Middle East exhausted, but ready to move forward in another direction. Whatever her motivation, Simone was consistent in her desire to achieve. Her previous undergraduate success earned her a select international scholarship to NYU's famed School of Law, where she continued her top-of-the-class performance. After graduation, she was recruited across the globe. Her language skills and school performance made her a highly attractive prospect to the largest and most dynamic organizations in the world. She had her choice in law, politics, and finance. She could have been an immediate vice president or fast-track partner. But she chose Faultline Technologies. Certainly not a bad option, but definitely a strange one. Sebastian must have offered her something beyond her highest expectations. It all left Jacob wondering.

Simone had intimated to him at their meeting that he would come calling, and soon. He picked up the phone and dialed her number first thing the next morning.

7.

Early computer games didn't interest Jacob the way they did so many others, but he played them in high school just the same. To him, the storylines were trite, the characters under-developed. But they were full of programming possibility, and programming had become his obsession. In sparse moments, he adventured through the elementary landscapes of medieval fantasy or futuristic badlands, all the while meeting other gamers online. Some of them he perceived as intellectual equals. And eventually those kindred minds introduced him to the gaming commune culture.

The communes closest to Jacob were up the coast, near Seattle proper. They were made up of teens and twenty-somethings with a shared interest in a video game or genre of game. Most of the communes consisted of eight to ten people, both men and women. That was one of the few aspects that attracted him. Living together in a house or condo, everyone would contribute to the expenses of life while endlessly playing the games they loved. Jacob considered it all a nerd version of 60s hippies. Not his style, but it gave him a place to land when he first stepped out on his own.

There were five men and four women in the "VW Compound." It had been named after the space-themed game *Vega Warning*, not a Volkswagen van, although that would have been fitting. The commune house was covered in tapestries for decoration and smelled of patchouli and marijuana. Jacob had met the head of the house online a few months earlier while playing the game. So when he decided to leave his hometown, he contacted the new friend, looking for a place to stay. "No problem, man," the gamer told him. "Just gotta pay your dues like the rest of us."

The others in the group welcomed Jacob with open arms. Soon enough, he was immersed in the collective's constant flow of gaming, drugs, and sex. He found himself most partial to the last activity in the list, but he kept up appearances by also playing the game as much as he could stand.

For money, Jacob had a plan. He contributed to the commune's expenses with an idea that he had concocted before he left high school. He had a friend who had graduated a year before him and moved north to Seattle. The friend was working in a music CD manufacturing plant in the city, which meant he had access to albums weeks before their record store release. His idea, to sell bootlegged CDs a week or more in advance, worked. Suburban teenagers were eager to pay a premium to have the exclusive music.

Jacob's trunk store music shop did better than he expected, in fact. And it also led him to a much bigger idea, although he wasn't the only one climbing that cerebral staircase.

When Jacob decided to leave the commune, two of the women went with him. They were young, and he was charming. Whatever they may have mistaken for love, it was enough for them to follow him. The three traveled into Seattle and found an apartment. He convinced them to support his musical experiment, with a huge payoff for all of them if it came to fruition. The girls worked and paid the bills, while Jacob programmed day and night.

The idea that he soon realized was not just his own was a computerized extension of the music he had been selling out of his car. When the music industry had shifted their focus to the cheapest-of-them-all compact disc, they had inadvertently created a much easier way to reproduce their product. They had digitized it. And Jacob was smart enough to take the next step.

By now, the story of Napster is digital history. Music in the form of downloads is the norm. But when Jacob first got to Seattle, the concept was outrageous. He worked tirelessly to construct a platform that could support the music files that he was able to transfer from CDs. But he couldn't quite do it in time. Not before Napster was everywhere.

He sulked for a long while. But then he decided to dig into the program that had beaten him, to seek out why it was better. For two months, he burrowed through it, looking into every coded corner. Then he tore it apart. He broke it down to see if he could. He wreaked numerical havoc and caused viral destruction. And what he learned was a simple truth on which he began to base his life: Jacob Marsh was meant not to create, but to destroy.

8.

Simone arranged for Faultline's private jet to pick Jacob up at a small regional airport outside of Seattle. He flew to California in modest luxury. She was waiting with a car when he landed.

"Mr. Sebastian will see you immediately," she told him as the car sped them away from the airport. "We will have someone take your luggage to the hotel...after we take you directly to Faultline."

Jacob didn't flinch. He knew this was probably part of a stress-test, the beginning of some new-wave interview process. But he wasn't there to interview. He was only there to relieve his curiosity. "No problem," he replied. "I'm looking forward to it."

The three-story building was a non-descript dark gray with mirrored windows across its face. One small sign that read "Faultline Technologies" stood just outside the main entrance. Most dot-coms and tech companies were ostentatious in their office structures. They inhabited lavish buildings with huge lettering at the top announcing their greatness to the world. For Jacob, they were yet another example of appearance over substance. But Faultline seemed different. *"At least Sebastian doesn't seem to be suffering from that form of delusional deceptiveness,"* he thought.

Simone led him through the small lobby and down a long hallway on the first floor. They stopped at the second-to-last door on the right.

"Are you ready?" she asked, wrapping her fingers around the metallic doorknob.

"Listen, Simone, this is all a bit dramatic, isn't it?" Jacob responded. "I mean, c'mon. You guys are taking yourselves a little too seriously."

She turned quickly, stopping with her face not more than six inches from his. "Why exactly do you think Sebastian brought you here?" She paused, but not long enough for him to answer. "This is more serious than you could ever imagine."

Then she opened the door to the small blue room.

Salvador Sebastian wore a charcoal gray suit, tailored to fit his tall slim body. The collar on his white button-down shirt was left open to the second button. His thick black hair and darkened skin left no question about his Latin-American heritage. The luck of being born with natural good looks has always been an advantage in society. When Salvador smiled as he entered the small blue room, Jacob felt very much at ease.

"Mr. Marsh," he said, with a casual air. "Such a pleasure to meet you. Let me say, I have admired you from afar for a long time now." The way he said these first words was with esteem, but they held a deeper meaning. He was informing Jacob that he had been able to surveil him, even as hidden as Jacob thought he had been.

"I see, Mr. Sebastian. My work precedes me. But that begs the question...how do you know that it's *my* work?" Jacob had recognized the veiled power-play, and his tone suggested that he would defend his secretive territory with vigor.

"Yes, Mr. Marsh, that is the question, isn't it? The best hacker in the country, if not the world. So good, in fact, that he is anonymous. Undercover. Utterly unknown. And yet, I found you." Sebastian sat down in the chair across from him. "First things first, Jacob, if I may call you that. I'm going to tell you exactly how and when I discovered your exploits. But under one condition." He raised an eyebrow and smirked.

Jacob relaxed in his chair and smiled. "And what condition would that be...*Salvador*?"

"That you listen to the rest of what I have to say, as far-fetched and wild-eyed as I may start to seem. That you allow yourself to think on a bigger scale than your mind has ever thought before. And that you accept the possibility that the entire world could be yours. Really, truly yours."

9.

Jacob could only assume that it was his two-month-long exploration into that first music file-sharing program that drove them away. The two women who had been supporting him were gone by the time he had satiated his destructive desires. If they had tried to say goodbye, he didn't notice. And, in the end, he didn't care. They were just a crutch for him by then, but their departure left him with a financial problem. He needed money to pursue his next computer endeavor, and he needed it fast.

He landed a telemarketing job that he could sleepwalk through, so that he could focus his off-time on hacking. It was horrendous work, inherently filled with abuse and rejection by way of constant hang-ups. But, more importantly, it was the two things that he needed it to be: mindless and anonymous.

His phone shift was weekday afternoons into evenings, from 2 PM until 10. He would hack at night, after work, until his eyes would begin to blur. After a few hours of sleep, he would pull his telephone shift, then back to the computer. Weekends were reserved for decompression, from hundreds of hang-ups and hours of hacking. And there was no better place in the world to decompress than Seattle. It was a city of rain, barbiturates, and experimental women. Jacob learned more in those few years of his existence than any college could have ever taught him.

After a year in the central call center, Jacob's manager allowed him to start working out of his apartment. In an industry where the average employment length was five weeks, he was the longest-tenured employee in the history of the company. So, he was given some personal freedoms. Once he was working from home, he was able to install his auto-dial program. It would make the phone calls based on the numbers he loaded into his computer at the beginning of each shift, using a pre-recorded introduction message. When a potential prospect would stay on the line for longer than 30 seconds, the program would sound an alert and Jacob would pick up the call. It was perfect for his greater goal. It gave him an additional eight hours a day to work on virus creation, encryption, and all of the other techniques a good hacker needed to have in his arsenal. Especially if he was going to hack his way to a fortune.

The computer scam that Jacob created in that time was simple in nature, and it eventually became commonplace within the hacking community. He never looked at it as stealing, because what he took wasn't important to him. In his mind, he was providing a service to the companies he was attacking by showing them just how unsecure their systems were. But showing them was just the beginning of the scam.

Jacob would build a virus specifically for the company he wanted to infiltrate, and that virus would mirror the company's systems administrator profile. It would act as that user. The same keystrokes, passwords, and so on. But it would hide itself, only logging into the system when that user was offline for long periods of time. Typically that would occur during overnight or weekend hours. Without someone investigating the logon times, the virus would appear to be operating just as the user might. But all the while, it was digging into the hard drives of presidents and vice presidents and CEOs and CFOs, slowly feeding bits and pieces back to its source: Jacob. Once he had copied the complete contents of the victim's hard drive onto one of his own, the virus was programmed to shut the system down, leaving no trace and no access.

It was a lucrative operation. Most black hats called it "hostage-taking," but Jacob justified his actions and slept quite well at night. He may have been demanding a ransom, but that didn't mean that he was going to hurt anyone. It was the fear of lost privacy, of secrets revealed no matter how trivial, that drove people to pay him. Most of the information he was able to obtain was company-related, but Jacob always believed the reason why those corporate giants paid him off was to keep their personal files from being exposed. He learned that people's depravity seemed to increase with the size of their bank account. He was just the one taking advantage of it.

10.

Jacob's file-stealing scam made him wealthy, but the real rush he got from doing it came from something else: control. Salvador already knew this about him. He seemingly knew everything about Jacob in their first meeting. But Salvador also divulged some secrets of his own that day. He had to in order to complete Jacob's recruitment.

Faultline housed a secret division underneath its legitimate web business. The division was small and agile and wickedly smart. They created viruses to infiltrate systems and servers, much like Jacob's did. But while their means were the same as his, their end was completely different. Their viruses were built to patiently lie in wait on a company or government server, only coming to life at the most opportune times. Their mission was information, and they collected it from every company and government agency with which they were contracted. Proprietary, personnel, patent, and so on. The viruses gave Salvador Sebastian knowledge, and therefore quiet power.

One of Faultline's viruses had discovered one of Jacob's while probing an insurance conglomerate that he had eyed to extort. The viruses that Jacob had created were virtually undetectable, but Salvador's group proved to be even more sophisticated. They traced Jacob's program back to him and, under Salvador's instruction, burrowed deep into his system with one of their own. The young hacker was oblivious to the viral mole on his hard drive.

"And that's how I found you, how I followed your work," Salvador finished. "Impressed, I'm sure?"

"Very," Jacob said. He thought for a few moments, while Salvador waited in silence. "But I don't get it. If you've gathered and stored all of this information, if you know so much about the inner-workings of these companies and agencies, why don't you do something with it? You're sitting on a goddam goldmine. There's got to be something more." Then it became clear in Jacob's mind. "You're planning something…*monumental*."

Salvador gave him an approving smile. "Good, Jacob. I was hoping you would get there. I like that word - 'monumental.' With your help, it will be exactly that."

11.

Before he presented his grand plan, Salvador described to Jacob what was going to happen next. "I know you, Jacob, even though we've just met. And I believe that I can trust you. But I need to know that what I'm going to tell you stays between us. That, should you decide not to participate, it will go no further. Understand?"

Jacob's curiosity was peaked. He was desperate to hear what Salvador wanted to tell him, and so he agreed. "Of course I understand."

"Good. Then this part shouldn't hurt one bit," Salvador said with a smile. "This room, Jacob, is my 'truth chamber,' for lack of a better term. Sounds like something out of a Bond movie, right? Sorry about that." He laughed a bit. He had stood from his chair and was pacing along the walls as he talked. "With no windows to provide distraction and its painted surfaces a cool blue, this room will ease you into authenticity. I've put all of my closest people through it, including Simone."

Jacob remembered then what Simone had said to him before he entered the room. *"This is more serious than you could ever imagine."* He was beginning to believe her.

Salvador continued. "I have to make sure you can be committed to me and this...'cause.' That term has become completely exaggerated, so I hate to use it. But that's what this is. A movement. Growing faster than you can imagine. I want you to become a part of the engine of that movement, Jacob. So I have to know that you can handle the power of it all."

Everything he said drove Jacob's imagination further. He had no idea what he might be committing to, but he wanted to commit nonetheless. "Understood," he replied.

"Ok, then, let's get started. First, I'd like to know about your family, how you were raised. Be as descriptive as you like."

Jacob tensed, unnoticeably he hoped. His family was far in his past, but not yet totally forgotten. The subject shouldn't have bothered him, but it did. "I was raised by my mother. Sorry, let me rephrase that: my mother was the only parent I had growing up. I can't say that she really raised me, because I feel like I did that all on my own."

"Do you know your father?"

"No," Jacob responded tersely. "Let me get to the quick of this right now, Salvador. My mother was an alcoholic, drug-riddled whore. If I believed in miracles, then I would classify my birth as one. But I don't. I always chalked my existence up to luck. I guess I'm an exception to the statistics of unsuccessful pregnancies. Rare, but they do exist." Jacob took a deep breath. He had never talked about this with anyone. "If she knew who or where my father was, she never told me. Granted, I didn't ask. It's hard to give a shit about a guy who obviously doesn't give a shit about me."

Salvador had stopped pacing. He walked over to the chair opposite Jacob and sat. "So tell me, how long has it been since you've spoken with your mother?"

Jacob was stunned by the question, only because it assumed what was true. That he had left home long ago and never looked back. He wondered if Salvador knew his answers before he gave them. "Years. After high school, I moved away from that hellhole and haven't thought about it again until right now."

"And tell me about high school, Jacob. You never attended college. How were your grades?"

"High school?" Jacob asked sarcastically. "How can I say this? The organized structure was a worthless waste of time. But in those years of my life, I fully realized how I could rein in the abstract thoughts that had been bouncing around my brain as a child. I know I'm smart. I knew it then. But I didn't care about grades or tests, and the teachers loathed me for it. It wasn't until I sat at the keyboard of a computer that I understood what focus and passion were. No teacher or class had ever done that for me."

"Do you regret not pursuing a formal computer education in college?"

"Not for a second. Not for what I do."

Salvador nodded. "And why, Jacob, do you do what you do?"

"Because I can," he replied. "Because I can make the most powerful people in this country feel powerless. Because I can take away any semblance of control from those who try to control the rest of us." Jacob's pride was getting the better of him, but he couldn't stop it. And something told him that Salvador liked it. "And until today - until you brought me here and told me about your operation - I thought I could do it better than anyone else in the world."

12.

Salvador stood from his chair, and Jacob did the same. He extended his arm and gave the young man a firm handshake. "Thank you for your candor, Jacob. I think you're going to be quite the asset for us. There is one last bit of questions. Simone will be handling those from here. Tonight, you will have dinner with me. And as long as this afternoon develops as I predict it will, I will lay out our plans then."

He walked to the door. When he opened it, Simone was there waiting in the hallway. Salvador leaned to her and whispered something that only she could hear. Then, before he left the room, he turned back and said, "Come hungry, hijo. People tell me I'm one hell of a cook." Jacob didn't understand the nickname, but he couldn't help but like the way it sounded.

The battery of tests that Simone administered were all psychological in nature. They had been designed by doctors hired by Salvador specifically for that purpose. He was recruiting some of the brightest minds in the world, but his scheme was scandalous. He needed to make sure his recruits were mentally fit and stable. And he needed reassurance that they could withstand the time and effort that it would take to complete the mission. His plan was to change the world. Weakness in mind and spirit would not do.

As late morning turned into afternoon, Jacob came to realize Simone's importance to Salvador. She was his second opinion, the left side of his right-thinking brain. Of course she was a brilliant legal and political intellectual, with credentials to prove it. But she was so much more. Jacob felt her analyzing him and his answers as they progressed through the examination. He had initially wanted to start a playful flirtation with her, but he quickly found that he didn't want to disrupt her work. It was a strange feeling for Jacob, something new. He respected Simone, unlike any woman he had ever known. So he allowed her to question him without interruption.

When they were finished, she thanked him for his patience. "Now, you'll be taken to your hotel. I suggest you take some time to rest. Tonight will be overwhelming. Dinner with Salvador will be at his home. A car will pick you up at 6 o'clock to take you there." She finally began to ease her strict composure with him. "And one piece of advice, Jacob - enjoy the sunset. From Salvador's place, it will be the best you've ever seen."

It was a full forty-minute drive from the hotel to the coastline, where Salvador lived. The last few miles of the journey took the car upward, around tight curves on a narrow roadway that gashed through dense California woodland. The twisted cypress trees began to thin as Jacob and the driver approached the summit of the small mountain they had been ascending. Houses had been scarce as they made the climb, and Salvador's driveway seemingly appeared out of nowhere. The driver pulled onto a dirt path that led a few hundred feet to the house and stopped when the car arrived at the front portico. Salvador was waiting there, and he led Jacob through the front door into his hideaway home.

Jacob expected something grandiose, but it wasn't. Instead, it was a reflection of the uncomplicated side of the man Jacob was just starting to comprehend. The house was a single-level Spanish-style structure. All of its floors were hardwood, its ceilings rustic with exposed redwood beams. It was furnished with hand-crafted tables and chairs, just enough for a single man who may host an occasional small group of guests. The central room was expansive but held only six leather chairs on a large oriental rug. Jacob noticed that one of the side room's four walls were lined from floor to ceiling with shelves holding hundreds of books. The kitchen was large, with every open space occupied by various utensils and tools and dishware. There wasn't a single example of modern technology throughout the home, which, to Jacob, seemed fitting.

"Follow me, hijo," Salvador directed as he walked toward the back of the house. Jacob had learned that the endearing word meant "son" in Spanish since the meeting. It made him feel carefree and comfortable with Salvador. "Let's enjoy the view from the patio before dinner."

Simone had been right. The scene was breathtaking, with the backyard abruptly becoming cliff after just a few feet of grass. There was Pacific Ocean as far north and south as the naked eye could see. And the sound of her white-capped waves pounding against giant rock was the only noise in the air. Jacob walked to the end of the yard. It felt as if he were standing on the edge of the earth.

"This...is...beautiful," Jacob whispered, almost to himself.

"Glorious, isn't it?" Salvador said as he walked up and placed a drink in Jacob's hand. "You spoke of control earlier. What you see before you is the definition of control. *Natural* control."

Jacob had never been an emotional person. Life had taught him that emotions could only get in the way of logic. But that moment brought unknown emotions to his surface. "Power," he said.

"That's right, Jacob. The most powerful force on this planet. I'm glad to see that you can appreciate that. Come on over, have a seat." There were two wooden chairs on the tiled patio, where they sat. "I've gotten the report from Simone on your psych evaluations. Very interesting."

"That doesn't necessarily sound good, Salvador."

"There's no good or bad on these types of tests. There's just you. And, for our purposes, you passed."

"I've got to say, you guys have done one hell of a job hanging me over a cliff. The suspense of this whole thing is making me sick."

Salvador laughed. "I know, and I'm sorry. We had to keep you in the dark until now. But I certainly don't need you to be ill before we eat - I've spent the entire afternoon preparing our dinner. So, where do I start? How about the part where you create the most vicious computer virus the world has ever witnessed?"

13.

Salvador described his scheme to change the world over a dinner of cioppino, a fish stew that he had made with fresh clams, mussels, shrimp, and crab. After he and Jacob finished eating, he opened a second bottle of wine and they returned to the patio. The bottle was empty by the time he finished relating his elaborate plan.

The idea had been hatched long ago, out of a distrust developed from the discovery of his family's past. More specific, a distrust of governments, and a disgust for the influence that money has over them. He told Jacob of his Cuban forefathers and how their self-made livelihood had been taken by their country. He talked of his father's futile fight to redeem the family name, and of his mother's abandonment under desperate American-bred circumstances.

He referenced past civilizations in world history. He asked esoteric questions, not looking for the actual answers. He just wanted Jacob to think differently, above his mind's mathematical sanctuary.

"Is it coincidence that, until now, the greatest of the world's societies have all collapsed or transformed?" Salvador posed. "Or was that natural order? What do we consider great about a society anyway? The Egyptians, the Romans, the Greeks.

Flashes in the grand historical pan. Shouldn't we be the same?"

The last thought lingered in the cool California night air before Salvador answered it himself. "Because our societies, our civilizations, are interdependent for the first time in the known history of this planet, one country's economy cannot exist without the others, and the group cannot let even one fail. The collapse of one would mean the collapse of all. And so, the corruption follows. The global economy controlled by a select few, who are in turn controlled by the highest bidders and the biggest contributors. We are long overdue for a cultural cataclysm, but technology has eliminated any chance of it happening naturally. So what do we do? Continue on the same path until the whole of us is eliminated? I say no. I say we use that same technology to make the cataclysm happen on our own terms."

The wheels of Salvador's change were already turning. The information that Faultline's secret division was gathering had already led to progress in the movement's foundation-building. Key personnel roles within companies and agencies were being filled by Salvador's people. His group influenced mergers, acquisitions, stock buys-and-sells. Even elections were being swayed on localized levels. And by creating the right computer program that could attack multiple secure servers simultaneously, he told Jacob that he felt like they were only a few years away from fulfilling the ultimate goal: complete global shutdown.

"Can you build that program for me, Jacob?"

Salvador had asked so many rhetorical questions in his presentation that Jacob didn't know if he expected an answer or not. "Hang on, Salvador. I'm still trying to wrap my head around all of this. After all, you don't come across as the evil mastermind type. What you're talking about is beyond anything anyone's ever conceived."

"Exactly as I forewarned you," Salvador quipped. "Don't get caught up in the details right now, Jacob. We will deal with those later. But the concept...can you build it?"

Simone had been right again. Jacob was overwhelmed. And a little drunk by then. But he was sold. It was logic in its most sensible form. Civilization was on a runaway steam train with no destination and no engineer, only firemen shoveling more and more coal into the engine. Salvador could become that engineer, even though he would have to derail the train to do it.

Jacob stood and regained a bit of his balance. "Of course I can, Salvador," he said with his innate confidence. "But you've got to tell me what we're gonna do once I burn this shithouse down."

"All in due time, hijo," Salvador said. He stood and went inside the house, and when he returned he held two long brown cylindrical shapes in his hand. He formed the infectious smile that came across his face quite often as he handed one of them to Jacob. "From my personal stash. To celebrate a new friendship. The best cigar you'll ever taste in your life."

14.

Jacob and Salvador sat silently listening to the Pacific Ocean slam herself into the California boulders below them. Salvador understood how life-altering his proposal to Jacob had been. He gave the young man time to take it all in.

Halfway through his Cuban cigar, Jacob spoke. "So you're telling me you've been planning this for years?" he asked. "And you've got people all over the world working for you in secret?"

"That's right, hijo," Salvador confirmed. "Revolutions take time. And organization."

"Well, I guess it's *time* for you to fill me in on the *organization*."

Salvador's secret division had begun as a simple social circle, formed to discuss philosophy and philanthropy in weekly meetings. He gathered friends from government and business inside Faultline's headquarters, where debates and arguments would arise and continue late into the night. Soon, he realized he had organized a group of similarly-minded individuals, each seeking a dramatic change in the country, if not the world. It was certainly not the first of its kind, but this group was different in that it had the means to actually affect a transformation. Salvador inadvertently found himself in a role of leadership at the gatherings, with everyone tending to agree with his broad-stroked ideas. The formation of ANTI- was a natural progression.

ANTI-'s mission from the beginning was to disrupt from within. Salvador inspired his new following to become a unit against the corrupted world and the sham its society had become with the rapid advance of technology. A unit from whom no one, no matter how powerful, was safe. ANTI-everyone and everything.

Recruitment for membership in the new division was quiet but aggressive. Throughout the world, unemployment and dissatisfaction was at an all-time high. And communication was moving easier than it ever had before. ANTI-'s leadership benefitted from it all. Then they began to reveal themselves, through protests and demonstrations. This only continued to increase growth among their ranks with people who sought liberation from a lopsided power-structure. And all the while, Salvador was developing something stronger than any protest, behind Faultline's closed doors. He was creating a group that could detach the world from what it had become utterly reliant upon: the technology that Salvador believed was slowly destroying civilization.

There were eight men and three women who made up ANTI-'s tech team. They operated invisibly and without affinity. Their programs, and their viruses, were sleek and inventive. Their actions were direct yet undercover.

"This is the group that you will join, Jacob," Salvador told him. "This is the team that you will lead."

"*Lead*?" Jacob asked with aversion. "No, no, no, Salvador. You don't understand. I work alone. Always have. I'm better that way."

Salvador leaned forward in his chair and stubbed out the last bit of his cigar in the ashtray next to him. "I told you earlier, hijo, that I know you. Believe me, I do. And I know you've got the strength that a leader needs, and the patience that this project will require. Trust me, and believe that you can be something greater."

Jacob felt inspired. And he was beginning to understand how Salvador's revolution had grown so large after all.

15.

For the first year of his employment under Salvador, Jacob shadowed each member of the ANTI-technology team. Collectively, the group had accomplished much in the few years since Salvador had assembled them. But individually, they could be better. Jacob silently watched their work, then reported to Salvador every few weeks. At the end of the year, Jacob was announced to the team as their new director.

Jacob's task was basic, but far from simple. He would need to design the program that would eventually infiltrate and overtake the servers of every developed country in the world. He designated the project, and the program, "The Domino Infection." His intent was to create something more organized than the typical computer virus, and he envisioned the infected servers falling in systematic rhythm like a series of dominos.

After Jacob took over the tech team, he met with Salvador monthly to review their progress. It was also because Salvador enjoyed Jacob's company. He saw a lot of himself in the young hacker, even though they came from such different places and times in life. Most of the meetings were long and detailed, and some developed into drawn-out discussions about the future and fulfillment of revolutionary destiny. In every meeting, Jacob reminded Salvador of the patience needed to write code and to program. The Domino Infection was going to take more time than even he had predicted. Salvador showed concern, but understood. And he could wait patiently because, unknown to Jacob, he had other projects that were moving forward much more efficiently.

Part of the ANTI- strategy all along was to place as many of their own into various company and government agency positions. "Inside" men and women throughout the world. Then, when it was time for action, they could overtake from the inside out. Salvador had been the original architect of the concept, and its execution was nearly flawless. ANTs, as the insiders had begun calling themselves, were entrenched and in disguise everywhere. The world would never see it coming.

It was in one of the Domino Infection meetings when Salvador told Jacob that something was happening within the hidden ANT strategy. Salvador was excited - Jacob could see it on his face.

"It's the financial world, hijo," Salvador said with lighted eyes. "Wall Street. Hedge funds. Investment banks. We know exactly what they're doing."

"Ok, so what exactly are they doing?" Jacob asked apathetically. He knew investment bankers were legalized frauds. So why was this so exciting?

"Let me back up, Jacob, and take it slowly. I know you're in a programming fog. But hear me out, because this could completely eliminate our need for the Domino Infection."

16.

Salvador and ANTI- didn't push America into the Great Recession, but he did see it coming. And he did all that he could to help make it happen. The ANTs he had in place across various financial institutions and investment banks sold derivatives and credit default swaps just like their co-workers. And their government counterparts had been signing off on less and less Wall Street regulation for years.

"This is it, Jacob," Salvador said with giddiness when they met that day. "The natural world is adjusting for the madness. The artificial pillars that this materialistic society has been building itself upon are buckling under the weight of its growing rapacity. I thought it would never happen."

"But what does that mean for us, Salvador? For ANTI-?" Jacob couldn't contain his disappointment. He wanted to be the ANTI- hero, the one to bring about the collapse.

"You don't see it, hijo? You don't see how much work this saves us? We are just as prepared to take over when the dust settles as we would be if this was our own doing. I have our people at the ready, across the planet, waiting for the moment when chaos emerges. Waiting to fortify, to defend, to create a new society." He looked at Jacob deeply. "ANTI- is the only thing that will survive the coming apocalypse. We may not be the cause, but we will still be the answer."

The global financial collapse didn't quite turn out the way Salvador was hoping. Government bailouts saved most of the banks and corporations that were determined to be "too big to fail." Money was printed and interest rates were lowered. Regulations were considered but eventually set aside. The income gap grew ever bigger. Jacob began to think that Salvador had been right all along. That there was no endgame except total extinction, unless some outside force intervened.

Transforming his disappointment into inspiration, Salvador started a new campaign of sorts. He kept his ANTs that were entrenched in place, but he began hyper-aggressive online recruitment for ground troop ANTs, too. He organized more protests. He siphoned more money to human rights groups. He staged more elaborate theatrical displays of government opposition. ANTI- expanded exponentially. The disenfranchised of the world joined the movement by the millions. And while all of it attracted more and more media attention, no one ever discovered what was really happening behind the ANTI- curtain.

17.

After the world avoided what would have been a natural collapse, Salvador came to Jacob with defiant determination in his tone. "Jacob, listen to me. We need the Domino Infection now more than ever."

Jacob felt renewed validation. "Yes, Salvador, I know. I won't let you down. But it will take time."

"Everything that's historic does, hijo. Don't ever forget that."

Jacob's tech team worked more earnestly than they had thought they could. They built replica government servers to exact specifications in order to match trial viruses against the security they would be facing. They studied the ways in which various countries defended themselves against cyber-crime. They destroyed each other's programs to learn their own weaknesses. In the end, they left nothing to possibility. Jacob demanded perfection, and when they were done, the Domino Infection was perfect. Once Jacob and his team had completed their years-long work, he went to Salvador and told him that it was ready.

"Wonderful, Jacob," he said approvingly, much like a proud father would have. "That means we can put the rest of our plan in motion. It won't be long now."

Jacob sent Salvador a short message on the day after the dominos fell. It represented the proudest he had ever felt about anything:

Salvador,

The Domino Infection is complete. Total electronic shutdown has been achieved. ANTI- is in control now.

Thank you for everything.

FtSoH
Jacob

PART THREE: GETTING OUT

Judd Vowell ◊ OVERTHROWN

1.

It doesn't hurt as badly as you might think. Getting shot, that is. I found myself focusing on a fly that kept buzzing past my face. Every few seconds. Zzzew one way. Zzzew the other. I don't know why that was my last mortal thought. A nuisance housefly. But it was.

2.

Jeff had to be restrained. The two Leftys he had been stationed with on the grid's border that horrendous morning held him down and zip-tied his wrists and ankles. They told Daniel that it had been a miracle they caught him before he made it down the stairs of the building where they had been positioned. And after watching the ANTs murder his brother Paul, there was no doubt that he would have attacked them once he got to the street, blinded by familial loss and vengeful rage. At least we had saved one life that morning.

I, on the other hand, wasn't as violently reactive. After Daniel stopped my instinctive effort to get to my children, I was consumed by despair. I collapsed on the fifth floor of that abandoned building in a heap of helplessness.

I had known in my heart that it was a bad idea. But I let Daniel and Anna convince me otherwise. Jessica and Henry, too, even though they weren't old enough to distinguish between courage and wisdom yet. Hell, I had pushed aside a portion of hard reality for the entire expedition. Truth be told, the chances of us getting the medication for Meg and then getting it back to her in time were slim at best. I knew that all along, but I had ignored it. Maybe that's what hope really is.

Daniel had instructed the other groups along the border to rendezvous two blocks west if anything went wrong, at the same building we had used as a rally area the night before. I had no idea how much time had passed when he began to shake me from my daze to tell me it was time to move.

"Gordon! Gorrr-dooonnnn!" His voice sounded far away, but I could hear it. Everything had been a silent ring up until then, much like I imagined one of those flash grenades would induce upon explosion. "Gordon, snap out of it! We have got to move!"

I wasn't fully cognizant, but I suppose Daniel felt like I was alert enough to make it the two blocks. He and the other Lefty soldier stood me up and dusted me off. "Gordon, we're going to walk now. Down the stairs, back to the rally point. Stay on my ass, step for step. You got it?" I muttered something that must've sounded like an "OK."

When we arrived at the rendezvous, one of the other groups was waiting. Within a few moments, a single Lefty from Jeff's threesome appeared. He related the situation with Jeff, and how he had left him at their position with his counterpart. I was beginning to see and hear clearly again. Daniel was calm and direct.

"No second-guessing at this point, everyone. We still have three people inside that grid. Still alive and in need. Priority now becomes getting them out of there. But we have to be smart." He paced a bit, thinking deeply. "Three of us will stay here, keep the grid under surveillance. The rest will head back to Overlord and regroup. We need to get Jeff and take him with us. Keep him subdued if needed." He walked up close to me. "Gordon, I promise: we will do everything in our power to get your kids out of there."

I had gathered more of my senses and emotions while Daniel spoke. My despair had grown into something more tangible: controlled fury. "You bet your ass you will, Daniel. I don't know what kind of war you've been planning, but I know this: it starts right here, right now."

3.

We double-timed our way back to Camp Overlord. Jeff had calmed himself and agreed to go with us. He walked in silence. We all did.

We reached the camp by early afternoon, and Daniel set to strategizing immediately. "Give me an hour, Gordon. I'll talk with my best people, and we'll come up with something. Go eat, shower, sleep...anything to keep yourself occupied. I'll run the plan by you as soon as we're done." He gave me a firm handshake, then took off into the former prison's interior.

I went to the room where the twins and I had set up our living area. I laid down on the steel-framed bed and closed my eyes. Flashes of Jessica and Henry's faces appeared, then Meg's. Smiling, happier faces. Then the image from the street that morning took over. The black hoods being thrown onto their heads, the shackles clasped around their wrists, their bodies tossed into the waiting vans. I forced open my eyes to cancel the thought, temporarily erase the memory. But then something hit me. I shut my eyes quickly, bringing the last part of the morning memory forward again. Two vans. I saw them take Anna toward one of them. And then I saw it, and I felt a hint of excitement. It was something I had been too overwhelmed to notice before. Jessica and Henry had been put into the same van.

I sat up in bed as I understood what that meant. Wherever the ANTs had taken them, wherever they had been imprisoned, they were together. And the one thing I knew better than anybody else: Jessica and Henry were good in their own ways by themselves, but they were great when they worked as a team.

Goddam hope. There it was again.

4.

Daniel showed up in the doorway to my room an hour and a half after he had left me. "Sorry for the delay, Gordon," he started. "Turns out we had a lot of opinions on how to handle this situation. Needless to say, it's complicated."

"I understand, Daniel, that it's complicated for you. But it's rather simple for me. I'm going to get my kids back, or I'm going to die trying. I just feel like I need to be clear about that before we continue."

He took a breath before he spoke. We both sat down. "I had a feeling that's what you were going to say. And believe me, that holds weight with us and our plan. And you need to understand something, too. Anna is the best asset I have here. Maybe one of the best in the whole Lefty organization. She's as important to me as your kids are to you right now."

Good. We were on the same page. "So, what have you got?" I asked.

"As we see it, there are two obstacles we're facing. One: the ANTI- force at the grid is entirely too powerful for us to attack head-on. Just so you know, we were never planning on attacking the ANTs directly. We had hoped to develop a series of electronic disruptions over time to introduce ourselves, then draw them to us here at Overlord when we were prepared. That would give us the advantage in a battle. But none of that matters now."

"And the second obstacle?"

"That one's a little more complex. You see, we don't know where Anna and the kids are located inside that grid, which is not a small area. Even if we do manage to get in, we'll be lucky at best to find them."

"You say that as if you're going to do it anyway..." I said, trailing the thought into a question.

"It's the only shot we've got, Gordon," Daniel said, almost dismissively. "It's risky and it's stupid, but Anna's worth it to us. And your kids are worth it to you, I imagine."

"You're damn right, they are."

"Well, alright then. The strategists are finalizing the details as we speak. I only have one question left to ask, as if I don't already know the answer." Daniel stood up from his chair, as did I from the bed. We stood eye to eye. "Do you want in?"

I responded emphatically. "Daniel, there's absolutely nothing you could do to stop me from saving my kids. Just tell me when we head out."

5.

Camp Overlord's strategic minds laid out their plans to those of us who were tasked with the rescue mission just as dusk was settling. We didn't have much time, they explained, so we would only go through them once. It was imperative to listen closely, as there were multiple layers to the formulated operation.

There were eighteen of us involved. Daniel would lead us, as he had the night before. The entire group would trek to the grid, at which point Daniel would meet with the Lefty soldiers who had stayed behind to keep watch over the border. If they had any new information, Daniel would use it accordingly. If not, which was expected, two groups of four Leftys each would travel north half a mile, then separate to designated positions.

At 5:30, one hour before dawn, the two northern groups would provide distraction. They would detonate C-4 explosives at the two locations, each a former auto repair facility. The explosions should create significant shockwaves and aftermath fires and smoke, with the facilities containing leftover oil, chemicals, and tires.

Next would come the point in question. How would the ANTs react? The predicted response would be investigation. If the ANTs reacted as the Lefty planners thought they would, a significant number of them would leave their posts to scrutinize the explosions. That action would leave a vulnerability in the border, somewhere. It was up to the rest of us to exploit that vulnerability.

Timing was critical. There should be just enough darkness left before dawn to use as cover getting into the grid. But we would need daylight once inside to locate Anna and the kids. It would be up to us to conceal ourselves as we searched. We would split into five teams of two and hunt. We would rally at sunset at the central-most point in the northern border, at a designated intersection, with the hopes that one group would have rescued the captives.

At this point, the eight Lefty soldiers who had set the explosives the night before would be waiting on the edge of the grid's northern border. They would then directly attack the ANTs in that area with small arms fire, luring them out and away from their posts. This should provide the rest of us a brief gap in the border to escape into the streets outside the grid.

We were set to leave in one hour and directed to eat and suit up beforehand. I pulled Daniel aside as the meeting broke up. I was apprehensive.

"Daniel, I'm gonna do this no matter what. You know that, and I know that. But, I've got to say, this sounds like a suicide mission for most of these guys."

He responded with an air of clarity beyond normal comprehension. "You may be right, Gordon. But sometimes we have to go forward on faith, even when we know what the outcome will be."

6.

The eighteen of us moved through the darkness along the same path we had taken the night before, except faster. We passed the same empty gas stations and strip malls, the same deserted office buildings. But this time they seemed even more ominous than just twenty-four hours earlier. They seemed alive with warning and trepidation.

Daniel stopped us at the same rally point, two blocks west of ANTI-'s pulsating power grid. It was 3 AM, two and a half hours before we were set to put the mission in motion. He instructed us to hunker down and wait while he and another soldier went to meet with the Leftys watching the border.

I found a spot to myself and sat on the ground, resting against a large pillar that was helping support the monstrous building's marble canopy. The others broke off into small groups and talked to pass the time. I watched them, admired them. They were young, like all of the foot-soldiers in the history of the world. Experienced men always made the decisions, but adventurous kids made the sacrifice. I silently thanked them for what they were about to do that day.

I had dozed into a light sleep by the time Daniel got back. I had not thought about how tired I was. Daniel told us that the surveillance team had not seen anything out of the ordinary since we had left that morning. They had no information on Anna and the kids' location inside. The ANTs were still heavily manned along the western border, and we surmised that to be the case along the other three.

"Ok, everyone. The mission is a go as planned. The two groups heading north will need to move out immediately. We've got a small window of time, so get those explosives set and ready to blow at 5:30. Those of us going inside will establish a launch area just outside of the grid, underneath the surveillance team's vantage point. They'll send a runner down with intel on the weakened location in the border once the ANTs leave to investigate. That's where we sneak through. Got it?" Everyone nodded. "Good. And remember: nobody do anything crazy...unless you have to. Let's go."

7.

When you come to a moment in your life when you are prepared to die, it's like the weight of persistent tension is lifted from your body. That tension that appears out of nowhere at some point in adulthood. It disappears. And what's left is uninhibited freedom. And I don't mean on your deathbed, with your family gathered about you, waiting to gasp your last breath. I'm talking about the willingness to give your healthy and able life if that's what it takes. It can open your mind to so many wonderful thoughts.

I believed that I was prepared to die when the twins and I set out on our journey to save Meg. But I wasn't. No, that was more like blind bravery. And in the hour before the explosions went off outside the grid, I recognized that. Because, in the pre-dawn of my second-to-last morning on earth, I reached that apex that so many never achieve. What I like to think of as true enlightenment.

8.

I didn't know the first thing about C-4. But while preparing for the mission back at Camp Overlord, I had curiously asked how much the Lefty soldiers would be carrying with them. Five brick-shaped blocks for every backpack, eight backpacks. While I assumed that was sufficient, it seemed like a small amount for two buildings in my naïve mind. I realized at the zero hour of our rescue mission just how naïve I had been.

The explosions went off almost simultaneously. There were two succinct shockwaves that I felt milliseconds before I heard the giant roars of destruction. We were positioned inside the loading dock of a large downtown department store, just across the street from the grid's border. Our view of the upheaval created by the Leftys who had gone north was blocked by the corner of the building, but we could hear it. ANTs shouting and moving haphazardly. We waited.

In the short time I had known Daniel, I learned that he didn't reveal his emotions easily. An important characteristic of a good leader. But as the minutes ticked by rapidly and the sun seemed to push its preliminary rays through the city corridors in front of us, I saw him show impatience. Then frustration. One of his men leaned into his ear and said, "We're losing our cover, sir."

Daniel responded tersely, "I know, dammit. But we can't go in there blind." Then he looked up and said to the sky. "Come on, guys. Give me a way to go."

Then, just as the second leg of our rescue mission looked to be falling apart before us, one of the Lefty spotters came around the back corner of the building. "South," he said, catching his breath as he spoke. "Three streets south. But you haven't got much time."

"You heard him, everybody. We stay a block behind the line...and we run." Daniel was already moving as he was saying it. We followed.

9.

The intersection where we would try and slip into ANTI-'s grid was deserted. The ANTs stationed there overnight had moved north in curiosity, just as their counterparts one street south had done. That gave us two unguarded intersections and still enough darkness to conceal our entry. We could see a large group of ANTs gathered north of our new position, all with their backs to us and watching the huge infernos burning half a mile away. First step in the mission - distraction - accomplished.

We had divided ourselves into teams of two at the rally point earlier that morning. Daniel had instructed us then that we would cross the border one team at a time, so as to limit our visibility. Two people can be nearly invisible compared to ten trying to move in rhythm across an open space. I was paired with Daniel, and we were set to cross second.

The first team silently made it from one side of the intersection to the other, trotting in a crouched position the entire way. Daniel and I waited for a few seconds. I held my breath. I could feel my heartbeat in my ears and my chest. I heard Daniel whisper decisively, "Go!"

We were off, into the street and moving ever closer to the enemy grid. I had my eyes trained on the small of Daniel's back, shifting as he did, keeping the same pace. I was so focused on him and on getting across undetected that I almost missed it. Two streaks of movement in my peripheral vision to the right. Across the empty intersection one street south of us. It happened just as we were reaching the edge of the ANTI- territory. And even though it was just a glimpse, a blur of motion, I knew exactly what it was.

10.

I grabbed Daniel by the shoulders the instant we were concealed by the buildings on the ANTI- side of the street. I turned him around and almost fell into him as I slowed my momentum.

"I saw them, Daniel." I tried to control my breathing. I felt a huge rush of adrenaline flowing through my body.

"Saw who?" Daniel asked, concerned.

"The kids," I barely got out of my mouth. I closed my eyes and focused on calming my nerves. The third pair of Leftys reached the relative safety of the corridor.

"What the hell are you talking about, Gordon?" Daniel pressed. I suppose he could see how critical the information was.

"I saw my kids. Crossing the street a block south. In the opposite direction. *Leaving the grid!*" I stressed. Now the fourth team was crossing.

"Wait a second. You saw your kids...how in the world?"

"I don't know how, but I saw them. I know it. We have to go back!" The final team of two was starting their run. Dawn was coming on fast.

Leaders of men have to trust their instincts more often than not in time-critical situations. I could see that Daniel's gut was telling him to believe me. As the last pair of Lefty soldiers made it safely into the grid, he adjusted the mission. "Change of plans, guys. Johnson and Carter, you two stick with Gordon and me. We're going back across. The rest of you, proceed with location and extraction, same as before. But you're only looking for Anna now."

Carter spoke up, "But, sir, the sun. We'll be going back in almost broad daylight."

"Then, Carter, I guess you'd better do it quickly. On my mark!" And before I had time to think, we were running back across the gauntlet, with no more night left to hide beneath.

11.

Daniel peered around the corner of the former department store to make sure we had not been spotted. He turned to us and said, "We're good." Then he gave the three teams across the intersection a thumbs-up, and we saw them scatter into the grid. "Now to find those kids of yours."

He directed Johnson and Carter to split from the two of us at the next corner and move a block south, then to continue west. We would all move in that direction with the assumption that Jessica and Henry did, too. One good thing - we didn't have to keep our eyes out for ANTs, like we would have inside the grid.

We moved swiftly. Daniel on one side of the street, me on the other. We checked in doorways and underneath overhangs, on porches and inside below-ground entrances. You could never imagine how many subtle places there are to hide along an empty city street. The rising sun helped to illuminate our search area, but the taller buildings still cast dark shadows along alleyways and storefronts.

The church's broken glass caught my eye about twelve blocks into our hunt. There were plenty of busted windows in the city from the early manic days of the Great Dark, but the stained glass next to the church's giant wooden door looked freshly smashed somehow. For whatever reason, it begged me to investigate it.

The church was a grand structure, occupying most of a city block with its parish offices and fellowship halls and Sunday-school classrooms. It was a beautiful dark brown, with copper roofing covering its sanctuary and spires. It looked proper and out of place, all at once. I thought to myself, *"If I was looking for a safe place to rest in the middle of this deserted concrete landscape, this would be it."* I hoped I was thinking like Jessica and Henry as I crawled through the shattered window.

I found myself inside a small vestibule with another doorway on the opposite side. The room was dark, but I could see that the door was halfway open. I eased into the giant sanctuary. It was better lit, with shades of blue and green and red laying across the pews and hardwood floors. The morning sun coming through the pastoral window scenes brought about a sense of serenity. But that sense faded as I walked down the center aisle.

I saw the first body a few rows down. Prostrate on a pew, it was long decomposed and looked like some bad prop out of a bygone horror movie. But I knew it was all too real. There were more as I kept walking. I guess those poor souls had sought spiritual refuge in their last moments. I felt sorry for them.

I reached the altar at the front of the sanctuary with no sign of the kids. I started to think my instincts had been wrong, that I was wasting time looking in the church. I decided to call their names, if only just to hear myself say them again. "Jessica...Henry..." The sound of my voice echoed throughout the room.

Then, barely audible to me, she spoke. "Dad???" It came from behind me, I thought. The second time was louder and stronger "Dad!" I turned around and saw Jessica's head rising above the pews at the back of the sanctuary. My heart leapt.

I ran back up the same aisle I had just come down. But when I got to the last pew, my excitement evaporated instantly. Jessica was kneeling, looking frazzled and scared. And Henry was lying flat on the floor, unconscious and unaware that I had found them.

12.

I wanted more than anything to trade places with him in the back of that church sanctuary. To let me be the one unable to wake. Most parents can relate. It comes with raising kids and bringing your own blood into the uncaring world. Unfortunately, the world had become something even less than uncaring. Downright cruel and unusual, goddammit. I just wanted to end the chaos and save him, no matter what it might take. And yet, there was nothing I could do to help Henry in the back of that church sanctuary.

13.

"We were running so fast, Dad. So much faster than I've ever seen him run. And then he said he had to stop, to catch his breath for a moment." Jessica was a mess. She was sobbing as she told me how they ended up in the church. "We saw the church and decided to break in. When we got inside, he collapsed. I dragged him over here to the corner. I didn't know what to do."

"It's ok, honey. It's ok."

I put my hand on his chest and prayed for the involuntary function of breathing. I had never been much on prayer, but it felt appropriate in the surroundings. They were there. Deep long breaths. Better than short shallow ones, I told myself. I grabbed his wrist and found his pulse, although I had no idea what a good pulse might feel like. But it was there, too. Strong and steady.

"I don't know what to do either, Jessica. But he's breathing. And he's resting." I'm not sure why, but I had not hugged her. "Come here." We embraced for a long moment. I needed it as much as she did. I could feel her calming in my arms. "Now, listen. I have to go outside and let the others know that I've found you, ok?"

"Yeah, ok. Wait, hang on. What others?"

"You guys created quite the uproar back at camp. Daniel sent a whole crew of soldiers to save you." I managed a small smile. "There are three of them with me. Let me go get them. I'll be back before you know I'm gone."

"Ok, Dad. But please...hurry."

Daniel was waiting for me outside the church. He said he had seen me go inside.

"They're in there, Daniel. But Henry's out cold. Some kind of exhaustion or something. I don't know what to do." I had held it together in front of Jessica, but I broke down right there in front of Daniel. "I just...don't know what...to do." I fell to my knees.

He knelt down beside me and put a hand on my shoulder. "Alright, Gordon, it's alright. You *found* them. That's all that matters now."

I knew that Daniel was right, even though my heart kept reminding me that everything was so very wrong.

14.

Daniel had rounded up Johnson and Carter and brought them back to the church. They stood in the vestibule and discussed our options. I sat with Jessica next to Henry, still motionless and asleep.

Daniel came in and asked to speak to me outside. "Whatever needs to be said can be said in front of her," I told him. "She's as much a part of this as any of us now."

"Understood," Daniel said as he walked over to us. "Here's the situation. We need to get back to Overlord. Simple as that. We've got doctors for Henry there. We've got resources. Plus, if everything goes as planned, at sunset there's gonna be one hell of a shitstorm nearby. We need to be long gone by then."

"And how do you propose we get Henry back there?" I pondered.

"Easy. We carry him. Johnson and Carter are constructing a makeshift stretcher now. Between the two of them and the two of us, we should be able to make it back before dark."

I understood we couldn't stay there. It didn't make any sense. But I didn't know what was wrong with my son. And I didn't know if moving him would make it worse.

Daniel felt my apprehension. "Gordon, it's the only choice we've got. You stay here and wait for Henry to wake up, and you risk everything. We'll take care of him, I promise. But we've got to get him out of here."

I turned to Jessica. I needed family support. I needed reinforcements. "What do you think, Jess?"

She had become very serious since Daniel had come over to us. She answered with conviction. "He's right, Dad. It's the only choice we've got. Let's give Henry a chance." Then she reached over to a backpack that was propped up against the wall behind her. She unzipped it all the way, revealing twelve small boxes of the medicine that I had become so familiar with over the last few years. She wiped the remaining tears from her face and looked up at me. "Let's give Mom a chance, too."

15.

Henry didn't stir the entire trek back to Camp Overlord. I didn't know if that was good or bad. We arrived just minutes before the sun disappeared below the horizon we had been walking toward.

Daniel had the former prison cell across from ours cleared and set up for Henry as soon as we came through the gates. He sent one of his people to alert the doctors at camp of our situation. He did all that he could.

Jessica and I sat with Henry while two doctors examined him. When they were finished, they conferred outside in the hallway. One of them came back in and related to us their lackluster diagnosis. "We can't find anything wrong. Heart rate, respiration, body temperature. All normal. Near perfect, to be honest. But please understand, we don't have all the tools we need. There's no way to tell if his brain is ok."

"Do you know what happened to him?" I asked.

"Unfortunately, no. We don't think it was exhaustion or heat stroke. His vitals are too stable. It's almost like he just went into some sort of deep sleep that we can't rouse him from. I hate to even mention the word coma, but I think we're in that realm of possibility."

I had been down this vague road with doctors before, but I understood his limitations. I couldn't press him much further. "So what do we do now?"

"We wait." The doctor took a moment before he continued. "Look, we'll keep monitoring him and watch for any changes. I'm sorry. I wish we knew more."

I couldn't respond. I was exhausted and dazed.

Jessica's voice cut through the fog in my head. "Come on, Dad. Let's go lay down, if just for a little while. They'll wake us if anything happens."

She was right. I needed rest desperately. We got up and stumbled across the prison corridor. I was asleep before my body hit the mattress.

When I woke up, I didn't know how long I had slept. I could see through the crisscross of steel bars in our room's only window that it was still dark outside. I sat up and saw that Jessica was awake, too. She was sitting at a small table in the corner of the room, writing. I rubbed my eyes and stretched my arms and back. The rest had done me good, even though I felt like I could go back to sleep for two more days.

I cleared the REM-induced phlegm from my throat. "What are you doing, Jessica?"

"Just writing it all down."

"All what?"

"I don't know. Just everything that's happened to us. I don't want to forget this. When we make it through and save Mom and the lights come back on and we get back to normal life, I don't want to forget."

I knew then that she needed to talk. She and Henry had been through something horrible, I was sure. "Jess, you want to tell me what happened in there?"

She stopped writing and raised her head, looking at the blank wall above the table. She waited a minute or so before she spoke. "I was so scared, Dad. I thought for sure they were going to kill us. And maybe they would have, if it hadn't been for Henry."

16.

As Jessica told the story of her escape from the grid with Henry, I could see her independence, her adulthood, taking shape before me.

"We didn't know where we were at first. After the van ride. They kept the hoods over our heads and the handcuffs on us. We were in there for a long time, then they came and took me away. They put me in a room and uncuffed me, took the hood off. There was a woman there, sitting across a table from me. She was pretty and tried to be nice, but I didn't trust her.

"She apologized for everything that had happened, said something about Paul being a necessary sacrifice. She said that they wanted to believe us, and they needed to frighten us to do that. That they wanted to make sure we knew how strong they were. 'Paul's death will assure you tell me the truth, you see?' she asked. 'You have to understand that we won't stand for deceptiveness. We do not need you as much as you need us.' She was so warped, Dad. They all were.

"I stuck with the plan, with the story that we had learned. It was so hard to keep it straight, but I think I did. They took me back to the room where Henry was afterward, and they took him away. That's when I almost lost it. Alone with my thoughts."

Jessica got quiet. She wasn't visibly upset, but I could tell that going back to that place was difficult. I pushed her through it. "So, Henry came back?"

"Yeah, they brought Henry back. Who knows how long it had been. Too long. No more handcuffs and hoods, thank God. We hugged and cried. Then Henry got serious. 'You stick with the story?' he asked. 'I tried to. Did you?' 'Yep. That should help. I think they're giving us a break because we're kids. But that's their mistake.' He was so confident, Dad. He said he could get us out of there, but that I needed to be ready. I told him I was."

Then she asked me something that I didn't see coming. "Dad, did you know that Henry could pick locks?"

The question took me back to a flurry of memories. A series of episodes in parenting that had left me bewildered. Kids have a way of doing that. Sometimes I'd find a scene of moderate destruction or minor injury and never get a straight answer about how it happened. I longed for those scenes instead of the ones we had been facing since the Great Dark had begun.

The subtle events that had jumped to the surface of my brain at Jessica's query occurred when Henry was eleven. It was only for a summer, but Meg and I had been confounded by it. And it was soon forgotten with all the other minute and mundane details of daily life. Henry began locking himself in rooms all over the house. Bathrooms, bedrooms, closets. Between Meg and me, we found him at one point or another self-imprisoned in every space with a lockable door. Not to be saved, mind you. Exactly the opposite. Every time I discovered a voice behind a locked door - "No problem here, Dad. Just working on something new."

The symbolism of the moment wasn't lost on me. For I realized in that transformed prison cell exactly what he had been working on during that summer years ago. Just another of his mind-growing experiments: the art of picking locks.

"No, I didn't know that, Jess," I said as a reminiscent smile crept across my mouth. "But I certainly should have."

17.

"Henry went to work on the door lock with a pick set that he had. He said he carried it with him always - just in case. 'You know what this place is?' he asked me while he messed with the deadbolt. I didn't. 'It's the city's utilities headquarters. I could see the power control room through my hood as we walked past it earlier. That means we're probably on the underground floor.' I always knew Henry was smart, Dad, but this was just weird. How did he know so much about that place?" She asked it rhetorically. *"He's smarter than any of us can imagine,"* I thought to myself.

"After he unlocked the door, he checked the hallway outside. Nobody was guarding us. 'Told you they were giving us a break,' he said. We went down the hall until we found a stairwell, avoiding the control room - 'Too much activity at the brain of this operation,' Henry had said. We made it up the stairs easy. I couldn't believe how easy it actually was. We sneaked through the first floor halls, hiding behind corners when we needed to. We got out through a back exit door that led into an alley. 'Need to lay low until dark,' Henry said. 'But we also need to get away from this building,' I replied. Henry agreed.

"And that's when it got so strange, Dad. When we got to the edge of the alley."

"What do you mean?" I asked.

"Life inside the grid. It's the same as before. People are just going about their business like nothing's changed. Stores are open, the streets are clean. I didn't remember how nice things were."

I hadn't thought much about it myself. About what the ANTs' existence was like inside their protected blocks across the world. Secretly I had hoped they were living like we were. But that wasn't the truth. Jessica's revelation was hard to hear, but not surprising. After all, humans have a knack for being sadistically amnesic when a superiority complex is at stake.

"I know, honey. People can be cruel without knowing it when they choose to be ignorant." I was trying to make her feel better about the whole thing. That's what fathers do when their children are learning the bitter realities of life. We didn't need to dwell on it. "How did you guys get the medicine?"

"Right, the medicine. We were able to find a good hiding spot in a parking garage. That's one thing we didn't see - cars. I guess not everything is the way it was. So the garage seemed like a perfect place to take cover. We hid there until late night. On the city map we had with us, we located the hospital, then the pharmacy building. We got there after walking the streets for a long time. Whenever we thought someone was near, we had to stop and hide. It was nerve-racking. We didn't know if they had found out we had escaped. We were looking over our shoulders the whole night.

"The pharmacy building wasn't guarded. It was locked, but Henry had that covered. Then it was just a matter of finding Mom's medicine. Once we did that, we moved south through the city. Henry thought it was best to get as far away from the place where we had tried to enter as possible. Then I guess it was just luck. We heard those explosions. The ANTs at the border did, too. We just happened to be in the right place at the right time. We saw the ANTs leave their patrol area at the intersection we were next to. 'It's now or never,' Henry said, 'but don't leave me, Jessica.' Turns out that was a funny thing to say. Like I told you before, he ran faster than I'd ever seen him run. And we didn't stop until we got to that church. And now Henry's..."

She couldn't finish her last thought, but she didn't need to.

We sat silently. It had been a harrowing experience for her to re-live. But I was thinking that Daniel needed to hear it for himself. Their escape story contained valuable information for the Lefty movement. For some reason, I was starting to feel more of a connection to Daniel and his team. After seeing the ANTI- modus operandi, it seemed like the Leftys were the only chance the world had. I started worrying for Anna.

"What about Anna, Jessica? Did you guys ever see her on the inside?"

"No, we didn't. But you know what Henry told me when we were hiding in the garage? He said he could've sworn he heard her behind a closed door as they were leading him down the hall. He said her voice was 'unmistakable' - that was the word he used. That it had the same tone as that first day we were here. In the orientation meeting. When she told that guy off that questioned her. Henry said she was in that utilities building...and she wasn't taking any shit." She looked at me apologetically. "Sorry, but that's what he said."

"That's ok, honey." I gave her a wink and a smile. "And I bet Henry was right. I can't imagine Anna taking shit off anyone, especially the ANTs." Our circumstances had become much more dire with Henry's condition, but I was trying to ease the emotions of it all. In the back of my mind, I had begun mulling over our options on getting back to Meg. They weren't good unless Henry recovered. And soon. "I need to talk to Daniel, ok? We're going to be alright, Jess. Triumphs forever, remember?"

She nodded slightly, keeping her head bowed and her face partially hidden. I stood and walked to her, pressed her head against my chest and kissed the top of it. There wasn't anything left to say.

As I let go of Jessica to go find Daniel, he walked into our room, startling me. He had a frantic look on his face. It was a look that I hadn't seen in the short time I had known him.

"They're coming," he said, forebodingly.

"Who?" I asked.

"The ANTs. I don't know why, but they're coming."

18.

Daniel vanished as quickly as he had appeared. "Stay with Henry," I told Jessica. "Let me go find out what's going on here. I'll be right back." I was nervous and getting panicked. How could I protect Henry? How were we going to get out of there? How was I going to save Meg?

I ran after Daniel, but there was no slowing him down. We were in the central atrium of the camp before I caught up with him. The energy level throughout the camp was heightened. Lefty soldiers were running this way and that, equipping themselves with guns and grenades and various war gear while moving to their pre-assigned stations of defense. Although they hadn't planned for a battle this soon, they were surprisingly prepared.

"Daniel, wait! What the hell is happening?!?" He stopped. "Please," I asked, "just tell me what is happening."

He turned around and faced me. "The distraction team. The ones that were supposed to lure the border ANTs out and create a gap for the others to escape..."

"Yeah?" I answered.

"Well, they lured 'em out, alright. Too far. The ANTs wouldn't stop chasing them. I guess they were on edge after the explosions. Two of my guys got out after a vicious gunfight in the streets. They got back just a little while ago, badly injured but alive. We don't know how, but we guess they were followed. We sent out a reconnaissance team to confirm it."

"What about the guys on the inside of the grid? What about Anna?"

Daniel shook his head. "We assume they never found her. She wasn't with them when they joined the fight in the streets." He took a breath. "We lost 'em all, Gordon. All but the two that made it back to Overlord."

I started speaking my instinctive thoughts. "I have to get out of here. I have to get my kids out before they get here."

"No way, Gordon. There's no time. And think about Henry," he said as he grasped my arm to settle me. "Go hunker down with your kids, Gordon. Hold on to Jessica. We'll do everything we can to protect this place."

I believed him. But I wondered desperately if his everything would be enough.

19.

I ran back to our living quarters as fast as I could, dodging frantic Lefty soldiers along the way. The battle was set, whether either side wanted it or not. And there I was, with Jessica and Henry and my want for Meg, caught in the middle of it all.

There was commotion at Henry's cell as I arrived. I recognized two of our traveling companions, Beth and Madeline, standing in the doorway. That journey seemed like ages earlier in life, but it had just been a few days. As I got closer, I could see through the vertical lines of prison bars more people inside the room. There was Jeff, looking much better than the last time I had seen him. He had regained his color and spirit. And Anthony was there - Paul's friend and the last of our fellow journeymen. Jessica spotted me coming and turned my way with a broad smile and tears on her cheeks. The others parted and made room for me to enter. And that's when I saw Henry, sitting up on his bed and grinning.

"Hey, Dad."

I couldn't let go of him. As much as I may have been concerned about his health and injuring him any further, I couldn't stop squeezing him.

"Come on, Gordon, let the boy come up for air," Jeff jokingly said over my shoulder.

I reluctantly eased out of my embrace, but held Henry's arms in my hands and looked at him. "Good to see you, son. It's so damn good to see you."

"I know, Dad. Been sleeping a while, huh?"

Jessica laughed. "Yeah, Henry. Understatement of the year." Still siblings...and still fifteen.

"Yeah, buddy. We were worried about you," I said to him. "How you feeling?"

"Pretty good, I guess. All I remember is being so tired. I couldn't stand any longer. I couldn't keep my eyes open. But now I feel better."

"Good, son. Good." I turned to Jeff. "Looks like you're feeling better, too." I stuck out my hand to shake his. "Glad to see you. And sorry."

"Thanks, Gordon. It's been a tough time. Thank God for friends." He nodded toward Anthony and Beth and Madeline. "If I want to honor Paul, I've got to fight back. These guys helped me realize that."

"Well, it looks like your opportunity is almost here. The ANTs are on their way."

"Yeah, that's why we came down here," Anthony said. "To check on you guys. Make sure you were ready. And to make sure Henry was protected."

"Thanks for that," I said.

"You need a secure spot to ride this thing out, Gordon," Jeff instructed. He was definitely feeling back to his old self, with his natural leadership coming through. "You got a plan?"

I didn't. It was all happening so fast. Now that Henry was awake, things were easier. And we had the medicine - the whole reason we had come in the first place. Maybe we could make a run for it before the ANTs attacked. Maybe we could save ourselves and actually get back to Meg.

"No, Jeff. No plan," I said. "But if Henry's up for it, we could try and make a dash for the road west." I felt a surge of excitement at the prospect of escape. I asked Jessica and Henry, "You guys want to get the hell out of here and save Mom?"

But before they could muster an answer, we felt the rumble of an explosion, heard the screeching of stone and mortar breaking apart in a fiery instant. And I knew our chance for escape was gone.

20.

The state penitentiary that became Camp Overlord in the midst of the Great Dark had originally been constructed in the 1920s. The county's largest landowner had left the land to the state in his will, having no children interested in the annual feast-or-famine of farming. His intentions were clear, those being that the land be used for agricultural research. But in typical government fashion, the legislators and governor claimed a funding appropriation and deemed the acreage an ideal fit for a new, larger prison. To ease their consciences, I suppose, they made the prison a working one, utilizing a section of the confinement for growing crops with the hands and backs of prisoners. It occupied a significant amount of land, and it was situated nearly a mile from the highway.

Natural barriers were positioned on two sides of the donated land, helping to diminish the prospect of escape for any adventurous inmate. On the west side, there were thick woods with heavy underbrush for miles. On the east, the local fast-paced river flowed, reaching a width of seventy-five feet alongside the prison. On the north side, the creative minds of the state commissioned a dig-and-fill project for the area between the prison and the highway. They dug up two feet of topsoil and filled it with water from the river. With sparse trees varying in height and form, the section became a swampy marshland that made wading to the highway nearly impossible. All that was needed for fencing on those three sides was chain link topped with barb wire. The few prisoners through the years that made it over the fence didn't make it much further.

    The road that delivered supplies and visitors and freshly-convicted criminals to the confines led south from the highway alongside the river until it met the prison's single entrance drive. The driveway ran beside the south barrier, which needed to be stronger than fencing, it lacking any physical obstruction gifted from nature. The prison designers built a stone wall twenty feet high with a steel gate in the center of it. On the four corners of the complex and dotted throughout were watchtowers, each large enough to hold four well-equipped men comfortably. Every tower housed a rotational spotlight, for after-dark escape attempts.

    It was a prison of near-perfect design. But it seemed to me an even better military base. The ANTs that early morning were about to put that opinion to the test.

There was no way to know how big the ANTI-force might be that was coming. I looked out the barred window in Henry's room to see if I could gain any knowledge. It was still dark outside, but the moon was bright and there wasn't a cloud in the sky. I located the source of the explosion we had felt. It was at the south wall, very near the corner of the complex on the river side. That was the only direction the ANTs could approach from unless they took the highway west for many miles and go around the heavy woods on that side. Advantage Lefty.

Although the explosion had sounded destructive, the wall was only moderately damaged. The Lefty soldiers stationed in the watchtower at the southeast corner were beginning to fire downward. They were unloading on the ANTs below them, hidden from my view by the wall. And then they were gone. The tower and everything in it disintegrated into fire and smoke and particles behind some launched rocket.

I had seen enough of the early battle, and fear began to propel my actions.

21.

I may have done things differently in the hours leading up to my death. There's that overused but accurate saying - hindsight's 20/20. I always thought it meant that we can see the mistakes we made and learn from them. But it's not just mistakes. It's choices - good, bad, or indifferent. It could be something as simple as leaving work at 4:45 instead of 5:00. Or eating the salmon instead of the steak. I didn't know that until I was dead. When everything about my life became even clearer than perfect vision.

22.

I had always heard war veterans, old and young alike, talk about "the heat of battle." Interviews, documentaries. Turns out there are a lot of ways to describe what it's like inside the throes of human-to-human mass murder. Heat is as good as any. Everything around you is happening with such intensity that it seems white hot.

I turned away from the window and saw Jeff and the others leaving through the doorway. He stopped and said, "Find some cover," on his way out.

"Jeff," I blurted out. "Don't be stupid out there." He nodded his affirmation and disappeared.

I didn't like where we were located inside the camp. Too close to the point of attack. The smell of smoke was beginning to find its way into the room.

"Henry, can you move?" I asked him.

He eased off of the bed and stood warily, testing his balance. "Yeah, Dad, I think so. Maybe slow, but I can move."

"Ok, good. Jessica, go gather everything we need. Make sure to get the guns and packs we brought with us." She took off before I was finished. "And the medicine!" I yelled after her.

"Got it, Dad..." I heard her say from the other side of the corridor.

I wanted to move us north and west inside the hallways. To get as far away from the ANTs' point of attack as possible. I had begun to realize that we still might have a chance to get away with their limited access to the camp. If we wanted to risk the wooded area to the west, we may be able to escape. There wouldn't be any ANTs in that direction.

I helped Henry get dressed. He was weak, I could tell. That was going to be our determining factor, the answer to our fate: would Henry have the strength to make a run for it?

Jessica came back with everything we needed tightly secured in three backpacks. She had her rifle and three handguns for each of us. And the large knife I had carried with me throughout our journey. "Where to, Dad?" she asked.

"Just follow me, guys," I replied. "I've got a plan."

23.

We made our way through the cell-lined halls of the camp, with me in the lead and Jessica last. I told Henry before we started to stop us if he needed to rest. Or if he couldn't go any further at all. I just didn't know what he was capable of doing yet. But he kept up. And he didn't complain. Neither his leg nor his condition seemed to be slowing him down much.

We reached the central section of the prison. It was the area that opened up into dining, meeting, and training facilities. What had been a bustling hub of activity just a short time earlier was quiet now. All of the Leftys were in their defensive positions. The sounds of war being waged outside were growing louder by the minute. But they were still only coming from the south.

I veered us down the corridor that led closest to the northwest corner of the facility. I could feel the battle behind us, trying to wrap its arms around the kids and me. I moved as quickly as I thought we could, but the hallways were long and serpentine-like. It seemed to take hours and yet move in a blur.

At the end of the last hallway was a large iron door. In its prison years, the door had been locked using an electronic seal. Although Lefty had managed to generate its own system of electrical power, they had not been using it to keep the doors locked. I hoped that had not changed as we approached our possible escape hatch. I stopped us at the door to try and assess the situation and come up with our next step.

"How you doing, Henry?" I asked as we all knelt down.

"Ok, Dad." He was winded, but not exhausted. First assessment: check.

The outside gunfire and explosions were more distant than before. We had outrun the battle. Second assessment: check.

I needed to get a visual of the area on the other side of the door. Then I could decide what we should do next. I grasped the lever that kept the door shut and closed my eyes, hoping for no resistance. It turned with ease.

"Guys, I've got to take a look outside. Don't move," I directed the kids.

I cracked the door and peered through the slight opening. I saw nothing in my limited scope of vision. I opened it further and still saw no movement. Third assessment: check.

In the distance I could see a medium-sized storage garage. Whether it had housed prison vehicles or farming equipment in its former existence, I didn't know. But it sparked an idea in my head. I had been worried that the three of us couldn't make it over the barb-topped fence even if we got the chance. But I was betting that garage still held tools. Industrial-strength tools capable of cutting through meshed steel wire.

I muttered to myself as I stared off toward it, "We just might not have to go over that fence after all."

24.

I eased the iron door closed behind me as I came back through the opening. Jessica and Henry were waiting, wide-eyed. "Well???" Jessica asked impatiently.

"We're clear," I said. "And I think I've got a way to get us out of here. Out of the whole God-forsaken place."

I explained the storage garage. I told them it was a few hundred feet away. We needed to get to it first, then get inside. "But it's probably locked. Henry, that's where I'm going to need you. Can you get us in?"

He turned to Jessica. "You pack my picks?"

She nodded. "Yeah, I got everything. They're in the front pocket of your backpack."

Henry unzipped the pocket and pulled out the pick set. It was a small leather sleeve. He opened it and shuffled his fingers through the numerous metal picks. "Yep. All here." He looked up at me. "Dad, as long as it's a standard locking mechanism, I can get us in. No problem." I was seeing the confidence in his demeanor that Jessica had described.

"Good," I said. "Then let's get ready. We haven't got long until sun-up."

Jessica led us across the expanse toward the garage. I followed behind Henry, keeping my head moving back and forth. I knew we were far from the action at the south wall, but I didn't want any surprises. As we crossed, I noticed two of the watchtowers looming ahead. One was just on the other side of the garage. The other was further away at the northwest corner. They both had their spotlights trained on the battle in the distance, but they weren't engaged in the fight. Yet.

We made it to the garage quickly. There were three large roll-up doors for vehicles. Each was locked from the inside. As we got to the last one, Jessica moved around the corner of the building. She leaned back and whispered, "There's a regular door over here."

Henry got to it and pulled out a small pen-sized flashlight from his pack. He took a few seconds to look at the locks on the door. There was a door knob lock and a deadbolt. He went to work on the deadbolt first, using precise wrist and finger motions to click each hidden tumbler into place. The lock on the door knob didn't take as long, and we were inside the garage within two minutes.

I pulled out my hi-beam flashlight and used it to explore the large space. It became obvious that the garage had been used in its prison time for farming equipment. There were still two tractors inside, although useless. The rest of the space contained organized stacks of military clothing and gear. Lefty was using it for storage. There wasn't much room for walking, and I began to doubt that the tool I needed was there. But when I finally made it to the far side, there they were. Along the wall behind one of the tractors were all sorts of farming and carpentry and mechanical repair tools of every shape and size.

I knew what I needed, and I knew it would be there. I ran the beam of my flashlight up and down the wall until I saw it: a bolt cutter strong enough to cut through the wire of a prison fence. I grabbed it up with excitement and made my way back to Jessica and Henry, who were waiting by the door.

"And here it is," I said, as I held up the cutter proudly.

Henry spoke up, "We're gonna make it out, aren't we, Dad?"

"This is the last piece of the puzzle, Henry." Then a surreal vision came into my head. "I never in my life thought I'd be breaking out of prison." It was absurd. "But that's exactly what we're about to do."

25.

The fence that separated us from the woods stood a long distance away from the garage. We could hear the battle at the south wall growing. I looked through the tinted glass on one of the roll-up doors. The Lefty soldiers in the watchtowers throughout the southern section of the camp were all firing now. It appeared that the ANTs had spread across the entire south border. There were residual fires burning along the length of the giant stone wall. As my eyes moved down the wall, I thought I could see gunfire and grenades beginning to explode at the southwest corner, then up the fence-line. The ANTs were coming around the south border and attacking at the much more accessible chain-link fence. The same fence we were about to use for our escape. Our window of time was closing fast.

"Ok, guys, this is it," I said to Jessica and Henry. "We get to the fence as fast as we can. I'll cut a hole large enough for us to crawl through, then we head straight into the woods. We'll get as far as we can from this mess, then rest. Good?"

"Good," they replied in unison.

"And don't think about what's happening around us when we get out there. It shouldn't take me long to cut the wire. And it's still dark enough for us to be invisible. Just stay calm."

"Don't worry, Dad," Jessica said. "We've made it this far, right?"

Henry put his hand out. Jessica grasped it in hers, then I put mine on top of both of them. "Triumphs forever," he said.

I held their hands in mine for a few sacred seconds, then I opened the door and led them to the fence.

26.

I ran as fast as I could. I knew that Henry would be slower, but Jessica was with him. And I needed to get working on the fence as quickly as possible. I glanced over to the battle that was continuing to extend itself toward us. The exchange of gunfire was now constant and close. I could see that the spotlights from the two watchtowers nearest us had moved. They were focused on the fence-line that I was fast approaching, but further south.

I got to one knee at the wire mesh and started working the bolt cutter. It took more strength to operate than I thought it would. But I squeezed and pulled as hard as possible. Jessica and Henry weren't far behind. I told them once they were kneeling beside me, "Keep your eyes peeled, guys. This may take a few minutes."

Pressure and time. Those are the two aspects of stress. How one can handle pressure under time constraints. The pressure of three lives relying on my efficiency was more stress than I could ever try to explain. But the funny thing is, I believe it fueled me. As the gunfire and explosions grew louder in my ears, I quickened my pace. And then, when I began to hear voices of soldiers on both sides, shouting orders or yelling in pain, my determination heightened.

"Come on, Dad," Jessica said in a hushed voice. "They're getting closer."

I cut the last piece of wire that I thought needed to be detached. I pushed on the section of fence that would become our salvation hole. It gave halfway, then hung. I pushed again. It pushed back. I had been able to see enough by moonlight to cut the fence, but now I was blind to why it wouldn't separate from itself completely. I had not wanted to use a flashlight. We couldn't afford the probable attention it would bring. But I was desperate in that moment. We were so close to leaving that horror behind.

I slung my backpack off one shoulder then the next. "Almost there, guys," I said. "Gotta shine a light for just a second. Get ready to crawl through when I say." I found the flashlight and made sure to turn it on facing the woods. I shined the beam along the cut-line in the fence. As the light moved across the area where I had been working, I saw it in the background. There was a large fallen tree just on the other side, with a huge branch that rose high into the air. The branch was strong and keeping the cut fence section from budging any further.

The fallen tree was immovable. But if I could sever the branch from it, even just a little, we could have enough room to slide through. I pulled my knife from its sheath at my side. I reached around the leaning fence piece and began hacking. It was an awkward position, but it was working. I pushed the fence as I hacked, and I could feel it begin to give more and more.

"Get ready, Henry. You first." The opening was big enough for him and Jessica. I would get them through while I continued to work on the branch. Then I could make it. Henry threw his backpack through the hole. He followed behind it with ease. "Your turn, Jess." She did the same. Backpack first, herself next.

As Jessica finished her passage, Henry said something that I didn't understand. "What?!?" I asked him as I finished hacking at the branch. There was finally enough room for me to slide through.

"Dad, look!" He said it with a certain intensity. It wasn't fear – that emotion in him seemed to be gone.

I looked in the direction he pointed. A bright beam from one of the watchtower's spotlights was tracking its way up the fence-line toward me. I had been worried about ANTs, but a different sense of dread sneaked up on me in that moment. What would we look like to a nervous Lefty soldier manning one of those watchtowers? Might we look like a group of ANTs trying to break through? The thought was instantaneous, and I frantically began to push my way through the hole. I was halfway through it when I felt the blinding light hit me.

27.

No. Not yet. And to be up front, there is no blinding light. No light at all really.

The first shots thudded into the ground a foot to my left. Eight rapid-fire successions. Dirt and grass flew into the air, some of it landing in my eyes and mouth. I yelled at Jessica and Henry a simple directive. The same one I had told them I would use in case of danger before we left Meg's farm. Before we set out on what kept feeling like a doomed mission. "Ruuunnnn!!!"

I tried to dig my feet deeper into the ground to propel myself faster through the fence hole. But they were slipping. I told myself to calm down, be deliberate. The second succession of bullets landed above my head. Some hit the fallen tree, sending pieces of bark upward. They had either seen the kids, were bad shots, or both. I didn't want to find out if the third spray would be more accurate. I bent my right knee, pushed my boot against the earth, and threw my body over the horizontal tree trunk and into the deep woods.

But the third spray of bullets met me there. Not all of them. Just one actually. Unfortunately, one was all it took.

PART FOUR: CONTROL

1.

The government servers didn't stand a chance. Jacob knew they were vulnerable, but not to the extent that they actually were. The only two problems occurred in Germany and Japan, which didn't surprise him much. Both of the countries had a history of ingenuity and protectionism. Each of their systems held on longer than Jacob had expected, but they eventually succumbed like the rest. The Domino Infection completed its takeover in eighteen hours and twelve minutes.

Once the world's electronic infrastructure was disabled, it was only a matter of time before the rest of it fell apart and ANTI- could take over. Countries grounded their commercial transportation almost instantaneously. At first, it was out of security fears. After all, if the attackers could so easily hack into their government systems, what would keep them from bringing down a jet airliner? Or even worse, bringing down an entire airspace of airliners. By the time they realized Salvador wasn't that kind of terrorist, it was too late to recover.

Salvador had predicted how the world would view him when he stopped it in its tracks, but terror was never his intent. It was certainly a side effect, but only because humans didn't know how to live without technology anymore. In fact, they were terrified of life without it. No, Salvador was never a terrorist in his own mind. He was something very different.

Twenty-four hours after Jacob's virus had finished its infiltration, the engineering ANTs moved into position. They invaded the utility headquarters of pre-designated cities across the planet. Once inside, they were able to reprogram the software that provided power to each of those cities, creating an electrified and fully functional grid in each.

Meanwhile, the more militaristic-minded ANTs cleared the grids for the rest. It was an ugly operation, but it was all part of the plan. Besides, Salvador had given everyone in the world a chance to join him in his revolution. The ANTI- mindset was simple – if they hadn't chosen to follow him, it was their own fault.

The grids became safe havens for the millions of ANTs throughout the world. The places where they would live their lives for the years it would take the rest of the population to destroy itself. There would be no way to know how long that process would take, but Salvador had prepared them all to wait it out. And the ANTs had proven to be patient already, slowly building their movement over many long years to reach their victorious climax.

But there was one other concern, another thing that Salvador had warned his ANTs about – the inevitable backlash from the outsiders. Even still, none of them saw the Sector 3 revolt coming as soon as it did. Not even Salvador.

2.

Communication between the powered grids was vital to the new ANTI- existence. A separate set of engineer ANTs was assigned to the configuration of fiber-optic telecommunication systems connecting each of the new communities. Access to land-line based telephones was virtually immediate, while Internet and cell phone capabilities took a couple of weeks to recover. There were some complicated obstacles to overcome, especially in the lesser-developed regions of the world, but eventually ANTI- was online, just as before. The new Earth looked like its own spherical constellation from an interstellar vantage point. A hundred or so stars lit up and dotting the land masses, invisibly interconnected by underground communication cables. The teams assigned to space satellite control would ultimately transmit images that confirmed just that.

Jacob was stationed at North America Sector 1's grid, located in Philadelphia. It was ANTI-'s unofficial capital, strategically chosen for its proximity to the largest cities on the continent, while distant from possible government backlash in Washington and the geographical complications of New York. When Salvador came out of his bunker, he joined Jacob there, as did Simone. They were able to monitor the progress of the takeover from that grid. Jacob was left in charge of the Domino Infection, tasked with fending off any counter-attacks against it. But there weren't any.

As soon as all of the power grids were up and running, Salvador made sure to communicate his message to the ANTs, his revolutionaries. He looked to continue his cause, and make an inspirational appearance before them. The speech was thoughtful and invigorating. It was broadcast from a former TV studio inside Philadelphia's tallest building, sent out across the new ANTI- network. Some watched on personal computer screens, while others crowded repurposed sports bars and restaurants. Most of the grids were in large cities, and ANTs gathered in the streets to watch him on giant media screens. It was propaganda for sure, but the people of ANTI- viewed the message as absolute truth.

Salvador spoke with conviction and purpose. "Welcome, my fellow pragmatists, to the new world. The world that is yours and mine now. The world that we can make into something so much better." He paused for effect. He was dressed in his typical attire: dark tailored suit with white button-down shirt. He was the definition of dapper. The camera focused on his entire profile from a distance, as his custom was to walk as he talked.

"By now, you should feel secure in your new environs. Our plan has progressed as predicted. We have complete control. The rest of Earth's population is in the dark, literally and figuratively. They are lost. It's only a matter of time until they become desperate. And desperation will lead to decimation. But that should not be your concern today. Today is a celebration." He held for another few seconds. ANTs cheered throughout the ANTI- populace.

"Many of you may ask, 'Where do we go from here?' Or, more succinctly, 'Now what?' It has always been part of our strategy to only give you the information you need. For your trust in me, I thank you." Salvador paused and bowed his head in thought. He looked up and straight into the camera's lens, emphasizing his next few sentences. "The 'where we go now' is up to you. We have no government, no policy, no directive. We only have each other."

No one had known what Salvador was going to say in the speech, not even Jacob or Simone. He was a true island. And at this point, Jacob began to question the course of Salvador's thoughts. But he should have known his leader better.

"No directive," Salvador continued, "but that's not to say we will become a society with no direction. And direction begets navigation. I will be your navigator. You, the people, will choose the path of your society - I will be there to make sure the path is clear and straight. You, the people, will control your destiny - I will be there to manifest it."

He began to smile. Salvador had an amazing affinity to loosen the mood of a situation with a simple gesture or subtle shift in emotion. Jacob watched him lift any remaining tension that may have been lingering over the ANTI- nation in that moment.

"I leave you with this today. Something I learned long ago. Something my family taught me. If you believe in something close to your heart, and someone takes it away - you fight and you take it back. We've taken our civilization back today – now we've got to hold on to it. And make it stronger. For the Soul of Humanity."

3.

Before the global attack, ANTI- had people on the inside of everything. Police, military, government - they were entrenched. That was the linchpin. Without the ANT insiders, they couldn't have pulled it off. There would have been entirely too much to overcome.

As soon as the servers went down in their respective countries, the ANTI- insiders attacked. It was calculated and synchronized. There were skirmishes, especially at the armories and arsenals and bases. In Moscow, they lost over a thousand ANTs in a battle that lasted for two days. And the Australian military proved to be remarkably resilient, fighting for a week before ANTI- was able to stamp them out.

The large metropolitan police departments were as big a concern for the ANTI- leadership as the established armies. Most had been equipping themselves like an arm of the military for many years prior, especially in the United States. And the majority of them were headquartered inside or very near the ANTI- grids. When the attack commenced, the police ANTs took control of the departments and ordered patrols back to their respective stations and headquarters, where the ANTI- clearance teams were waiting. In the end, it was much easier than the various military takeovers.

Once they had the police and military threat contained, protection of the grids was simple. They had the equipment, and they had the manpower. There were invasion attempts for months, but the grids' security ANTs were vigilant and hyper-protective. At times, Jacob thought too much so. But Salvador would remind him in those moments that revolution is a bloody proposal. And that, no matter how much he hated it, theirs could be no different.

4.

Salvador made sure that life inside the grids was as stable as possible. He made sure that basic provisions were accessible, and that money became a device of the past civilization. Every ANT had shelter and access to food and water. There was electricity, phones, and computers. Eventually, excursion teams were formed to maintain supplies inside the sectored habitats. These mercenary-style convoys would trek into the grid surroundings every two weeks to re-stock from the abandoned outside world. It was utopian, on the inside.

Every ANT had a job, regardless of pay. It was part of the revolution's mentality. Everyone worked to keep the society progressing and that progress was the reward. In effect, it was socialism. But Salvador didn't like to talk about -isms and -archys and -ocracys. "ANTI- is above definition, hijo," he would say in philosophical discussions with Jacob.

There were occasions when a member of the new society had to be removed. These instances were rare, by design. After all, there were only two choices once the Great Dark began: life inside the powered, protected grids or life outside them. It only took a few banishments to drive this point home to the ANTI-populace. Everyone worked, or else suffered the darkness.

There was leadership within the new society, although Salvador worked to keep it subtle. "People need guidance," Salvador told Jacob once. "I don't have a title, and I don't want one. But have no doubt about my position - I am at the top."

Each grid had its own upper layer of directorships, for lack of a more ethereal term. The directors were well-established members of Salvador's decades-old operation. He held daily briefings via video teleconferences, where developments were reported and decisions were made. But, on the whole, he let the new society, divided into separate communities, breathe and grow on its own. It entertained him to watch his ANTs become whatever they were going to become.

Jacob had told Salvador in one of their first meetings so many years before that he didn't see the man as some evil mastermind. And he wasn't. But good and evil can become blurred together over time. In the end, the perspective all depends on which side you're fighting.

5.

Salvador had never been one for egotistical representations. Instead, he chose Philadelphia's tallest building to be his headquarters because of its basic physical attributes. The tower was fifty-eight stories high and afforded him miles of visibility. That's what was important to him. He could look out upon all four corners of the new world he had created.

The building had been the centralized offices of a former national corporation, with residential space in its top eight floors. It was a spectacle of modern architecture. The exterior was covered in mirrored glass upward to its tapered tip, where its final four floors sat like a separate metallic cube that some giant had placed there as a finishing touch. Its lower office space was occupied by Salvador's staff, including Jacob and the programmers that worked for him.

The residences in the upper portion of the tower were spacious and luxurious. Jacob was furnished an apartment two stories below Salvador, who lived and worked at the top. He had transformed the entire floor into his own personal sanctuary, and he rarely invited visitors. The day he issued Jacob's new assignment to him, they met there.

The building's elevator glided up through the center of the structure. When its doors opened on the top floor, Jacob found himself in the middle of a large room, with sky and clouds just a short distance away. He stepped out and saw Salvador to his left.

"Unnerving, isn't it?" Salvador asked, with his signature smile.

"Yeah, a little," Jacob said. As he looked around, he could see that the top floor was one gigantic open room. It was enclosed with floor-to-ceiling glass on all four sides. The glass was the clearest he had ever seen, almost invisible.

"I've gotten used to it by now," Salvador said. "You should see it at night."

"You definitely don't disappoint on views," Jacob said. "It takes me back to that first night in California."

Salvador was walking over to a bar that was set up in a far corner. "Right, California. Now that's something I miss. The ocean, the trees." He closed his eyes and turned his head upward to the ceiling, as if he could smell and hear the nature of his old homestead all of a sudden. "Someday, hijo. Someday we'll be back there." He released the memory and turned to Jacob. "What are we drinking today?"

"Depends on why I'm here, I suppose." Jacob had a feeling that the meeting's purpose was to define his next mission, and he didn't want things to get too cloudy too quickly with alcohol. "How about whiskey?" he offered. That was something he could sip on without indulging too much.

"Whiskey it is," Salvador replied. He started pouring the drinks, and Jacob took the opportunity to survey their surroundings. The space was eerily similar to Salvador's west coast house. There was very little furniture and decoration, and it made the outside skyscape seem even more invasive. Jacob felt as if the room was floating in midair. "Come sit down," Salvador said as he handed Jacob his drink. There were four leather chairs in the center of the room. They chose two across from each other.

"Thanks for this, Salvador. I've got to say, we're a little overdue for a celebration."

"Yes, hijo, we are." He held out his glass half-filled with ice and whiskey. "A toast. To saving the world from itself." Jacob raised his in return, and they each took a pull. "I couldn't have done it without you, Jacob. I want you to know that."

"Thank you for bringing me on the adventure. To say you changed my life would be a little cliché, considering. But you did. You made me better than I ever imagined I could be."

Salvador's face filled with satisfaction. "Exactly what I wanted for all of us. To be better than we thought we could be. So far, so good."

Jacob considered the statement. It was something he had known but not given much credence. The big picture of Salvador's intent was becoming more vivid and defined. "So what's next for us?"

"Honest answer? I have no idea. Don't misunderstand me. I have my predictions. And I certainly won't let things revert back to the way they were. But I don't want to interfere too much."

"Interfere?" Jacob asked.

"With the experiment. All I need to do is keep everyone in line until enough of the outside world is gone. Then we can start all over again. Or maybe we can't. That's what we'll find out. And that's what this whole thing is about."

6.

Salvador walked to the bar and poured another round of whiskeys as he introduced the next phase of Jacob's contribution to his ANTI- experiment. It was an important moment in their relationship, with Salvador showing that he thought of Jacob as more than just a hacker. He wanted to entrust Jacob with something different, but obviously big. And the Domino Infection having finished its job, Jacob was hungry for something else.

"What do you think you should do now, hijo? Now that your virus has destroyed the modern world?" Salvador asked as he handed him his second drink. He was doing what he always did with Jacob - what good leaders do. He was pushing Jacob to think outside of his comfort zone.

"It's funny you ask, Salvador. I've been considering the possibilities. The Domino Infection has been my life's focus for so many years, it's hard to imagine doing anything else."

"Of course it is. But, Jacob, you're like an artist. When you finish one project, you move on to the next. You have to. It's in your DNA."

Jacob stood and walked to the edge of the room, to what felt like the edge of the heavens. He took a long drink of the ice-cold whiskey, holding it on his tongue and letting it slip down his throat slowly. It was smoky with a slight burn. He looked out over the broad distance that the height of the tower afforded, and it came to him.

"You need eyes, don't you?" Jacob asked. He could feel Salvador's approval from behind him.

"I certainly do, hijo."

"Right now, you're near-sighted. Blind to what's happening outside of the grids."

"That's right. I am."

"You need to know how quickly the outside population is devouring itself." Jacob turned from the glass wall and faced his mentor. "And you need to make sure everything is going as planned."

"I don't need any surprises, Jacob. In order for this experiment to continue unabated, I can't have any unforeseen opposition. I need more than just sight. I need knowledge."

Jacob began to realize something that Salvador had known all along. That they weren't done fighting. That there would still be obstacles in forming their new society. That certain human wills might not give up too easily. There was no calculation or statistic that could determine it. It was one of the few things in nature that was beyond mathematical presumption, and therefore beyond Jacob's logical mindset.

Salvador continued. "I'm not concerned with the small random invasion attempts that we're seeing now. No, that's just desperation at work. What I need to anticipate is the organized attacks. The groups of people that will inevitably develop a strategic challenge to what we're trying to do."

"It won't be easy, Salvador."

"I know it won't. But that's why you're the one to do it. We've got time. These types of revolts won't develop quickly. But the sooner you get me those eyes, the better. Simone will help. She's good with information. Getting it and analyzing it. But you know that by now."

Jacob did know that. He had become somewhat enchanted with Simone's persona ever since the invasion, and ever since the Domino Infection wasn't occupying all of his time. She was skilled in so many ways, and he enjoyed watching her work. "Ok then, we'll get started tomorrow," Jacob said as he finished the last bit of whiskey in his glass. "I'll get it done, Salvador. Trust me."

"Of course you will, hijo. It's who you are: the straight line that connects my abstract dots."

7.

The ANTs who provided security for the grids were frightening, even to those on the inside. They appeared at the onset of the attack, seemingly out of nowhere to the other ANTs. They had been designated as a separate division from the rest of ANTI-, and they were the most hidden secret of Salvador's revolution. They were known as the Omega XT.

They were the same group that cleared the grids before the other ANTs moved into them. Their tactics for removal were ruthless and unemotional. People who were living inside the pre-determined grid boundaries were given one chance to leave peacefully as the Great Dark began. But instead of then forcefully pushing them out if they refused, the Omega XT would simply eliminate them, without question or regard for human dignity. It was one of the hardest things for Jacob to accept about the takeover. He could see the logic in it - these people were going to die in the darkness anyway. But he couldn't hide his distaste when he heard stories of eliminated children. He told himself that the Omega XT were saving them from future suffering, and most of the time it helped him sleep at night.

With access to the inventory at military bases and police departments, the Omega XT were able to equip themselves with hi-tech weaponry and advanced-tactic vehicles. They used all-terrain jeeps, humvees, and armored trucks, each upfitted with high-caliber machine guns or rocket launchers. And every Omega XT ANT carried an assault rifle and wore two crisscrossed utility belts filled with grenades and ammunition. They were highly trained, although their origin and training grounds remained a mystery to most other ANTs, including Jacob.

They dressed themselves in black and gray camouflage with full-scale military body armor, and they wore tinted goggles and dark face masks under tight-fitting helmets. They were completely anonymous and resoundingly intimidating. Salvador had explained to Jacob before ANTI- compelled the Great Dark upon the world that there would be necessary horrors that came with it. Jacob trusted him that the Omega XT were necessary. And he never had any doubts that they were truly horrific.

8.

Simone and Jacob met to discuss the plan for their next project the morning after his top-floor meeting with Salvador. What started as an informal breakfast turned into lunch and then early afternoon drinks as the discussion flowed without pause. He had always been impressed with her intellect - it was rare to find someone who thought on the same level as he did. It immediately felt to Jacob like they were meant to work together, even though they had never had the chance.

Their mutual flirtation from years ago had not subsided either. Jacob held a deep respect for Simone, but he couldn't deny the sexual tension that existed between them. Simone felt it, too. They both left it unacknowledged and simmering underneath their interactions. And they let it fuel the creativity that they needed to help Salvador further his revolution.

"The goal is intel," Jacob said in that first meeting. "You'll know what to do with it. But first things first - we've got to get it."

"Exactly," she replied. "The problem is that we're dealing with total blackout. They're in complete darkness out there - but once we cross that grid line, so are we."

They kicked around all sorts of ideas. Spy planes and helicopters. A network of satellite bases with dedicated reconnaissance teams. They even came up with a crazy system of tunnels dug throughout the land masses of the earth. "A human-sized, globalized ANT farm," they laughed. That one came after the first round of cocktails. By the last drink, no strategy, no matter how absurd, was off the table.

But their initial brainstorming that day turned fruitless. They had inevitably run into the same problem with all of their ideas: they each involved ANTs roaming outside the grids, something that they learned Salvador wanted to avoid at all costs. He told Jacob that having their people journey deep into the Great Dark was not an option, no matter what.

"There's no hope out there right now, Jacob," he said. "None at all. But helicopters, planes, cars, trucks...*us*...that would create hope. Do you understand?"

Jacob did.

"The excursion teams that we use to re-stock our supplies are one thing. They never travel more than a few miles out."

That was right.

"But if we become even moderately visible with the same technology we have taken away from the rest, all we would do is inspire and excite them. And give them hope in a hopeless world."

Jacob nodded.

"Come up with something else."

For Jacob and Simone, it was back to the proverbial drawing board.

The answer came to him while he was sleeping. It was a real eureka moment. Jacob awoke reminded of the math of Archimedes, while mentally kicking himself for not thinking of it that first day with Simone. It had been right in front of him without his seeing it.

He jumped out of bed and reached for his phone. When he touched the screen, it read "2:38 AM." It was the deep recesses of REM sleep that had led him to it. He pressed the circular button and said, "Call Simone." She didn't answer at first. Jacob was wide awake by the fourth ring, when her voice finally came through the phone's speaker.

"Jacob, what the hell are you doing? Sleep is precious to me, goddammit."

"Simone, just shut up. I've got it."

"Got what?"

"The answer to our problem. The way we can see the world."

"Oh yeah? What is it?"

"One word: Drones."

9.

The Omega XT became overtly emboldened in certain grids. Salvador had predicted it would happen at a certain level, as aggression tends to follow a sense of power. He maintained as much control of them as possible, and the vast majority of his leadership across the globe was mindful of the importance of their subtle supervision over the elite soldiers. But the logistics of keeping that many people in line across an entire planet were nightmarish. There were grid directorships that lost the respect of the fighting force, and the stories of the violence that followed were hard to comprehend.

The worst instance of unchecked power gone wrong occurred in Eastern Europe Sector 5. Jacob was on the conference call with Salvador as he was briefed on the situation.

"They have run amok, Salvador," one of the directors from the grid was explaining vehemently. "We were never supposed to be real terrorists, were we? Our own people are scared of them! The ones that are supposed to be protecting us!"

"Wait, slow down, director," Salvador interrupted. "What exactly is happening?"

"Our Omega XT - they're off the rails! They've taken a group of kids, Salvador. Kids! Maybe 12, maybe 13 years old. Over twenty of them. All they were doing was looking for food, I think. They let them get close, acted as if they might help them." The director was on the verge of breaking down. His voice cracked as he continued. "Once they were close enough, they grabbed them up and slit their throats. One by one. A few tried to run, but they mowed them down with the .50-cals. Cut them to pieces."

I heard Salvador sigh under his breath. "Oh, hell."

"And then the others. It was barbaric. I can't believe it still." The director hesitated. "They hung them up by their feet from the light poles over the street. Like hogs in a slaughterhouse. They bled out in front of all of us." He took a breath, and then stunned us out of our shock, "Kids, Salvador!"

"I know, I know."

"I don't know that you do. I never signed up for anything like this!"

Salvador raised himself from the crouched position in which he had been sitting during the horrid tale. He spoke sternly, powerfully. "What you signed up for, director, is some form of leadership. A form of leadership that seems to be missing right now, as far as I can tell."

The director fought back. "Listen, Salvador, I don't know where these guys came from, but their methods are downright inhuman and sickening. This is not what I thought it was going to be."

"You let me handle the methodology of the Omega XT from here. But you've got to get yourself under control, dammit. This is not going to be perfect. And your people will look to you as an example. You can do this, director. There's nothing to fear. Make sure you and your directorship display exactly that sentiment. Got it?"

There was silence on the other end. Finally, the director replied. "Got it. Nothing to fear."

Jacob left the call wondering what Salvador could really do to rein in that group of Omega XT on the other side of the world. He also began to wonder if they would allow themselves to be reined in at all, there or anywhere else.

10.

Drones were everywhere before the Great Dark, constantly hovering above the world's people. The United States used the most by far. The classic American defense budget rule applied: if one is worth the money, then build a thousand. Russia and China had been using them, too. And a number of other developed countries were exploring the multiple ways in which a drone program could be effective.

On a more localized level, the U.S. government had developed an extensive network of drones for use across its homeland. Various agencies were watching the nation's citizens, under the guise of protection. Most people probably wouldn't have cared had they known about them. But to Jacob, that wasn't the point. The more he learned about the U.S. drone program, the more he understood what government overreach meant. And it made him feel more justified than ever in what he had done.

America's use of unmanned aircraft had begun during the Vietnam War, although it was highly classified. Those first drones were limited to straight-line or circular flight paths, and therefore only employed for surveillance. More sophisticated ones were used with success in the Gulf War, which led to interest and money flowing into their research and development throughout the 1990s. By the time the Global War on Terror was declared, drones were ready to bear the brunt of battle. Armed and agile, their missions of assassination and destruction became the U.S. military norm.

The country's history of self-spying, and the tactics utilized in it, wasn't quite so clear. Some of ANTI-'s military insiders said it had started soon after the 9/11 attacks. Some who had been embedded deeper said it was in place long before then. Satellites in orbit and streets full of cameras were a large part of it. But drones provided such flexibility. They could be flown wherever and whenever needed. And with the technological advances in video occurring at a hyper pace, there was eventually little left that a drone couldn't see.

For the job Jacob had ahead of him, they were the perfect tools. He just had to learn how to fly them.

11.

Simone and Jacob focused their drone team on North America, planning to test the program in Sector 1 first and then outward. If they could make it work there, they would roll it out across the world with ample supply of the unmanned aircraft and the facilities needed to operate them. Salvador approved. The drones by their very intent would be invisible to the people they were observing, just as he wanted. Equipped with advanced high-definition video cameras, they could fly at an altitude high enough to be silent and out of sight while still being effective.

And to top it all off, their team could be centralized, commandeering the flights from a single headquarters and eliminating confusion of their purpose. America's spy program against itself was based in one place, with drones remotely controlled out of a solitary underground room. And that room was housed a short distance from the Sector 1 grid, just outside of the former nation's capital. Jacob and Simone organized a group of pilots and engineers and made their way to the former military complex where it was located. It would become their home for the next few weeks. Home of the Omni Operation.

Jacob poured himself into the various training manuals that described both operation and capability of the aircraft. He was obsessive about that kind of thing. There wasn't a number or word that he thought he could afford to miss. The people he and Simone had assembled acted the same, whether by nature or impression. He didn't care, as long as they created a successful program for Salvador. Jacob saw the end game, and they just needed to help him get there.

Simone worked differently. She was much more personal, much better dealing with people. It didn't matter if she were interrogating a threat or having lunch with a colleague, she always got what she wanted from the person through interaction and conversation. Jacob envied her for that.

She quickly grew bored with the analysis of the machines and how they worked. "Go back to the grid," Jacob told her after a week. "There's nothing for you here yet. Besides, you can keep Salvador calm in person much easier than from afar."

"How long before you'll be ready to send them out?" she asked.

"A couple more weeks, at least. You know me - I don't try anything without absolute confidence. Don't worry, I'll send for you before we get started." He hated to see her go, but he hated to see her restless even more. That was a new feeling for Jacob - caring about someone else's happiness. He was becoming very fond of Simone, in a way that he had never experienced with anyone else. He felt apprehensive about it, but he couldn't stop its effect on him.

"Ok, Jacob. But you make sure I'm here for that first flight. I don't want to miss out on anything you might find. And Salvador doesn't want me to either."

"Whoa, hold on a second. That might have sounded like a threat if I thought about it too much."

She laughed under her breath. "You don't have to think about it at all, dear boy. That's exactly what it was."

Jacob smiled. He knew he was going to miss her.

12.

ANTI-'s first full-scale drone flight was successful. Jacob's team had prepared well. They could see what they wanted with clarity. Simone had brought Salvador with her when she traveled back for it. He was pleased, even though that first mission produced a harsh reminder of what they had truly done.

The aircraft flew for two hundred miles, where Jacob paused its flight so that it could hover over a small town. "This should give us good detail on how easily we will be able to collect information from people on the ground," he told Salvador.

He instructed the pilot, who was sitting at a control platform just across the room, "Move over the area slowly. Keep it above the pre-determined flight deck." Then he turned to the head engineer. "Make sure you record video of everything."

The picture feed coming through the giant video screen in the underground control room displayed houses lining subdivided streets. Some had backyard pools filled with brownish-green water. Others were partially burned out from long-ago fires, missing roofs or walls or both. There were more of those than Jacob could have anticipated.

The video feed was clear. From the control room, they didn't see anyone for several minutes as the drone surveyed the outskirts of the town. But as it moved closer to the city's center, Jacob's video engineer spoke up, "Starting to see movement, sir."

Images of the townspeople appeared as the drone moved over the central square. It showed a gathering of sorts, outside a large building that appeared to be the town's former courthouse. "Hover here," Jacob told the pilot. "And zoom as close as you can," he directed the video engineer.

"What is it?" Simone whispered.

"I can't tell," Jacob responded.

Salvador leaned in to the two of them and said in a soft voice, "It's a trade market. Just like they had in the third world."

Jacob started to discern some sort of organized pattern of tables and goods. Most people were moving around quickly and haphazardly. Some were slowly milling through the large crowd, while others weren't moving at all.

"What are they trading?" Simone asked.

"Hard to tell," Salvador answered. "But it looks as though everyone wants food."

He was right. They could make out the goods by then. The food was mostly vegetables, fruits, and breads. A few tables held small dead animals, skinned and prepared for cooking. One older man stood at a table with buckets of water on it. He held a shotgun in the crook of his arm.

It became clear that there were more people without items to trade than there were with. Most of the crowd seemed to only be looking, with nothing to barter for much needed food and water. Jacob spotted a man with a bullhorn standing on the steps of the building, just above the gathering of sad souls. He had one arm in the air, as if he were directing traffic as he spoke. Jacob thought he looked mayoral, even though most of the crowd seemed to be ignoring him. It was a depressing scene of want and despair.

Jacob decided that they had seen enough. He was giving his pilot the instruction to start his flight back when suddenly he saw the man with the bullhorn on the ground. He had fallen so abruptly that Jacob thought he may have had a heart attack. But then he saw the pool of blood forming around his splayed body. The crowd began to panic, and what had been a fairly rapid but peaceful pace around the event turned into pandemonium, with people running randomly this way and that.

A man with a raised handgun slowly walking through the madness appeared. Jacob told the engineer to focus the camera on him. He seemed to be moving from table to table, taking aim at the people who had the most goods to trade. He had shot the man with the bullhorn first, and then a woman at a vegetable set-up. His next victim appeared to be a woman with baskets of apples. But as he aimed his pistol to shoot her, the older man who had been offering buckets of water walked up beside him. He raised his shotgun to the shooter's stomach and fired. The shooter fell to the ground and grasped his midsection, and Jacob could see his face break into an expression of agony. The man with the shotgun straddled the shooter and took point-blank aim. From the control room, the voyeuristic ANTs saw the blast come out of the shotgun's muzzle and the shooter's head come apart.

There was a hushed moment in the room until Salvador spoke. "Fly the aircraft home, pilot," he directed. Then he turned and left the rest of them in silence.

13.

The Omni Operation continued on schedule for the next three weeks. Jacob tested multiple drones over varying distances, collecting mostly useless information on each flight. Still, his team was diligent in their record-keeping and maintained extensive logs on the performance of the unmanned aircraft. He was preparing to launch the second phase of the project in the next two sectors when Salvador called him back to the grid. It was almost a year to the day since he had unleashed the Domino Infection. Jacob thought that maybe it was time for an anniversary celebration, a new independence day of sorts.

An excursion team picked him up from the military complex and drove him back to the grid for the meeting. They arrived at the tower in Philadelphia at dusk. Jacob expected a chance to relax and get some sleep before he saw Salvador, but waiting in his apartment when he walked through the door was a handwritten note on the kitchen counter. "Refresh yourself and come up to the top floor. Quickly. We need to talk. - S."

The elevator doors slid open to a dimly lit room. When Jacob walked out into the open area, he noticed that the only light was coming from around the tops of the four glass walls. The edges of ceiling held a strip of ambient lighting, and it created just enough glow for him to see the shape of the room and the few hazy forms inside it. It also provided unfettered views of the outside night, with its design avoiding a single instance of glare.

Jacob saw a figure standing near the glass, facing south: Salvador. "Hello, Jacob," he said, without turning away from the view. "Please, make yourself a drink."

At the bar in the corner, Jacob saw a bottle of scotch sitting away from the other liquor. He poured two fingers into a short glass and walked across the room to where Salvador was standing. They stood silently, looking past the lighted grid into the never-ending darkness for a while.

After a few sips of scotch, Jacob spoke. "Everything ok, Salvador?"

Before he answered, he pulled in a deep breath through his nose and held it. "It's been a lot tougher than I thought, Jacob. It's affecting me differently than I thought it would."

Salvador wasn't drunk, but Jacob could tell that he had been drinking. His demeanor was confusing. He wasn't himself. "What do you mean?" Jacob asked.

"I haven't been able to get that image out of my mind. The one described by that Eastern Europe director. The kids. The Omega XT and what they did to those kids."

Jacob tried to reassure him. He wanted to bring back the man whose stoicism he had grown to respect more than anything about him. "That was a random thing, Salvador. No need to dwell on it. And besides, didn't you tell me that some of what happens with all of this might not be too pretty?"

"Yes, hijo, yes I did. But that wasn't us, Jacob. It wasn't what I set out to do with ANTI-." He thought for a few seconds, as if considering whether he was going to say something else. Then he did. "And it wasn't as random as you might think."

"Not random?" Jacob was starting to feel concerned and anxious. The lighting, the urgency of Salvador's note, and the man clearly at odds with himself in that moment had Jacob reeling.

Salvador continued staring into the night. "I've gotten more reports than I'd like to admit. The Omega XT seem to be relishing their power in some areas. And they're brandishing it with more and more unnecessary violence. I feel like I'm losing control of the experiment before it even has a chance to begin." He finished the drink he was holding in one large gulp and closed his eyes.

"Shit, Salvador. I don't know what to say." Jacob thought for a few seconds, dumbfounded. Then he proceeded anyway. "You have to have somebody to do the dirty work, right? I guess it's like having a guard dog in your front yard. You need him to be vicious, but he's got to know his place in the pack."

"Good analogy, Jacob. You're right." Salvador turned to him and his mouth curled up on one side. It was almost a smile. "Problem is, I've got over a hundred front yards with thousands of guard dogs." He laughed sarcastically and put his hand on Jacob's shoulder. "But that's not your problem, hijo. And that's not why I called you here." He walked across the room to the bar and poured himself another scotch.

"Ok, then," Jacob said. "I'll bite - why exactly am I here?" He had relaxed since Salvador's mood had lightened, but the feeling didn't last long.

"It's Sector 3, Jacob. We have a situation."

14.

The situation at Sector 3 was strange, more than anything else. But Salvador's instincts had stirred at the information he had received from the directors there. They were telling him to be curious and to investigate. With so much at stake, he didn't want anything slipping by him.

Located south in Nashville, Sector 3 had been picking up electronic signals close to its grid, meaning within 50 miles. There had been sporadic electrical activity across most of the planet for the past year, typically weak radio waves. But the Sector 3 signals were different. They were steady and strong. And for Salvador, they were too close to the grid there. His explanation to Jacob seemed to hold an element of anticipation. And Jacob had come to know Salvador as a man with very good predictive skills.

Salvador wanted Jacob and Simone to go there, monitor the activity, and investigate anything unusual. He was vague about it all, but concerned. Above anything else, he needed more knowledge.

"How close are you with the drones?" he asked Jacob.

"Not close enough for Sector 3. I was just getting ready to test into Sector 2, but 3 is so much further away."

"That's what I thought. And that's why I need you and Simone to go there. We can't let anything slip through the cracks. I want you two to see and hear everything that comes through. You're the best minds I've got."

Jacob thought before he spoke. He knew he would go on the mission, no matter the risk. "Ok, Salvador. To Sector 3, it is. And I'll have my team continue working on Omni while I'm gone," Jacob told him. "I'll tell them to start preparing for flights to Sector 3. But it will take them some time."

"Very good. And Jacob, listen closely. If this is what I think it might be, you and Simone have to stay away from it. I just want you to be my eyes and ears. Nothing more. I'll handle our reaction from here." Then Salvador moved close to Jacob to make his last point. "I can't afford to lose either one of you now."

Jacob returned to the Omni Operation early the next morning. He needed to spend a few days there adjusting the drone rollout and delegating the updated workload. He also had to explain to Simone the plan for the two of them, and that they would be going to Sector 3 within the week.

"Going where?!?" she asked. She was flabbergasted, much like Jacob had been when Salvador told him the same thing.

"Sector 3. Nashville. Orders from Salvador. You and me."

"Wait a minute," she said. "Salvador told *you*, to tell *me*, that I'm going to Nashville. *Nashville!* What the hell?!?"

Jacob knew she felt slighted, like maybe she was losing some ground to him within Salvador's power structure. He tried to reassure her. "Don't worry about that, Simone. Look at the bigger picture here. Something's happening, and it's got Salvador scared."

She calmed herself down. "I know, I know. It just seems a little risky, don't you think?"

"Yeah, I agree. But Salvador says the situation warrants the travel risk. And, don't worry, we'll have an escort for the trip."

"Let me guess - the Omega XT?"

"You got it."

Simone shook her head in disbelief. "Goddam, Jacob - this must be some situation."

15.

The convoy to Sector 3's grid consisted of five vehicles: two converted jeeps and three military-style humvees. The jeeps, positioned in the front and rear of the pack, carried three Omega XT members each: two in the cab, and one who manned the rotating .50-caliber machine gun that was mounted in the back bed. Four ANTs rode in each humvee, with Simone and Jacob traveling inside the one in the middle of the group.

They had planned for an overnight trek, when there would be less chance of being spotted or encountering outsiders in the dark. The trip would take most of the night, even with traveling on fairly open roads at maximum speed. The Omega XT escort wore night-vision goggles to avoid using headlights. Besides the sound of the vehicles' engines and the roar of the all-terrain tires against pavement, the convoy was invisible.

Simone and Jacob talked about what they might find at Sector 3 when they weren't trying to sleep. "So, Salvador didn't give you any specifics about what's going on at 3?" she asked him.

"No, not really."

"And you didn't press him about it?" She had a way of changing the tone of her voice with questions when she already knew the answer. She was trying to make Jacob feel like he had missed something obvious. But Jacob didn't let it get to him. He had wanted to make his own interpretation of the situation once he got there, and anything Salvador would have told him would have been assumption and conjecture. He didn't need that to fog his own analysis.

"No, Simone, I didn't. Why would I? He doesn't truly know. That's why he's sending us."

"Oh, he knows, Jacob," she said with absolute confidence. "Don't think for a second that he doesn't. But that's what I don't get. This has got to be big. Or else he wouldn't want the two of us to be there."

Jacob turned his face to the humvee's window and let the noise of the rolling tires drown out the conversation. Simone was right. Salvador had to know more than he was letting on. But he had also said how important they were. Jacob couldn't imagine that Salvador would be deliberately leading them into danger. In fact, he trusted his mentor implicitly, but one of his remarks kept repeating in Jacob's head - *"If this is what I think it might be, you and Simone have to stay away from it."*

If he had only known then how significant those instructions really were, everything might have been different.

16.

Jacob fell asleep soon after his conversation with Simone about Salvador. She woke him up by shaking his shoulders. "Jacob, get up. Something's happening."

He knew the humvee was motionless immediately. The two Omega XT were missing from the front seats. He leaned to the center of the backseat and looked through the windshield, but his view was blocked by the vehicle ahead of him. "Come on," Simone said as he was trying to alert his senses from deep sleep. "We've got to see what's going on."

He followed her out of the humvee's passenger side back door. That was another thing Jacob had learned about Simone: she was fearless. As they walked to the front of the stopped convoy, his eyes adjusted to the pitch-black darkness. The other vehicles were empty, too. When they got to the jeep that had been leading them, all of the Omega XT were gathered together there, watching something in the distance.

Jacob eased up next to one of them. He tried to ask with levity, "What exactly are we doing here? Sight-seeing?" It didn't elicit the response he had hoped it would.

"See for yourself," the Omega XT soldier replied. He took off his night-vision goggles and handed them to Jacob.

Ahead on the highway, maybe two hundred yards away, was a herd of humans. It was the only way Jacob could qualify the sight, as humiliating as that sounded. With the limited detail Jacob could discern through the goggles, they all looked beaten down and tired, with ragged clothes and dirty faces. Some were shoeless. There were older ones and younger ones, children even. And too many of them to count. They were slowly trudging toward the convoy on the highway, seemingly walking without purpose except to move forward.

Jacob handed the goggles to Simone. "There's a large group of people walking this way. Blocking the road," he told her. She put the goggles on and looked for herself.

"Well, that's just sad," she said dismissively. "What an awful-looking bunch."

"Don't worry," one of the Omega XT said in response. "We'll take care of it."

What transpired without warning in the next few moments took Jacob's breath away.

"Hit the lights," one of the soldiers said, and the driver of the front jeep turned his hi-beam headlights on. The band of vagabonds froze, each one like an animal about to take the brunt of a speeding pick-up truck might. It was apparent that they couldn't see the source of the light. Most of them held their arms up to their foreheads to create some shade over their squinting eyes.

"Lock and load," the same voice instructed. And before the realization of what was happening finished completing its synapse in Jacob's brain, the soldier ordered, "Fire!"

The Omega XT at the .50-caliber machine gun in the back of the jeep shot first. The others joined him within seconds, creating a cacophony of rapid-succession gunfire that was deafening. Jacob put his hands to his ears and ducked instinctively, but he knew where all of the bullets were going.

The human herd didn't have time to react or to run, and it was all over in a minute's time. "Cease fire!" the voice sounded over the glorified firing squad. The aftermath was hard to see through the haze of machine-gun smoke. But Jacob could soon enough make out the lifeless bodies, some stacked on top of others. Some were missing limbs or separated from their lower half.

"Holy shit!" Jacob yelled out instinctively. "What the hell was that?!?"

The Omega XT standing next to him said plainly, "Clearing a path." He grabbed the night-vision goggles from Simone. "We put them out of their misery, if you ask me."

The voice that had directed the massacre gave one last order, to everyone. "Load up. Time's-a wasting. Got to get moving."

Simone and Jacob walked back to the middle humvee and climbed into the backseat without words. He laid his head back and closed his eyes. And as the vehicle bounced over the freshly-dead bodies sprawled across the highway, he silently questioned Salvador and his experiment for the very first time.

17.

It was just before dawn when the convoy entered Sector 3's grid. Jacob quickly arranged a meeting with its directorship for the afternoon. He and Simone were shown their living quarters in the meantime. The Nashville hotel that would become their temporary home had previously been one of the most notable in the country. It was classic and traditional, with high vaulted ceilings and ornate fixtures throughout. There were large murals painted on the walls of the massive atrium that served as both lobby and late-night social lounge. They depicted scenes of well-known American battles, famous for their heroic history.

Many of the Sector 3 ANTs lived in the hotel, and enough of them worked there to maintain its original intent. Simone and Jacob were led to their rooms by a young man dressed in a suit and tie. He was well-spoken and cheerful. Jacob felt as if the two of them were on some former-life vacation with each other, until they split into their separate rooms. They agreed to rest first, and then meet for lunch before their meeting with the directors.

Jacob took a long hot shower and tried to wash away the memory from the night before on the highway. But it was deeply set in his mind, like a blood stain on a white shirt. As much as he scrubbed the darkness of it out, he couldn't keep its faded imprint from leaving his mind. He had not talked to Simone for the rest of the trip. He didn't feel comfortable expressing his opinions in front of the Omega XT in the front seat of their humvee. He didn't know what she was thinking, but he assumed it was something similar to his own thoughts. Thoughts of astonishment laced with fear. But she was better with emotions, fleshing them out and giving them definition. He spent the hours leading up to lunch analyzing their options for regaining control of the Omega XT, even though he hoped Simone would somehow allay his concerns.

  They ate at a restaurant close to the directorship's headquarters. Soup with fruit and bread. Jacob still found amazement in the food that ANTI-maintained inside the grids. Their meal was delicious and refreshing, and it restored a small bit of Jacob's faith in Salvador and his grand scheme. After all, there he was in a still-modernized yet self-contained area of the world hundreds of miles from the next one like it, eating a fresh meal and staying in a luxurious hotel and living a civilized life. People were cooking soup and cleaning rooms and working. Not for themselves, but for the society. What Jacob hadn't considered until last night was, at what cost?

He didn't hesitate to broach the subject as soon as they sat down at their small corner table. "So, last night, right?" he asked. "That was insane."

"I know," Simone replied, examining her meal with a look of hungry excitement. "Hard to see something like that up close." She stabbed a large piece of watermelon and shoved it into her mouth. It wasn't the reaction Jacob was expecting.

"Here's the thing," he said, "Salvador was telling me the other night about the Omega XT. That they were becoming emboldened, independent. Taking matters into their own hands. And not in a good way. I didn't like how he was talking about it. He sounded...regretful."

Simone cocked her head to one side. "Really???" she asked sarcastically. "What did he think was going to happen with the Omega XT? That they were just going to ask the outsiders to stay away from the grids nicely? With a pretty please or something?" She leaned over the table and lowered her voice. "Jacob, what you saw last night is all part of the plan. Most of the people outside of the grids aren't going to survive the next few years anyway. C'mon - Salvador knows that. And you should, too."

She was so blatant and defensive about it. She was almost angry at Jacob's ignorance. He began to think that he needed to harden himself to what they were really doing with ANTI- from here forward. "I don't know. I guess it's just the barbaric ways in which they're going about it. Hell, Simone, they were so disconnected last night. If I didn't know better, I'd say they damn near enjoyed it."

"And?" she mumbled as she chewed. She finished her bite and drank from her glass of water.

"And, I'm a little shocked that you're acting the same," Jacob said accusingly.

Then he saw a look of realization come into her eyes. "You don't know who they are, do you?"

"What are you talking about?"

"The Omega XT. He didn't tell you." She sat back in her chair and threw her hands up in the air. "Of course. You were preoccupied with the Domino Infection. So you don't know."

"No, I don't. And, frankly, maybe it's better that way." Jacob's head was beginning to swim. He hadn't foreseen Simone's demeanor, much like he hadn't with Salvador a few nights earlier.

She leaned forward again. "Listen, Jacob, and listen closely. The men who make up the Omega XT are mercenaries, plain and simple. Their name says everything - 'End-All Exterminators' - and they've been training for this for years. They were trained to be *barbaric*, so get used to it. In the end, it's the only method that will work. We need the world's population gone, nil, destroyed. The Omega XT exist to ensure that will happen."

He didn't understand why she was being so confrontational.

"And one more thing," she said. "Don't you dare let Salvador sway you to think he doesn't know what they are. Or why they're doing what they're doing the way they're doing it. He knows." She looked down at her plate, thinking for a second. Then, with her gaze still downward, she said, "And if he doesn't - you, me, the whole damn lot of us - we're all screwed."

18.

The Sector 3 directorship was made up of nine ANTs, as it was in all the grids. There were men and women, and the uneven number meant no decision was ever left in a stalemate. The people who served as directors of Salvador's grids were his oldest followers. Most of them had been with him for more than two decades, in some form or fashion. Their loyalty to him and to ANTI- was unwavering.

Jacob and Simone met with them in a large conference room that occupied the majority of the bottom floor of the grid's headquarters. The building was historic, made of red brick and not even ten stories high. It felt archaic compared to their Sector 1 home in Philadelphia. Inside, they were greeted with the typical smiles and courtesies that always precede those kinds of meetings. Jacob's hatred of small talk was ballooning because of his antagonistic lunch with Simone, but he tried to remain pleasant as the others made their way through the pointless chatter.

Jacob's mind was roaming through probabilities and possibilities. Why had Salvador led him into thinking he was worried about the Omega XT tactics? Was he setting Jacob up for something? Was it his way of controlling Jacob? Or was all of this Simone? Was she the manipulator? He couldn't figure it out. The intricacies of human behavior still eluded him.

He heard Simone's voice through his fogged thoughts. "Jacob?"

"Yes?" he replied hastily. Jacob shut down the confused portion of his brain. Instead, he focused on the reason he was there, no matter the whys of it all. He would work on that later.

"Are you ready to hear the directors' report?" Simone asked, with a curious tone. Jacob's distraction had not gone unnoticed.

"Of course." He put on his good face and classic charm. "Sorry, everyone. It's been a long few days." He turned to Simone and gave her a nudge with his elbow. "Plus, traveling with this one is no picnic." The room smiled and relieved itself from most of its tension. "Now, please, tell us exactly what's happening down here."

Sector 3's engineers had first picked up the steady signal three months prior. It was electrical, no doubt, but its location and source of power remained a mystery to them. The one thing that they all seemed to agree upon was the size of it. It was providing for something large. Not city block large, but definitely bigger than what might be supported by a simple generator. This was no house of resourceful outsiders, tapping into some dormant powerline just to see if they could. This was more, and it had them worried.

There were all sorts of theories being thrown about by the directors. Most centered on a formation of rebels somewhere, organizing an attack. "We've also intercepted some strange radio transmissions," one of the directors said. "They don't make much sense to us, but they seem, at the very least, to be consistent with one another." Jacob succinctly informed them to shelve their opinions. He and Simone were there to investigate and determine the answer, and they would be in charge of the theories moving forward.

He hated to be short with the directorship, but he couldn't help it. He was seething throughout their entire presentation, and he was feeling claustrophobic. He was mostly upset with himself for being so trusting. He thought he knew better. But he was also disgusted with the way he had acted so weakly in front of Simone. *Never again*, he told himself.

He and Simone wrapped the meeting once the directors had finished presenting the intelligence they had gathered up to that point. Simone told them that she and Jacob would develop a strategy for analysis of the information and action based upon it. She thanked them for their candor.

Jacob walked briskly out of the headquarters. Simone had to rush to keep up. "Jacob, what are you doing? Those were some of Salvador's closest friends in there. You need to get your shit together," she said forcefully as she trailed after him.

Jacob agreed - he did need to get his shit together. And he planned to do exactly that over the next twenty-four hours. He stopped and turned back to her. "I know, Simone. Sorry, I'm just not feeling well. Maybe it was lunch. Or maybe I just need some sleep." He tried not to betray his anger with everything that was happening, but he also knew how perceptive Simone was. The first thing he needed to do was get away from her. "I think I'll call it a day. Get some much-needed rest. Can we start fresh in the morning?"

"Yeah, ok," she said slowly. "In the morning it is."

Jacob started walking across the street to the hotel, ahead of her. She called after him.

"Hey, Jacob - if for some reason you can't sleep tonight, you know where to find me."

He stopped in the middle of the street and looked back over his shoulder at her. She looked small and helpless all of a sudden, the way so many women do when their desire outweighs whatever moral obligations they may carry with them. When, more simply, they are offering. But Simone didn't have moral obligations. Jacob knew that now. He laughed so that she could see him laugh, but also because he couldn't help it. No woman had ever outwitted him before. Simone was certainly trying to do just that, and for the moment, she was succeeding.

"This is about to get very interesting, Jacob," he whispered to himself as he turned his head back around and walked away.

Jacob slept restfully through the night, having come up with a way to deal with both Salvador and Simone on a personal level before he shut his eyes. He knew that he had been too gullible with both of them. And even though he still didn't know either of their intentions, he had decided to be more alert and aware of their possible manipulations. To watch and listen closely to every word and gesture. He should have known that to Salvador he was merely a valuable tool in his worldwide workshop. From that night on, he did. Jacob still believed in the grand ANTI-experiment, but he recreated the protective barrier around himself that had disappeared long ago. Against Salvador, Simone, and anyone else. He had forgotten that lesson he had learned so early in life: there's no one in this world worth trusting.

He knocked on Simone's door at 6 AM. "Get up, Simone, time for breakfast!" he gleefully shouted through the door to her. "I hope you didn't wait up on me last night. See you downstairs." He didn't wait for her to answer, but instead went to the elevator smiling.

The old Jacob was back, and the game was on.

19.

Jacob and Simone spent the better part of a week analyzing the electronic signal and studying the geography and population of Sector 3. He confirmed the strength and consistency of the signal, but he couldn't decipher the exact location. One of many limitations that they were experiencing in that sector was the lack of sourcing technology to pinpoint distant electrical outputs. Jacob was able to eliminate certain directions: north-northeast, east, and south-southeast. But that still left a significant amount of ground to cover.

The geography within fifty miles of the remaining directions was rugged, but generally flat. It consisted of dense woods throughout and the occasional gentle rise and fall of a nearby mountain range's foothill. The city's outskirts spread for approximately five miles outside of the grid, just at the limit of Salvador's tolerance for ANT exploration. Past that was the unknown. The people of the region were not unlike most in the country, but the area was more rural than most places. And one thing that jumped out at Jacob from the statistics: the prevalence of gun-owners. It was higher than the other sectors. He jotted down a note on that.

Once they had exhausted their research efforts on those fronts, they began the interviews. The interviews occupied another week of time, but thankfully led to a breakthrough of sorts. Jacob and Simone talked with each of the directors separately, the engineers who had been receiving and recording the signals and transmissions, and the Omega XT members stationed around the borders. Jacob let Simone control the interrogations. It was her specialty, after all. She was imposing, but delicate. Her techniques for getting information were honed and practiced. There was no wasted time during an interrogation. Even her compliments and niceties were intended to glean intelligence. And all of that with the people on her own side. Jacob hated to think what she might be like with a known enemy.

The most in-depth questioning took place with the Omega XT that made up the excursion team for that grid. They were the ones who had been outside the borders to restock supplies, and they were the ones who may have observed something, even if they didn't know it.

Excursion teams were required by one of the few ANTI- sector rules to stay within a five-mile radius of the grid. It went along with Salvador's reasoning behind his nixing Jacob and Simone's manned surveillance ideas before they came up with the drone program: ANTI- couldn't give the outsiders hope by letting them see ANTs roaming around in vehicles. If a few witnessed it, it would have to be, but within five miles only. Anything more was unacceptable.

Simone didn't have any luck with the excursionists until she questioned the last one of them. He wasn't talkative at first, much like the rest, so she had to work to get anything out of him. But once she knew that he had seen something unusual, she started pushing.

"I've asked everyone on your team these same questions," Simone started. "Standard stuff, just making sure we've got everything we need to move forward. Please, answer the questions with as much detail as you can. How long have you been going outside of the grid on supply missions?"

"Seven months," he answered dryly.

"And how often?"

"Every other week."

"And is the team always made up of the same group of men?"

"Of course. If something works, why change it?" It was more than a simplified answer. Simone noticed it immediately.

"Right. So, on the excursions, do you go in a different direction each time?"

"Typically, yes. We're always looking for fresh resources."

"Some of the grids have started farms outside of their borders to replenish their food. You guys doing that?" she asked.

"No."

"So then, your team is pretty important around here, huh?"

"Just doing what's required."

She was trying to boost his ego, just enough to open him up if he'd allow. It hadn't worked with the other Omega XT, but she was persistent in her ways. Plus she saw a crack in this one - time to start pulling it apart.

"Have you ever had to do anything to protect this place? To preserve the integrity of the grid?" She was leading him now, but he didn't know it.

"Nothing out of the ordinary."

"Aw, c'mon. It's been over a year since you started taking care of these people. And you're saying that there's nothing worth telling me? I don't believe it."

He hesitated. It was difficult to read the emotions of the Omega XT because they never removed their masks. It was part of their mystique to be anonymous, and it was certainly making Simone's job harder. But she and Jacob both noticed a relaxing of this one's shoulders. They could almost see a smile on his hidden face.

"Ok, there was one thing, early on. Before we formed the excursion team. My group was on guard duty one night, on the southwest corner of the grid. It had been quiet that night. Most of the random attacks had all but disappeared. Anyway, I'm patrolling, watching for anything strange, when I saw a flash in the building across from us. A few stories up. I put the scope of my rifle to my eye and could barely make out the silhouette of somebody with a gun pointed at my group. I fired immediately. The others saw where I was shooting and unloaded on the area with me. When they investigated it, they found three men with sniper rifles and pipe bombs. Three dead men, that is."

"And if you hadn't seen that flash...," Simone said, acting impressed.

"They would have killed my entire patrol. No doubt about it."

That was more talk than she had gotten out of the other excursion team members combined. Simone was making progress.

She pressed. "I'd say that was pretty damn heroic, wouldn't you, Jacob?"

Jacob nodded and said, "Pretty damn heroic is right."

The Omega XT responded with a twinge of pride in his voice. "Just doing my job. Doing what's required."

"I understand," Simone continued. "And we thank you for that. Just a couple more questions, then you can go."

"Shoot," he responded, loosening up.

"You can obviously spot things *unusual*, right? You proved that on the night with the snipers, huh?"

"No need for glasses, if that's what you mean."

"Yeah, that's what I mean. Now tell me, have you seen anything *unusual* on any of your excursions? Anything at all?"

"Don't take this the wrong way, miss, but everything outside of here is unusual."

Simone laughed lightly. "I know. What I mean is...anything we should be concerned about? You and I both know something strange is going on somewhere out there. I just need to know if you've got any clues as to what that may be?"

He thought for a minute. He was considering not speaking anymore, but he did. "Maybe there was something. I didn't think much about it when it happened, but it stuck with me. We were out a few weeks back, to the west. We were at the five-mile limit, loading up some food supplies from a grocery store. I was the only one on watch. I was looking down the main highway that leads out of the city. Just off the road, hiding almost, I saw this group of people. Five or six of them. I reached for my rifle and raised my scope to the spot. They were watching us through binoculars, and they took off as soon as I got a good look at them."

"Something tells me that's not the first time you've seen outsiders on an excursion," Simone said.

"No, not the first."

"So why did it stick with you?"

"It's hard to say. Maybe it was the way they were dressed, all alike in military-type clothes. And they looked healthy, something we just don't see anymore out there. And the way they moved when I spotted them. It was like they were trained. Like they were on a mission. I haven't seen outsiders act that way since the takeover."

Simone turned to Jacob with a look of accomplishment. They had been hunting a lead, and she had just found the first one.

She turned back to the Omega XT. "I'm gonna need to see that spot on the highway as soon as possible, soldier."

20.

They left the next morning with the Sector 3 excursion team to search the area where the Omega XT's strange sighting had occurred. They spent an hour there, but it became obvious rather quickly that whatever they were looking for was further west, further out on the highway.

"We need to see what's down that road," Simone said. "I've got a feeling there was something to that sighting."

"I can't say I disagree," Jacob told her. "But this could get dangerous. What if, by some crazy chance, it is a rebel force out there. What are we supposed to do then?"

"Observe," she replied. "And that's it. I'm not going to screw this up, Jacob. Trust me."

"You've got three miles, Simone. And then we come back and re-double our efforts on the electronic side of this. Got it?"

"Yeah, sure." Then she turned to the excursion team. "Listen up, guys. Here's what we're doing..."

As he listened to her bark instructions, Jacob hoped that three miles would give her what she wanted. But it didn't.

She and Jacob took one vehicle with a driver and gunner from the excursion team and sent the rest back to the grid. The plan was to stay on the highway and look for anything suspicious as they rode in the back of the jeep. They would stay underneath the gunner and his machine gun, from where they could hopefully see anything that might be noteworthy. But by the eighth mile, they had seen nothing.

"We're going back, Simone. That was the deal," Jacob stated as emphatically as he could, yelling over the wind noise from the moving jeep.

"Listen, Jacob, there's something out here. I can feel it. Let's go a little further," she yelled back.

Jacob leaned into the jeep's open cab and instructed the Omega XT driving to stop. He didn't truly know who outranked who between Simone and himself because Salvador had never spelled that out in definitive terms. But he was about to exert the authority that he felt was needed to preserve their overall mission.

"No way, Simone. Absolutely not."

"C'mon, Jacob, what are you worried about? This is what we're here to do. You think Salvador's going to come down here and give us a lecture or something?"

She was doing that thing again with her questioning, trying to make Jacob feel small and stupid. But they were way too far outside the grid in his opinion. They had ridden eight miles by his count. He could feel the trip getting riskier with every rotation of the jeep's wheels.

"No, I don't," he said with authority. "And stop with the 'smarter-than-thou' act. It isn't attractive." He finally knew how to push her buttons. "What if we go another three miles and nothing? What then?" She didn't respond. "We're turning this ignorant adventure around, right now."

And, under Simone's silent protest, they did. She was angry and frustrated, and she didn't try to hide it. When they arrived back at the grid, Jacob told her, "You know it would have been foolish to continue, Simone. We had to come back."

She didn't respond until after she had climbed down from the jeep's bed. She looked up at him and said, "Yeah, it may have been foolish, Jacob. And yeah, we had to come back. But the reason we're in Sector 3 right now is out on that highway. I know it is."

Before he could say anything more, a familiar voice rose up from behind them. It was one of the directors. "She's right." Jacob turned around and saw him holding a piece of paper in his hand. "And now we have proof."

21.

Jacob read the printed email that the director had given him twice before Simone grabbed it out of his hands. She skimmed over the short message, then once more like he had done. Her face was bright with excitement when she raised her head from the piece of paper.

"This is it, Jacob," she said. "This is the break we needed."

His analytical nature tempered his reaction. "We need to make sure it's authentic, but I have to say - at first glance, this looks like an attempt to infiltrate the grid."

"There's no way it's not a play, right? This is them. This is contact, Jacob. And they think we're stupid enough to fall for it, but they've actually given us the upper hand."

Her elation was infectious. Jacob found himself nervous about what do next. This had become actual espionage, and he and Simone were controlling it. It was as exciting to him as watching a computer virus spread, but the difference was detachment. He had always been a spectator in the hacking world. This time, he was playing in the game, and the risk was exhilarating.

He took off toward the Sector 3 headquarters, yelling as he ran. "We've got to formulate a response quickly. Let's go!"

After looking at every angle he could imagine, Jacob determined that the probability of the email being a ruse was high. Combined with the strange electronic signal, the surveillance sighting, and his gut feeling, he decided to treat it as enemy-produced. He had not thought in those terms before then, but it was part of his recent wake-up call. These outsiders were his enemy because that was how he had to view them. And because he was coming around to the new world's brutal realities that Simone had been so casual about. If the email happened to be real and four people were sacrificed innocently in the name of protecting the ANTI- revolution, then that was just part of the war they had begun waging.

The email represented its author as an ANT named Paul who had been injured in the early days of the takeover. He had missed his opportunity to live in the grids, and now he wanted inside, along with a relative and her children. He would be awaiting instructions on how to gain access.

"Paul" passed verification, but just barely. He matched the profile of a low-level ANT who had not been seen since before the Great Dark. And his membership then was minimal at best. He had been involved in a few protests, but that was it. The whole thing was transparent, even without deep analysis.

After Jacob had sat with the email for an hour, he created a response to bring the outsiders in with little to no suspicion:

> ID: HQ-5051
> SECTOR: NA-3
>
> Re: Grid Access Instructions
>
> 2-370-552 -
>
> Your transmission has been received. Welcome back. You and your companions who seek refuge are instructed to meet at the northwestern corner of the grid at sunrise tomorrow morning. There will be a group of us there waiting.
>
> FtSoH

It was short and direct, but encouraging. Jacob wanted them to approach the next day with as little caution as possible. The ANTs needed to catch them off their guard possible. He hoped the style of the message would help do that.

Once the email was sent, Simone presented the plan for the group's arrival to Jacob and the directors. A group of Omega XT would be stationed at the corner with two vans. Paul, the former ANT, and his companions would be stopped just outside the grid and told to kneel. Four of the Omega XT would approach the group and begin a frantic interrogation of Paul: the first step of fear. No matter what he answered to any of the questions, one of the Omega XT would draw his pistol and shoot him dead.

One of the directors spoke up, asking exactly what Jacob was thinking, "Forgive me, but is that necessary?"

Simone darted her eyes at the questioner. "For us to determine why this group truly wants to be inside, it is absolutely necessary." She started pacing across the front of the room. "I want everyone to realize something right here and now. This is a threat. There's no doubt about it. And these four people most likely represent something much bigger. We can't afford to not know what that is anymore. We have to scare information out of them, quickly. We kill the strongest one," she stopped and looked at everyone with assurance, "and the others will talk."

She went on to explain that the woman and two children would be taken separately to the grid's utility station. There, she would begin questioning them, specifically the woman. No interrogation tactic would be off-limits with her. But the brilliance of the plan was what she had in store for the children.

She held up something small and black between her thumb and forefinger. It was the size of a quarter, and it blinked a dull blue light. "This," she said, "is how we find out the real story."

22.

What Simone showed the directors and Jacob was a tracking device. She went on to explain just how she planned to use it. While transporting the children back to the utility building, the ANTs would plant a pair of the devices on them, either in their clothing or the lining of any packs they may be carrying. Simone would proceed with a light interrogation of them, and then they would be left together in a locked room. At some point after, one of the ANTs would check on them and leave the door unlocked, seemingly as an act of incompetence. Anticipating the children would be astute and aggressive, an attempted escape would be imminent. And Simone would let that escape happen without challenge. She would let them lead ANTI- back to their starting point, and back to what she predicted would be the home of the strange electronic signal.

"Any questions?" Simone asked.

"What about the woman?" a director wondered. "What do we do with her?"

"I'll get as much from her as I can. But if the children lead us to the answers, then she becomes useless. And I don't have time for useless people." Jacob understood what she meant. He was understanding just how callous she could be the more he worked with her. But it wasn't turning him off. Not yet. She continued, "Alright, everybody. That's it. Meet back here at 5 AM. See you then."

As the roomful of directors stood and broke into small conversations, Jacob went to Simone. She had been confident and powerful in her presentation, strong without qualms. That was the Simone he liked, and he was strangely feeling very attracted to her at that moment.

"Hell of an idea you've got here," he said. "Think it'll work?"

She smiled. "Of course it will work, Jacob. I don't come up with bad ideas. Right?"

He followed along. "Like endlessly driving into the unknown without considering the consequences? Nah, you never have any bad ideas."

"Thanks for that, by the way," she said. "You were right. That was dangerous."

"Look at this," he said sarcastically. "You're about to walk yourself into an apology, Simone." Jacob moved in closer. "Watch your step."

"No, I'm serious. Thank you." She gave him that look again, the one from the street. She was weak and wanting. And it was working.

That night, before the battle that would change everything, Simone and Jacob shattered the sexual tension that had been building between them for so many years. It was the most engagement he had ever experienced with a woman. It was soulfully invigorating and physically debilitating, all at once. They replenished their energy often, and used most of the night to continually satiate themselves.

Jacob had always mocked the term "making love" - to him, it was a greeting-card description of chemically-charged animal behavior. But it made sense in his head and heart that night. As he and Simone breathed simultaneously and moved in tandem, he understood what it meant. Never-felt emotions began to overtake him. If this was love, he was having a difficult time processing it, but he didn't mind trying either.

He got up at 4:30 in the morning to take a quick shower and prepare for the dramatic day ahead. She roused as he was about to leave, and looked up at him from the bed, smiling drowsily. "We're going to have to do that again," she whispered.

"And again and again and again," he responded. He leaned over and kissed her on her forehead, then he left with a happiness he had never known.

23.

Simone wanted to watch the group of exiles approach in person, even though the ANTs had cameras set up to record their interaction with the Omega XT and the subsequent capture. She and Jacob found a vantage point inside a building just above the proceedings. As they were waiting for the sun to rise and the events to unfold, he wanted to say something about the night before. She did, too. He could feel it. But they remained professional, only swapping inside glances with each other until the outsiders appeared.

"On your toes, Jacob," she said when she saw them. "Here they come."

The email description from Paul, the former ANT, proved to be accurate. There were two adults, a male and female, and two children, a girl and boy. The children appeared to be teenagers. They were all dressed for hiking, and they each carried a backpack. While they appeared weathered from foot travel, they were not repulsive like so many of the outsiders had become.

The following few minutes went as Simone had explained they would. The group came to the center of the road and kneeled. Four Omega XT approached them and began questioning Paul. Not long after, the Omega XT in front of him shot him through his head.

The other three were seized, bound, and hooded, then thrown into the two awaiting cargo vans and driven away.

Simone turned from the window and said to Jacob excitedly, "Showtime!"

She had prepared two rooms in the grid's utilities building to use for interrogation. One for the children and one for the woman. Simone wanted to start with the children, interviewing them separately. For the woman, she instructed one of the directors to begin the questioning to wear her down a bit. ANTs had built a two-way mirror and placed microphones in one of the rooms, the one that would be used for the captured woman. Simone wanted to watch her before she interrogated her, analyze her behavior and develop a strategy for getting as much out of her as possible.

Once the prisoners were placed in their holding areas and Simone was ready, she went to the room where she would begin her process and asked for the teenage girl. "I won't be long with these two," she told Jacob before she left. "Wait here and keep an eye on the woman." So he did, watching her sit at the interrogation table without emotion until the warm-up director entered.

Within twenty minutes, Simone was back.

"How'd it go?" Jacob asked.

"As expected," she said. "Just a taste of fear, but not enough to traumatize them too much. Especially after what they just witnessed in the street. They're strong. No doubt in my mind that they'll try to escape. What about this one?"

"Not much yet," he told her. "She's been giving it right back to that director since he began, but not telling him a thing. She's a hellcat, Simone."

"Is she now? Well, let's see how long it takes me to tame her."

24.

When the door opened to the interrogation room, the director and the captured woman fell silent. They had been in the midst of a verbal showdown, with neither one of them relenting. Simone entered and bowed her head to the woman, as if to give a courteous hello. It garnered no response. Jacob watched and listened from the behind the two-way mirror while Simone went to work.

"Thank you, director. You may leave us now," Simone instructed the director. He left the room with an obvious sigh of disgust. "First off, tell me your name. Given only is fine."

"Why would I tell you anything?" the captured woman asked calmly, squinting her eyes with a hint of anger.

"Let me lay this out for you, clear and simple," Simone said. "You're in a real shitty situation here. We have zero need for you, even if your story is true. You can live or die, for all I care. But I make that call. You answer what I ask, and you've got a chance."

"Might as well kill me then."

"Now wait. I never said I wanted to do that. I'm a compassionate woman, and if Paul's email was legit, then I want to get to the bottom of it. After all, there's two kids involved here. None of us wants to see anything happen to them."

The captured woman glared at Simone.

"So, I'll say again: tell me your name."

The woman thought for a minute. She was smart. Jacob could almost see her brain's inner-workings moving feverishly to determine a strategy. He knew Simone well enough to know that she could see it, too.

"Anna," the captured woman finally said.

"Ok, Anna. Now we're having a conversation. So let's get right to it: why are you here?"

Anna's shoulders relaxed forward and down, and she lowered her head. She muttered something inaudible, even to Simone inside the room.

"What was that?" Simone asked.

Anna raised her face but kept her eyes focused on the table in front of her. "Drugs," she stated plainly.

The answer caught Simone by surprise. "Did you say, 'drugs'?"

Anna nodded.

"What do you mean by that, exactly?"

"It's my husband, the children's father. He's dying. And the only way we might save him is with a medicine that's inside the hospital. Which is inside this grid. Paul is...was a family friend. He offered to try and get us inside. And here we are." Anna displayed a beaten look on her face. She was resigned and tearful.

"So the email was a lie?"

"Yes."

"You have no intention of joining us?"

"No."

Simone walked over and put her hand on Anna's back. She began rubbing her consolingly. "Then I have to tell you this, Anna. No medicine is going to save your husband. He's going to die. Just like you. And just like your children."

Anna straightened her spine quickly and reached for Simone, but the restraints around her wrists kept her arms just a few inches from the table.

"I know the truth is painful, Anna," Simone goaded. "But you need to know it. Now, I'm going to leave you with your thoughts. And when I come back, you better have something else to tell me."

"Screw you," Anna seethed through clenched teeth.

"Your husband is as good as dead, Anna. The sooner you accept that, the better friends you and I can be."

With that, she left the interrogation and came back to the observation room and Jacob.

"If it isn't true, she's one hell of a storyteller," he said as Simone came in.

"I don't know. I think it's all an act. I'll work on her some more, but those kids are the key."

As Simone was finishing her thought, a knock came at the door. One of the directors opened it and leaned his head into the room. "The children," he said.

"Yes?" Simone asked.

"They're already gone."

25.

The two captured teenagers were locked in an empty closet-space in the grid's utilities building once Simone was done interrogating them. One of the Omega XT ANTs had been assigned to checking them every thirty minutes until he would be instructed to leave the door unlocked and precipitate their escape. But before those instructions ever came, he found the closet door open and the teenage children gone. He reported that they had picked the lock on the door from the inside, as there was no damage to the lock at all.

"Not bad," Simone responded to the director when he told her about the kids' clever escape, and then to herself, "Smarter than I expected." She hesitated, frozen in some deep thought.

"What should we do?" the director asked.

"Exactly what we planned," Simone announced. "Track them, dammit. The only difference is that we have to do it now rather than later."

"Understood," the director said, turning to leave.

Simone waited for the director to exit the observation room. Then she said to Jacob, "I'm going back in there. And I'm going to get aggressive with her.

We need to move quickly now. You come get me if there's anything that I need to know. Understand?"

"I do," he told her. As the day had unfolded, Jacob had become more excited, but also more apprehensive. Worry was something that had never distracted him before, but he cared for someone besides himself all of a sudden. And his worry was for her. "Simone, don't back down. Push her as hard as she can stand it. For the Soul of Humanity."

"So you're sticking with this 'dying husband' story?" Simone asked as she faced Anna again.

The captured woman gave her no answer.

"Aw, c'mon. We were doing so well. Don't give me the silent treatment now."

Still nothing.

"Ok, I guess I'll do the talking. Let me tell you a few things that I know as fact. One, there's a strong electronic signal that we've been picking up here at the grid. It's not far away. Just down the highway you came from, actually."

Anna remained silent.

"Two, we're organizing right now to send an army of ANTs out there to find the source. We're going down that highway tomorrow. And we'll find it, I can assure you."

Anna's face stayed emotionless.

"And three, your children."

With that, Anna looked up at Simone.

"That's right. The kids. They're gone."

Gradually, a broad smile spread over Anna's face. She started shaking her head and laughing. "Of course they are," she said, staring at Simone directly.

It wasn't the reaction that Simone was expecting, and it angered her. "Did you hear what I said? They're *gone.*"

Anna kept smiling. "I know what you're doing. You want me to think that they're dead. But they're not. Don't worry, I believe you. You're speaking with too much conviction. So, of course they're gone. But my guess would be that they've left by their own choice. By their own ingenuity. And that you don't have a clue where they are."

Simone returned the smile that Anna was proudly displaying. "Ok, Anna, you're right. They're not dead, for now. And they did escape. But only because I let them." She reached in her pocket and wrapped her fingers around something inside it. "But you're wrong about one thing." She pulled a tracking device out of the pocket and held it up in the air. "We know exactly where they are. And they're going to lead us straight to the answers that you refuse to give."

26.

Simone and Jacob went to the utility building's control room to investigate the kids' progress while she took a break from questioning Anna. She had not broken the captured woman yet, even after hours of interrogation. Jacob actually had begun to wonder if Simone could break her at all. Between Anna's mental strength and the children's clever courage, his worry about what they were facing had grown. He hated the feeling, and deliberately tried to bury it so that it wouldn't affect him. He didn't want emotions to get in the way of the mission.

Hanging in the center of the main control room wall was a large monitor, six feet long by four feet high. The Sector 3 engineers had created a digital map of the grid and the area surrounding it, and that's what appeared on the screen when Simone and Jacob entered. The map could be manipulated to focus on certain sections or show a broad view of fifty square miles. In the middle of the screen were two flashing blue lights: the kids. The tracking devices were working flawlessly.

"Where are they?" Simone asked as she and Jacob came into the room. There were several people there, including the grid directors and engineers at the controls.

"Holed up in a parking garage," one of the engineers replied. "Been there for over an hour."

"Good. Stay on them," Simone directed. She took Jacob's arm in her hand and said softly into his ear, "Follow me."

She led him to a private office down the hall and closed the door behind her. They grabbed each other at the same time and were on the floor before Jacob realized what was happening. "Make me scream, Jacob," she breathed from underneath him.

And he did.

The director who woke them was as startled as they were. They had fallen asleep on the office's couch, exhausted from the night before and the stress of the day so far. The office door swung open and the overhead light came to life, forcing Jacob awake in an instant. The director stood there motionless.

"Oh!" he gasped, when he comprehended what he was seeing. "Sorry. Didn't mean to disturb you." He tried to overcome his discomfort quickly and leave the situation. "You need to come to the control room. Both of you. They're on the move."

He left the light on, but closed the door behind him.

"Shit," Simone said. "That was stupid."

"I kinda thought it was great, myself," Jacob said with a grin.

She smiled as she slipped back into her bra. "You know what I mean."

They finished re-dressing and hurried down the hall to the control room. Jacob checked his watch: 11 PM. They had slept for a long time.

"Where are they heading?" Simone asked the engineers.

"West, but that's all we know for now."

"Ok. Let's make sure we're on top of it when they get close to the border. We need to alert the Omega XT to let them sneak out of the grid without incident."

Simone and Jacob watched the teenagers from the control room as they moved up and down the grid's city blocks. Occasionally the blue blips representing them would stop and hesitate for a few minutes. The duo was stealthy, apparently avoiding contact with anyone.

Jacob whispered to Simone at one point, "Why do you think they're walking so randomly instead of straight to a border?"

"I'm not sure it's random at all, Jacob," she replied perceptively.

Simone had been right. The teenagers' progress through the grid halted two blocks from the northwest border. They remained still for much longer than they had before.

"Zoom in," Jacob directed. "As close as you can." The map shrunk down to a city block size. He couldn't quite make out the building where they were positioned. "What is it? Where are they?"

Simone answered his question, with conviction. "It's the hospital pharmacy. Where the medicine is stored."

The two blue blips went inside the building and drifted through it slowly. They held fast after a few minutes, then moved rapidly back to the door that they had come through. Then they were moving again, toward the grid's western border.

"Anna's telling the truth," Jacob said to Simone.

"About the dying dad...maybe," she reckoned. "But there's more. And once I make sure those kids are out, I'm giving her one last chance to tell me."

27.

Observing the teenagers' progression through the grid occupied most of the night, and the sun had risen by the time Jacob and Simone shifted to the next phase of the fast-developing mission. The morning's daylight hours were spent preparing the group of Omega XT that would travel west on the highway following the children. The pair had moved south and then west after leaving the hospital, and they had crossed the grid's border just minutes before dawn. And something strange had happened not long before: two huge explosions far to the north, but inside the city. Even if Simone had not instructed the Omega XT to move away from the intersection where the kids were crossing, they probably would have anyway. The explosions were hard to ignore.

Jacob and Simone determined to let the children journey for the day before they would begin the pursuit. They were on foot, so they wouldn't be getting very far. And it would be better for the ANTs to advance under cover of darkness. They planned to leave the grid one hour after sunset.

Once the mission was set and preparations were made, Simone and Jacob went back to the interrogation room. Anna had not been moved. She had been there for more than twenty-four hours, sitting shackled to the table in front of her. Jacob went into the adjacent observation area to watch Simone pull as much information from her as she could. He was hoping Anna would relent, for everyone's sake. She looked haggard and dazed.

"Look alive, Anna!" Simone shouted as she came into the room. "Not much time now. I need you to be alert." She set a glass of water on the table within Anna's reach. "Please, drink."

Anna took the glass with both hands and raised it toward her mouth. Just as it cleared the table below it, she slowly turned it upside down, letting the water trickle to the linoleum floor until the glass was empty.

"Goddammit, Anna! It doesn't have to be this way. You help me, and I'll help you. Can't you see that?"

"You're not helping anyone but yourself. I know that. I also know how this scenario plays out, whether I talk or not." She was looking at Simone from sleep-deprived eyes, but they held a deep-set fire in them. "So I'm not saying shit, especially to you. There's your help - *Simone*."

She said her name with vengeance. Jacob was surprised that she knew it. He searched his memory for an instance when Simone had used it in her presence. But he couldn't find any moment when she had.

Anna continued. "That's right, Simone, these walls aren't exactly soundproof, in case you wanted to know. You make sure and tell that to Jacob, too."

She had also picked up on his name, and now she was toying with them. Simone remained composed, but she was raging inside.

"What does it matter, Anna? So, you know our names. I've told you everything else. Your kids are heading west, just as I predicted. And we're going after them. Tonight. You want to save them? You tell me what else we're going to find down that highway."

Anna laughed, like she knew something that they didn't. "Here's why it matters, Simone. Because now I know exactly who I'm coming after when I get out of these chains. Because I know the names of the people that I'm going to kill. You listen to me: if you follow those kids at all, you're going down. Maybe not ANTI- and maybe not Salvador. But you and your friend Jacob in there," she looked at the two-way mirror, "you'll be dead. I promise you that much."

Simone started clapping, over-dramatically. "Well done, Anna. I've got to say, I'm impressed. Here you are, starving and dehydrated and under my thumb, and you've got the gall to threaten me. But you know as well as I do that you're not getting out of this. I suppose that's something that hasn't completely disappeared from some of you outsiders: ignorant, blind, desperate hope. It's sad, really." She leaned over the table until her face was close to Anna's. "Now you listen to me - I'm saving you for later. After I finish with your children."

With that, she straightened and went to the door, hesitating when Anna said one last thing. "You come right back, Simone. I'll be waiting."

Simone walked out and slammed the door shut, never looking back to acknowledge Anna's challenge.

28.

During the afternoon hours, Simone and Jacob watched the flashing blue lights as they moved west along the highway. They had paused at a church for a long while only a few blocks from the grid. Jacob speculated that they may not go any further, but they eventually started traveling again. As the day was ending, they stopped, this time inside a large fenced-in structure. He cross-referenced the area with their ANTI- maps and determined what the facility was: a former prison camp. "That's it," Simone said confidently. "Now we know where we're going."

At sunset, an attack occurred on the northern border of the grid. It was a small group of outsiders, but they were using military-style assault rifles and grenades. And they retreated into the city's empty streets with purpose. It didn't matter. A group of Omega XT followed them, keeping them engaged for three blocks until they were decimated. The Omega XT's report said that a couple of them may have gotten away.

Jacob began to worry again. But, by then, it was a double-edged feeling. He was as concerned for their potential failure as he was for their success. He suppressed it like before, but it was much more difficult to do.

"Do you think this has anything to do with Anna and the kids?" he asked Simone after news of the attack reached them.

"No doubt in my mind, Jacob. That's why we're taking an army down that highway."

They left the grid's borders protected with a quarter of the typical-sized security force, taking all other Omega XT with them. There were over forty modified jeeps and humvees in the convoy carrying close to three hundred soldiers. They drove three-wide across the highway. It was an intimidating spectacle of power.

Simone carried with her a hand-held version of the tracking map that they had used to follow the teenagers earlier, in case they started moving again. "But they won't," she said. She checked the blue blips every few minutes as they rode, making sure that she was right.

The prison camp was approximately twelve miles outside the city limits. The highway would lead the convoy to it, but their intelligence showed it to be two miles south of the road once they arrived. Jacob could see two faint lines on the map that ran perpendicular to the highway on the east side of the prison. One was a river, running from north to south and then west for hundreds of miles. But the other was short and stopped abruptly. He showed it to Simone as they got closer. "That must be the road in," he said.

"What about the other side?" she asked.

"From what we know, it's all dense woods. Trees growing on top of each other."

"And between the highway and northern boundary?" She asked it as if she already knew it wasn't a feasible option.

"Man-made marsh. No walking, no vehicles."

"Leaves us no choice then, right?"

"Simone, with only one way in, we're putting ourselves in a precarious position. We could get bottlenecked in there. Then, if that camp is what we think it is, we'll be sitting ducks."

"You're forgetting one thing, Jacob." She raised one of her dark eyebrows. "The classic element of surprise - they don't know we're coming."

Jacob organized the assault on the outsiders' camp, sending three-quarters of the Omega XT force down the road to the prison's south entrance. He and Simone watched the attack from an elevated position on the highway's bridge that spanned the river. They had night-vision scopes that gave them as close a view of the action as they needed. Jacob felt like a general in battle.

They had no knowledge of what or who was inside the camp. For all Jacob knew, it could have been the two children hiding by themselves, but that made no logical sense. The former prison was too far off the highway and too difficult to access for use as an overnight hideout. Simone's hunch was that a gathering of rebels was taking place there, and Jacob's deductive reasoning had led him to the same conclusion. It was all confirmed as the first Omega XT vehicle reached the camp's south wall.

The rebels turned blinding spotlights on the ANTI- troops and began firing on them as they crossed the river. The first vehicles suffered heavy damage, and casualties mounted swiftly. But slowly, the Omega XT got through and were able to position themselves and return fire. There were watchtowers throughout the camp where the rebels were perched, giving them a great advantage. The frontline Omega XT ANTs finally took down the first line of watchtowers with rockets launched from the back of equipped jeeps. That gave them enough of an opening to move down the south wall and establish a strong offensive line.

"I don't know much about battle strategy, Jacob, but this looks pretty good so far," Simone said after an hour or so of gunfire and explosions.

"For not knowing what we were getting into, I'd say they're doing well. But if it turns against us, I'm pulling us out. I want you to know that."

"Don't worry so much, Jacob." He flinched, wishing she hadn't used that word. It seemed prophetic by then. "I guarantee you - Salvador is going to be proud of what we're doing here tonight."

Jacob thought that was a funny thing to say, but he appreciated it. It gave him a feeling of satisfaction. And what transpired over the next few hours did make Salvador proud. But it also changed Jacob's notion of the new world, and his obligation to it, forever.

29.

Simone noticed the movement deep into the night, after many hours of fighting. She had not checked the tracking monitor at all during the battle, distracted by the excitement of war. But what she saw on the screen made her crazed, and Jacob couldn't do anything to stop her.

"Look, Jacob," she said, as she pointed to the screen. The two flashing blue lights were outside of the prison's fences, on the west side in the thick woods. They were moving north and appeared to be making their way to the same highway where she and Jacob stood watching the battle.

"Yeah, ok. So what?" he replied.

"So they're getting away," she said frantically.

"Simone, forget about it. You've gotten what you wanted out of them. Look down there." Jacob motioned to the battle below. "This is why we're here. Not those kids."

"Some things you'll never understand," she replied.

He glanced down at the monitor again and saw the blue blips getting closer to the highway, maybe two miles to the west of their position. "Let it go, Simone. For me." He tried to express it as an intimate plea.

"No way, Jacob." She turned to a group of Omega XT waiting in a jeep for orders. She directed them to drive west and watch for the children as they escaped from the woods. "But don't act, you understand. Just find out who's with them and come tell me immediately." They sped off.

Jacob turned his attention back to the battle, but worry was trying to overcome him again. It was starting to cloud his focus, just as he had thought it might. He had never let emotions control his logical life, and yet here they were doing exactly that. He was angry with himself, but he was enraged with Simone. He didn't understand how someone could be so hateful. This revolution was never supposed to be personal.

The group of Omega XT that Simone had sent came back quickly. Jacob overheard one of them reporting to Simone. "Just the kids. Nobody else. They came out of the woods and turned in our direction."

"You're sure?" Simone asked. "Just the two of them?"

"Yes, ma'am."

"Did they see you?"

"No, ma'am."

"Very good," she said. "Very, very good."

Jacob couldn't believe what he was hearing. Simone sounded almost maniacal. This was vengeance for the sake of vengeance. And it was children.

"I'm not going to let you do this, Simone," he said as aggressively as he could. "You're out of your mind right now."

She laughed. "You don't have to *let* me do anything. This one is all on my own. This one's for that bitch Anna."

She leapt onto the back of the jeep that held the Omega XT she had just sent to spy on the kids. "Let's go!" she yelled at the driver. And before Jacob could say anything else, they were gone, on a renegade mission to kill kids.

He was nauseous. He didn't care anymore about the battle at the prison camp, or the group of rebels they were fighting. And as the sun rose behind him, and he heard the sound of gunfire coming from the western horizon, Jacob didn't care about ANTI- anymore either.

PART FIVE: GETTING BACK

1.

When we're alive, we tell ourselves that whatever comes next for our beings or souls is overwhelmingly joyous. That we are relieved of all the physical pain and limits instilled upon our animal forms. Maybe that we see the ones who preceded us in death. Or in our most morbid reckonings, that we stay in the world in spirit, appearing as ghostly apparitions to spook anyone invading our phantom territory. You've got to give it to the human mind: creativity abounds if it means we can make ourselves feel better.

Death wasn't all bad. I got to watch the kids. And Meg. No, I wasn't a guardian angel or anything like that. I was just present. In the energy. I suppose the cosmos or God or the soul's unwavering will allows us to see the ones closest to us. The ones we love the most as they continue with their lives. For a little while, at least.

But I don't need to get ahead of myself. First I have to tell you how I got there.

2.

The one bullet that invaded my body pierced through my back, at the bottom left side of my rib cage. It didn't stay long, exiting the front of my midsection almost as quickly as it had entered. Initially, there was a pulse of pressure followed by sharp pain. But the pain disappeared quickly. I had always heard of the human body protecting itself from physical torment through shock. That would be my first, and last, experience with it.

I knew it was bad. I knew there was flesh and bone and organs torn to shreds. But I tried to survive anyway.

I rolled over onto my back and reached down to the fresh wound with my right hand. I could feel the damp flow of blood coming out of my body, soaking through my clothes rapidly. It was difficult to comprehend what was happening. Life had become fuzzy and surreal.

The kids were suddenly kneeling over me.

"Dad, are you hurt?" I heard Henry ask. All I could do was raise my blood-covered hand to show him.

"Oh, no," Jessica said, covering her mouth. The next succession of bullets landed with muffled thuds in the dirt two feet beside her. I raised my head enough to see that the spotlight was slowly making its way to where I lay.

"Move me, guys...fast," I muttered.

"Under his arms, Jess," Henry instructed.

They took me by the armpits, each of them using the bend in an arm to hook me from behind. I could feel the sticky underbrush scraping my lower back and buttocks and legs as they dragged me. The forest was thick, but they managed to push through it swiftly. My kids, my heroes. I stopped them when I felt the euphoric death chemicals begin to rush into my brain.

I tried to convey to them as much love and direction as I could in the last moment of my life. But my thinking was cloudy. I felt like I was falling backwards through a long dark tunnel, the world getting further away with each labored breath.

"The...river," I said. "Get to...to the river. It will...fork. Get...out...at the fork." I couldn't tell if the words were even audible. Or if anything I was saying made sense. But I was coherent enough to remember the river that ran along the prison's opposite boundary. To remember that it was the fastest way out of that mess, it they could get to it. It flowed south for two hundred miles until it opened into a massive lake. But before that, a tributary broke in, bending from the west. Following it would lead them back to the farm. I could barely recall its image on the map, but I knew it was there. "Follow...the...fork. Follow...it...home."

Jessica's cries were becoming sobs. Henry was trying his hardest to remain strong in the face of inevitability, but tears had begun to well up at the corners of his eyes. Then they became too full, and a drop fell and landed on my cheek.

For the minute or two that remained, everything around me became abundantly clear. It was still dark, but I could see my children's faces with great detail. They seemed to become illuminated from within somehow. I loved them so much, and wanted desperately to stay with them. But I couldn't stop what was happening.

I was able to speak one last time. I repeated something that I had said to them on the morning of their capture, before I watched from a fifth-story window as they were kidnapped into the grid. Something that held a whole new meaning as I died on that forest floor.

"I'll be right above you, guys. Don't forget that. Triumphs forever."

As everything faded into dark gray and then black, my singular focus became that buzzing fly. I could hear the individual flaps of its wings distinctly as it flew back and forth across my numbing face. And then I was gone.

3.

I was no longer mass or weight or volume. I wasn't shape or size. I couldn't touch or smell or taste.
I just was.

4.

Jessica and Henry knelt over my lifeless body for a long time. They didn't say anything. But they cried it all out.

Henry composed himself first. He turned his attention back toward the prison camp, where the battle was still being fought. The watchtower that had been focused on us had transitioned to closer targets along the fence line. He and Jessica were in the clear.

She interrupted his study of the situation behind them. "What do we do now?"

He wiped a sleeve across his face, wiping the residue of grief away. "We move," he said. "We get to that river. And we get back to Mom."

"I know that," Jessica responded, "but what about Dad? We can't just leave him here, in the middle of nowhere."

Henry reached across my body and took her hand in his. "This isn't Dad anymore, Jessica." I wished I could tell him that he was right. "We leave this behind, just like he did. We have to."

She gave him a quick nod and wiped her own face clean. She took his other hand and gave it a hard shake. "We have to," she repeated.

He went to my backpack and unzipped the front pocket, where I kept the maps I had been carrying. I had picked up a new one since we had arrived at Camp Overlord: a prison guard's map of the property and the area surrounding it. There had been a few copies in one of the training offices at the camp's atrium, and I had sneaked one of them for myself, just in case.

"Here's what we need," Henry said when he found it. He spread it out on the forest floor and pulled out a flashlight to read it. He explained to Jessica what he was thinking as he studied it. "Based on the position of the storage garage here," he pointed, "we should be in this general area of the woods." He pointed again. "That leaves us a whole lot closer to the highway than if we went around the south end. I know that's backtracking, but it's the easiest path."

"Plus, most of the fighting is at the south wall," Jessica said. "If we go to the highway, we can avoid the ANTs."

"That's assuming there aren't more waiting. But it's worth the risk. There's only two of us. We should be able to stay hidden until we get to the river."

"And what exactly do we do when we get there?" Jessica wondered.

Henry thought for a moment and shrugged his shoulders. Matter-of-factly, he told her, "We float."

5.

If you'll allow, let me pause my story here. Because things are about to get strange, if they haven't already.

I cannot completely describe to you what happened to me. Your mind wouldn't comprehend it. Mine wouldn't have either when I was alive. The great mystery we humans have forever tried to solve. I know at least part of the answer now, but you wouldn't accept it if I told you.

So I'll keep the earthly restrictions in place. It will be easier that way. Do this: imagine me as a spirit, able to transport myself anywhere in an instant, floating invisibly above the action.

That'll help you understand how I got to see Meg again.

6.

The kids gathered themselves and said their goodbyes to my remains. Jessica kissed my body's forehead and whispered something that my mortal ears couldn't hear anymore. Henry took a blanket from my backpack. He crossed my limp arms across my chest and covered me with it, face and all.

They set off north, on a direct line to the highway. The night hours were fading quickly, and they knew it. The more progress they could make under cover of darkness, the better.

As they trudged their way through the dense woods, I felt I could leave them for a while. Their trek to the highway would take some time. And there was someone else I had to see.

She was just as we had left her, in the farmhouse's upstairs bedroom. She was lying on her side asleep. Her face was peaceful, but her cheeks and eyes were sunken. And her skin was an off-white pale, unnatural and translucent. But she was still my beautiful Meg, breathing and living and waiting.

I watched her for a long time, until she woke with a sudden jerk. She began coughing uncontrollably and writhing under the bed's sheets. It lasted for minutes. When she finally conquered the fit, she rolled onto her back and stared up at the ceiling above her.

Her glazed eyes seemed to look further, through the plaster and wood and shingles.

She was so tired and sick. I wanted to soothe her, to tell her that her extraordinary children had retrieved the medicine and were bringing it back to her. More than that, I wanted to hold her. One more time.

I soon needed to leave her, to go back to the kids. But before I left, she did something that made me think she may have felt my presence in the room with her. Just maybe. She smiled with solace and closed her eyes again, falling back asleep with ease.

7.

The twins had almost reached the edge of the woods when I returned to them. It was still dark, but wouldn't be for much longer. They wouldn't have enough time to reach the river before daybreak. And unfortunately, I didn't know what, if anything, lurked down the highway toward it. I could only follow their path. I could only witness what was going to happen to them.

When they got to the tree-line, they stopped. They both pulled out binoculars and peered through them in the direction they planned to travel. But it was still black night.

"I can't see a thing," Jessica said in frustration.

"Me neither," Henry replied. "But maybe that's a good thing. It means we've still got some darkness to protect us. Let's stay at the side of the road, in case we need to dart back into the woods." He started out of the forest.

"Hang on, Henry. Before we do this, I need to know - how's your leg?"

"Don't worry about me, Jess. It's never felt better." And he was off, leaving her no choice but to follow him.

They hadn't made it far when the noise of a vehicle coming toward them became audible. There were no headlights, and the sound disappeared as abruptly as it had emerged. Jessica and Henry continued walking. Had I been able to hear it and not them? I felt helpless.

Then the noise was there again. And this time the kids caught it. They ran to the woods simultaneously, crouching just inside the leading edge of trees.

"Did you hear that?!?" Henry asked excitedly. The screeching sound of an off-road vehicle turning around and speeding away quickly was undeniable.

"Sounded like a truck to me. Ahead of us."

"Yeah, that's what I'm thinking. But I didn't see a thing." He looked down, deep in thought.

"What's up?" Jessica asked him.

"We didn't see them, but they had to have seen us." He continued spinning the wheels of deduction in his mind. Suddenly, he raised his head to Jessica with a brightness on his face, happy to have come to the answer. But as soon as he said it aloud, the brightness went away. "Jessica, we're the reason they're attacking Camp Overlord right now. They've been watching us the whole time."

8.

Henry started frantically pulling items out of his backpack. Once it was empty, he ran his hand through the interior of it until he found something unusual. He reached for a flashlight and shone it into the pack. He turned the opening to Jessica, showing her what he had found.

Underneath the nylon fabric at one of the bottom corners was a small blue light, almost undetectable. Jessica reached in and felt it between her thumb and forefinger. "What is it, Henry?"

"Not sure exactly. But if I had to guess, I'd say it's some sort of monitor. Something that the ANTs put in there."

He took a knife from the supplies spread out next to him. "Hold the flashlight where I can see," he directed Jessica. He dragged the blade across the bottom seam of the backpack. Then he pulled the fabric back and took hold of the device. He held it up, Jessica following his hand with the beam of light. "I can't believe we did this," he said in exasperation.

"Did what?" Jessica asked.

"Led them to Overlord. To Daniel and Jeff and the rest of them. Do you remember how easy it was getting out of that utility building? And how nobody came looking for us while we hid in the parking garage? I should've realized it was too simple."

"Henry, we were just trying to get out of there. We couldn't have known about this. But now that we do, we've got to react." There was my girl, remembering the vehicle they had just heard. Knowing that it would be back.

"Right," Henry said. "We've got to get as far away from this as possible." He looked down from her face, to the straps over her shoulders. "Jess, is that the same pack you wore into the grid?"

"Yeah, why?"

"Because they're not dumb enough to only track one of us."

As if on cue, the same sound from before of a vehicle on the road ahead could be heard. The sun was beginning to break over the horizon in that direction, and the silhouette of a fast-moving jeep was barely visible.

"Quick, Jess," Henry yelled at her. "Give me your pack!"

Jessica looked at Henry, moving her eyes down to his leg. Then she looked back at the road, at the jeep speeding toward them.

"No time, Henry." She grabbed the tracking device from his hand before he could think to stop her.

"I'll meet you at the river. And if I don't, make sure you get back to Mom."

Henry didn't have a chance to respond before she was gone. She ran from the woods toward the highway, crossing over the pavement just as the jeep roared past him.

9.

On the opposite side of the highway was an unkempt field, wide and deep. It had once been a farmed acreage. Maybe wheat, maybe corn - it was hard to discern. In the year since the Great Dark had begun, it had become overgrown and interlaced with weeded grass and wildflowers. The foliage was at least five feet high throughout.

The jeep turned sharply to follow Jessica into the field, but stopped at the edge of it. She had disappeared into the thick vegetation before they could reach her. Henry was frozen where she had left him in the woods, just barely hidden from the growing sunlight.

He held the binoculars to his eyes. There were two ANTs in the back of the jeep. One was manning the large machine gun attached to the bed of the vehicle. The other was a woman, not dressed like the rest. She wasn't wearing the goggles and face mask like her comrades were. He could only see a portion of her profile from his angle, but I could tell that he recognized her. She was looking down at a device that she held in her hands.

The woman looked up from the device suddenly, yelling a direction to the gunner next to her and pointing to a distant area in the field. He unloaded a volley of bullets into the brown and green and yellow mixture of plant life. The sound of the gun was deafening and constant. He didn't stop until the woman held her hand up to him. Mechanical smoke and smell hung in the air as the machine gun whirred to a halt.

    I went to Jessica in the field, to be with her in whatever way that I could. She had not joined me in my unearthly state after the attack. I hoped that meant that she had survived it.

    I found her crouched and thinking. She was calm, considering her options. And above all else, she was unhurt. The gunfire had been aimed at a spot less than twenty feet from her current position. She had avoided their initial onslaught, but I knew they would be relentless. I guess, based on what happened next, she did, too.

    She stood and threw the blue light that Henry had retrieved from his backpack, landing it inside the newly barren area created by the machine gun's bullets. Then she took the rifle she was carrying off of her shoulder. She raised the scope to her dominant eye and closed the other. The top of her head was just an inch lower than the tallest stalks of former crop and wild grass, keeping her hidden from the ANTs' eyes. She was pointing her gun at the woman in the back of the jeep, which was raised enough to allow a clear line of sight. The woman was surveying the field with a high-powered scope, hunting.

Jessica pulled the trigger and shouldered the rifle in one movement. She was off and running through the thick field by the time her bullet had met its target. Jessica had aimed for a lethal head-shot on the woman. And her aim was true, as always. Only the scope that the woman was holding up to her eye kept her from certain death.

10.

The scope flew from the woman's hands and her head dipped violently backward. She lost her balance and dropped to the bed of the jeep, landing on her back. She raised herself to a sitting position quickly. She had instinctively put her hands to one side of her face, where her left cheekbone met the matching eye socket. As she pulled her hands away, blood poured from the wound. She screamed in pain and anger.

I caught up with Jessica, who was continuing to fight the field's vegetation as she tried to run. Her progress was slow and arduous. For some reason, intentional or not, she was angling back toward the highway.

As she neared the edge of the tall brush, I wanted to intervene. I wanted to push her back, to keep her hidden. But I was helpless again. An audience member, watching the drama unfold before me. Whether she knew that she was leading herself back into the open or she lost track of her direction, one thing proved certain. Her sacrifice that day was to save Henry and her mother - and she did just that.

11.

Parents are supposed to die before their children. Circle of life and all. I managed to go first, but it didn't make watching her execution any easier. She was still just a child, even though she did something more grown up than most adults ever consider. I was so proud of her, but I never got to say it.

12.

When Jessica broke from the field's vegetation, she turned to look back at the jeep. She was west of them, but not far. She stood there, not moving. As if she wanted them to see her.

The woman had regained her feet beneath her on the bed of the jeep and placed a large piece of cloth against her gunshot wound. She was peering down at the tracking device again, searching for the blue signals, visibly enraged. She looked in Jessica's direction with surprise, and froze for a moment in recognition of her prey. Then she yelled at the top of her voice's volume, "Fire!!!"

The jeep's gunner had followed the woman's eyes to where Jessica stood like a statue. She wasn't unable to move. I came to understand that. Instead, she was holding her ground with purpose. The gunner rotated the machine gun toward her. Jessica lunged to the highway just as he pulled the gun's trigger, and I expected a flurry of high-caliber bullets to fly toward and possibly into her. But the gun locked, stuttering itself into inability.

Jessica glanced over her shoulder as she ran, stunned like me by the fortuitous development. A smile crept across her face. Until she saw the wounded woman raise a pistol.

The woman fired until the gun's clip was empty, keeping overwrought pressure on the trigger even after the fact. She was half-blind and one-handed, forced to hold the cloth against her wound so she wouldn't bleed out. So most of the bullets soared past Jessica, finding distant trunks and branches and limbs to damage.

But there were two shots that met their target. The goddam luck of it all was impossible. Chance is a strange thing. It can change a life's direction forever.

Jessica went to the pavement chest-first. The rifle she carried fell off of her shoulder, making a crashing sound as it bounced on the empty highway. At first, I thought that maybe her backpack and its contents had taken enough velocity off of the bullets to save her. But there was no backpack. Instead, it was sitting upright and by itself on the side of the road. She had left it at the edge of the field, where she had revealed herself. *"But why, Jess? Why?"*

Her head rested sideways against the ground. The half of her face that was visible looked untroubled, with its one eye closed. There was still redness in her cheek and skin, but I feared that would disappear soon. Had I still been capable of creating tears, I would have cried my eyes dry.

The jeep's engine revved suddenly and its driver brought it next to Jessica's body.

"Pick her up," the woman commanded from above her.

Two of the jeep's ANTs got out and walked over to Jessica. One took her wrists, the other her ankles. She was limp as they raised her off the highway.

"Load her in," the woman said. "I want her mother to see what I've done."

Her mother? What was that supposed to mean? She couldn't have known anything about Meg. Unless the kids had said something about her back at the grid. But Jessica would have told me that, right? Then it dawned on me: Anna. Goddam Anna. Probably created some ruse about the kids being hers. She couldn't have known that her deception would lead to what had transpired. She couldn't have, right?

I didn't blame Anna for long. Death brings a specific awareness of happenstance with it. Besides, it's hard to hold a grudge in the afterlife. Not when you have other loved ones left to watch over.

13.

Henry had watched the whole scene unfold from his hiding spot just inside the forest's tree-line. He sat dumbfounded as the ANTs loaded Jessica into the back of the jeep and it sped past him, back to its origination on the eastern horizon. It took him a few minutes to recover himself. It was shock. Then I saw it turn to anger, and resolve.

He spread the opening of his backpack and began placing his supplies back into it. One by one, he packed them tightly and organized them to maximize the space. Blanket, flashlight, rope, handgun ammunition, extra pair of hiking pants, extra shirt, two pairs of socks, utility knife, canned food, water thermos.

The last item he picked up was something I didn't recognize at first. He had not had it with him before. He held it in his hands, staring at it and turning it over, considering something. Before he put it at the top of his pack, I remembered where I had seen its brick-like shape. Two places. The first time as we were preparing the mission to save him and Jessica from the grid. The team of Leftys that were going to provide distraction was packing similar bricks of explosive C-4 compound that morning when I mistakenly questioned their efficacy.

The second time was in Camp Overlord's storage garage during our escape. Where Henry must have picked one up and taken it with him. I had noticed a stack of them in one corner, along with the corresponding digital timers that could be used to set them off.

I was sure that Henry had grabbed one of the bricks out of precaution while I searched for the bolt cutters in the garage. But I was afraid that he had become filled with enough vengeance watching the attack on his sister to use it out of aggression. I just hoped he knew what he was doing.

14.

The map Henry consulted before he set off for the river showed him to be about two miles away from it. He could cross the highway and walk along the edge of the overgrown field to get there. That way, if anyone should come back down the road, he could slide into the tall stalks to conceal himself.

He left the cover of the woods carefully and slowly, straining to listen for another vehicle on the highway above the sound of battle in the distance. The gunfire and explosions had not subsided. He shook his head in frustration as he looked in the direction of Camp Overlord.

"It's not your fault," I wanted to tell him. *"You couldn't have known they were tracking you."*

As if he understood me, he adjusted his backpack and crossed the road with confidence. The sun was higher, shining from the direction he planned to walk. He pulled his sunglasses out from the front pocket of his shirt and put them on to shield his eyes. He took a deep breath and started his journey.

He had not taken ten steps when he stopped abruptly. He muttered to himself, "Shit - the medicine." Turning around, he looked down the straight line that marked the separation of the field from the highway. Still placed where Jessica had left it was her backpack.

It all made sense. Jessica had left the backpack there for Henry because she didn't know if she would make it to the river or not. She had been two steps ahead of everybody, including me.

Henry ran to the bag and unzipped it. Inside was the life-saving medicine for his mother. He looked up to the blue sky and said, "Nice work, Jess."

Nice work, indeed.

15.

Henry's hike to the river was uneventful. The field remained at his side, giving him a quick escape if the ANTs came back for him. But they never did. He had transferred his mother's medicine to his own backpack, removing a few of the items to make room. He left Jessica's pack where it was, at the side of the road. After all, it still had its tracking device inside. *"Good thinking, son."*

A few hundred yards from the water's edge, he stopped to survey what lay ahead on the highway. The road began to rise in front of him, separating itself from the earth by way of concrete supports. As it stretched across the river, Henry counted six braces reaching up through the water to the bottom edges of the road-turned-bridge. The supports grew taller as the bridge continued away from him to compensate for the higher ground on the opposite side. The bank there must have been thirty feet tall.

He could see a large gathering of vehicles and people on top of the bridge. He took off his sunglasses and put the binoculars to his eyes. The people were ANTs, dressed in the same military gear as the others he had seen that morning. They were watching the battle at the camp to their south. There were fourteen vehicles on the bridge, but the jeep that had carried Jessica away was nowhere in sight.

He swung the backpack off of his shoulders and opened it, taking the C-4 brick out gently. He placed it on the ground next to him and reached back into the pack, retrieving his utility knife. He carefully sliced the C-4 compound into two pieces, almost square. Then he unzipped the front pocket of the pack. From inside, he pulled out two of the digital timers that had been stored with the explosives in the Overlord garage. They each had two electrical prongs. Henry slowly pushed the timers into the separated compounds prong-first, and then wrapped them in the blanket he had with him.

Meg's medicine was vacuum-sealed in plastic bottles, but Henry made sure to create an added layer of water defense by folding it inside his extra clothes. That was my Henry: deliberate and thorough. He repacked his bag, leaving the blanket and its volatile contents at the top. Then he walked to the river and disappeared below the rising road.

16.

I didn't pretend to know Henry's plan that morning. If I could have talked to him, I would have told him to get into the river and drift away. Away from the Leftys and the ANTs and the war that had started between them. Away from the death and the violence. I would have told him to forget about what had happened that morning and the night before and the day before that. I wanted to protect him from any more pain. I didn't want him to risk it all when escape was so near.

But he wouldn't have listened. And part of me understood why.

17.

The fallen tree trunk on the river's bank was serendipity at work. Or karma. Or just sheer luck. Whatever it was, he deserved it.

I tried to put together the most likely scenario for Henry and his explosives. It had to be the bridge, but the one question that remained was *"How?"* Henry was a good swimmer, but the skills required to do what I thought he was about to do would take an accomplished athlete. How would he swim out to the bridge's supports, remove the C-4 bricks from his backpack, and place them while treading water? It seemed impossible. Until he discovered the tree trunk.

It had fallen some time ago, and it was partially dead. Why it fell didn't matter. But how it fell did. The tree had come down parallel to the river, crashing to the ground with enough force to crack into three sections. The middle section had dislodged itself from the other two, and it had rolled down the bank until it stopped just at the water's edge. It wouldn't take very much effort for Henry to push it into the river and use it as a float. Mother Nature's ageless helping hand.

It had been a towering oak when it stood. The circumference of its trunk was substantial. The log it had left at the water was about six feet long. Henry set his backpack to the side so that he could put all of his focus into launching his buoyant transport. It didn't take him long. He acted surprised at the log's momentum once he had forced it to move just a few inches from its stationary resting place. He quickly grabbed up his backpack and jumped onto the floating tree trunk, before the river's current had carried it too far away from him.

He straddled it, his legs stretching widely over each side. He laid down with his chest and stomach against the bark to balance himself. From that position, he was able to paddle with his arms.

The current was steady but not fast, allowing him to guide the log sideways. He passed by the first concrete support, then the second. As he neared the third one, he slowed the improvised boat down. Once he was beside the support, he sat up and reached for it, stopping his forward motion. He looked up to the bottom of the bridge. The support was at least thirty feet tall, maybe more.

He took his backpack off of one shoulder, then the other, and placed it on the log in front of him. He unzipped the bag and removed the blanket. Then he unwrapped the two separated explosives. On one timer, he set the number to "16:00." He took the C-4 compound and pressed it against the concrete. He closed his eyes and drew a deep breath. As he exhaled, he opened his eyes and pressed the button that started the timer. "15:59...15:58..."

He quickly wrapped the other explosive and placed it back inside his pack. He slung it over his shoulders and started paddling toward the fourth support. He counted to himself all the while. His mouth moved continuously, "1-one-thousand, 2-one-thousand, 3-one-thousand..." By the time he floated up to the next concrete brace, he was three minutes into his count.

At the fourth support, he moved with precision, performing the same motions as he had at the third one. He set the second timer for "12:00" to synchronize with the first, ensuring that the blasts would be almost simultaneous. He apparently didn't need the deep breath again. Instead he started the timer as he placed the explosive on the concrete. "11:59...11:58..."

Backpack secured, he turned the log south and laid flat. The river took him with it, underneath the bridge and then downstream. He remained still as he rode, hoping his dark clothes would blend in with the wet bark and camouflage him. His face was turned toward Camp Overlord as he floated by, and he saw the carnage continuing unabated. He muttered something before he was beyond the battle at the Lefty camp.

"I'm sorry, guys. I'm sorry for everything."

18.

There was no distinction between the two explosions. Henry had set the timers with near perfection. He watched from a safe distance south, turning and riding the log backwards to grant himself a full view as he drifted.

The fireballs shot out and up, creating a singular shockwave that made the bridge drift a foot higher and then back down. The air surrounding the highway seemed to vibrate from the explosions' sound and energy. The ANTs on the bridge were knocked to the concrete, deafened and dumbed.

One of the supports buckled immediately. It shifted once and then snapped with a screech. The ANTs and their vehicles slid in that direction as the bridge above it crumbled. The other support held for a moment, then gave way just like its counterpart. The section of suspended highway that existed in between them fell to the river dramatically, carrying ANTs and jeeps and humvees with it.

The explosions had created such an extreme level of heat that the vehicles remaining on top of the bridge soon caught fire and began melting. A few ANTs ran from them blindly, their clothing consumed by flames, until they stumbled over a mangled edge and plummeted to the water.

After a minute or so, other portions of the bridge began to crack. ANTs who had come to the rescue of their comrades found themselves atop a dissolving structure, with no time to correct their mistake. Huge chunks of concrete dropped like giant boulders into the water, crushing men and vehicles underneath. From Henry's distant vantage point, they appeared to fall in slow-motion, and the splashes they created looked like gigantic geysers shooting steam and vapor high into the atmosphere.

The fighting at Camp Overlord appeared to subside as the bridge slowly collapsed. Both Leftys and ANTs turned to the distraction, forgetting for a moment the battle they had been waging. The ANTI-vehicles that were positioned along the entrance road that ran alongside the river retreated back to the highway. And some of the ANTs at the camp's south wall followed.

The river's current carried Henry further away, and I went with him. Soon the partial bridge and Camp Overlord were specks on the landscape, only discernible by the plumes of smoke rising from them. Henry turned himself around on the log so that he was facing forward again. Facing the journey back home. He had a look of resolve and satisfaction, but also of sadness. He had just committed mass murder. But maybe he had also saved the lives of countless Leftys.

19.

Henry wouldn't reach the fork in the river before nightfall. He had pulled out his map and realized that. With some time left before sunset, he paddled with one arm and guided the log to the western bank. There were dense woods all around him, which would make sleeping easier.

He pulled the log out of the water and secured it with the rope he had, looping it on both ends and tying it to a large standing tree. He walked into the woods and found enough space to set up a small camp. He gathered wood and leaves and built his fire for the night. He opened a can of beans and ate. Before he tried to sleep, he went to his pack and unwrapped his mother's medicine. He checked the bottles for dampness and placed them back into his backpack. Then he spread his blanket on the ground and went to sleep peacefully.

I went to Meg while Henry slept. She was in her bed still, but awake and fearful. She held the pistol that we had left for her in her hands.

There were noises coming from downstairs. Sounds of rummaging and damage being done. Doors opening and closing, shelves being cleared of their contents, drawers being pulled and dumped. There were crashes and shatters. There was breaking in and busting open. Meg's fragile body was trembling.

I could follow the intruder through the bottom floor of the house based on the rise of fall of destruction as he went from room to room. Then I heard his footsteps begin the climb upstairs.

As the sound of his approach to Meg's bedroom grew louder, I had to decide something. Whether or not I would stay with her. I could only watch what was going to unfold. Her beating, her rape, her murder. It might have been too much to bear, but fortunately I never had to watch any of it happen.

The intruder opened the door to the bedroom and stood frozen. He was dirty and disheveled, with matted hair and beard. His surprise at finding Meg was obvious.

She lay still, playing dead as we had planned so long ago. She had put her arms and hands under the sheet covering her body, along with the gun. Her breathing was shallow and only visible to me because I knew that she was alive. *"Go away,"* I said into the ether. *"Leave her alone."* But he couldn't hear me.

He approached the bed slowly. He stood at its side and watched her for a while, holding a smile on his grimy face. Then he reached one of his hands into the front of his pants as his breathing got deeper. He took his other hand and reached over the bed toward

Meg's stomach. His fingertips had just begun pressing into the sheet on top of her when I saw her open her eyes. The gunshot was abrupt, and it echoed throughout the bedroom. The intruder grabbed his midsection, then fell to the floor beside the bed. He writhed there, grunting and moaning in pain, for many minutes. Then he grew pale and quiet, a large stain of blood forming around his body.

I stayed with her through the rest of the night, although I could do nothing but just be there. She was surviving, but barely. *"Hold on, Meg. Just a little while longer..."*

As the morning approached, I had to leave her. I needed to be with Henry. He had packed up camp when I got there, and was untying the log. Making the most of the daylight hours, just as I had taught him on our earlier journey.

I couldn't inspire or influence him. And I couldn't speed him up. But Meg wouldn't make it much longer. There was too much cancer and too many desperate humans.

Henry eased the log into the river and slid his left leg over it, climbing into his now-familiar paddling position. *"Hurry, Henry. Get yourself home,"* I wanted to say to him, but I had no way to express it. *"If only I could push you."*

Suddenly, a wind picked up from the north. The river's current began to build, enough that Henry looked over his shoulder with question in his eyes. But there were few clouds in the blue sky. He turned his head back around and leaned his body down, like he was the driver of a racing motorcycle. And the mysteriously powerful current carried him swiftly down the river.

20.

Henry arrived at the fork in the river at midday. It was a tributary that fed from the west, adding water and pushing the larger river to the southeast. He had tried to stay close to the west bank all morning in anticipation of it. When he saw the change in current approaching, he leaned to the right and turned the log to the river's edge. He floated up to the bank and reached out for a tree branch. Once he was confident in his grasp, he loosened his legs' grip and let the log go. It drifted to the middle of the river and flowed with the current, dipping in and out of Henry's sight. He watched gratefully until it was gone, then pulled himself over to steady ground.

He walked a few steps and sat. Time for rest and food and planning. The map showed the tributary meandering from the west and passing by a medium-sized city about fifteen miles from where he sat. I watched him trace his finger along a path to avoid it, then northwest, lining him up with the farm. It would lead him home in six days' time if he didn't meet any obstacles. I hoped that Meg could hold on that long.

The landscape Henry had to traverse was much like the first part of our journey to the camp. Thick woods and underbrush. He walked close to the river, using it both for guidance and because the vegetation alongside it wasn't as difficult to move through. His left leg's limp was almost unnoticeable. He was driven.

He made it to the city's outskirts before sundown the following day. He set up camp and went hunting. He wouldn't make it on the few cans of food he had left. Using the rope, he created a small animal trap by looping it in the middle. He tied one end to a tree and dragged it flatly across the ground. Near the loop, he placed a bit of tuna from a can he had packed. He went to the loose end of the rope and waited.

He heard the animal before he saw it. It crept slowly from a low-growing tree that had limbs hanging to the ground. It was a raccoon, much larger than what his improvised trap had been made to hold. The raccoon circled the tuna, then edged up to it. One of its hind feet stepped into the loop, and Henry yanked his end. The animal squealed as the rope tightened around its leg. It jumped about and tried to run, but Henry held the rope firmly. He approached the animal from behind and slit its throat.

The raccoon's meat, plus his canned provisions, would get him through the rest of his trip. He cooked the entire animal and ate. Then he packed the leftover meat deep inside his backpack and laid close by the fire so that he could stoke it throughout the night. He slept restfully again, with a full belly and one concern allayed.

The city he passed the next morning was deserted like most. There was no ANTI- grid in it, and therefore no ANTs. He stopped on a rise just north of it and took out his binoculars. He spent a brief time gazing into different sections of the city. Then he lowered the binoculars and stood solemnly above the decrepit buildings and empty streets. He had changed. He was no longer fifteen years old, because he was no longer defined by age. He was experience. He was confidence. He was my son, and he had become a man.

21.

Henry's walk became routine-like. One step after another. He would refer to his map every few miles, matching landmarks to maintain his direction. Meals were necessary, as was rest. The monotony of the trek was gratifying to me. It meant that he was avoiding conflict, in whatever form it might come.

There were a few close-calls. On the fourth morning, as he was putting out his fire, he heard human voices. A group of them. He steeled himself and listened intently. They were close. And they sounded like hunters. Like before. But they passed without discovering him, and he never saw them again.

That same day, in the afternoon, he crossed the path of a bobcat. He saw its fresh tracks in the dry dirt. Through his binoculars, he could see the animal in the distance. Creeping away from him. He adjusted his direction slightly and kept walking. Henry the journeyman.

As the sun set on his last night, he appeared disgusted and frustrated. He was only two miles from the farm, but he couldn't dare walk any further. The darkness would remove all advantage he had against the animal world.

He didn't sleep well that night. So close. *"She's alive, son. Just get to her tomorrow."*

He was packed as the first rays of sun broke through the treetops above him. He looked at the map one more time, but he knew where he was going. His surroundings had become familiar. He set off, walking faster for the final leg of his trip. So much had gone wrong since he had left home, but at least he could save his mother. At least he would have that to keep himself alive.

22.

Henry stood later that morning at the farm's gate, as if to absorb his accomplishment before it might be ruined if his mother was not still waiting. But she was. I went to her for the last time, and saw her lying in her bed, as she had been for so long. Frail and weak, but waiting. Her will was a marvel. I felt calm wash over my being.

Then I was gone again. And this time, I was gone forever.

EPILOGUE: STILL ALIVE

My head hurts. Not a sharp pain. Dull, but all over. I can hear a voice. A woman. She's saying my name, but she's quiet about it. I'm dreaming. I know it because I can see my mother. But it's not her voice. Even though it's so familiar. I try to connect the two. The image with the sound. But they don't. They won't. God, my head hurts. Maybe I can just keep sleeping and the pain will go away...

The one constant in my dream-state is sunlight. A lot of dreams happen at night. Like when you're being chased by someone. For me, that's always at night. But not lately. Everything has been during the daytime.

One was a picnic, with some of my school friends from so long ago. My brother was there, too. We were by a river that flowed so much faster than any river I'd ever seen. The boys started daring one another to jump in. To see if they could swim back to shore. I knew I could do it, so I stepped to the edge. Before they even knew I was there. I was getting ready to jump when someone else ran past me, splashing into the water. I thought it was him, but the scene faded away before I could tell for sure.

"Hey!" It's a man's voice this time. Hushed and wispy, but definitely a man. "Hey! Wake up!" I try to open my eyes. They feel like they've been sewn shut. And my head still hurts.

Then I hear the familiar woman's voice again. "What are you doing here? Leave her alone."

"I'm here to help," the man answers. "But I've got to make sure she's ok first. Got it?"

"Yeah, ok, got it. You're here, right now, to help us. I'll believe it when I see it," she says.

Who *is* that? Someone recent. I'm searching my ailing brain. If I could just open my eyes, everything would become clear.

I start to hear whispers from close by. The two of them are talking about something. Come on, eyes, open!

Footsteps. Hard boots echoing through a long hallway. Then the creak of a door opening, and the crash of it slamming shut.

I'm falling again. Another sleep. More daytime dreams.

The door is creaking back open. It wakes me up. It didn't before. Hey, my eyes are open. I blink rapidly to make sure.

I'm in a gray room. The first thing I see is the ceiling. It's painted cement, cracked in places. The walls are made of cinder-blocks, stacked and cemented on top of each other.

I raise my head. It's not hurting anymore, but my body screams in defiance at my movement. I look to one side, toward the noise of the door. There are horizontal bars, like our room at the camp. Camp Overlord. A sense of relief comes over me.

I try to sit up, fighting my body's instinct to remain still. It's like nothing I've ever felt before. Sharp pains in the middle of my body. I'm on my hands, struggling to inhale, but breathing. He appears outside the bars, in my peripheral vision.

"Good!" he says excitedly, but still in a quiet tone. "You're awake!"

He pulls out a key and unlocks the cell door, sliding it sideways.

"Take it slow with her," the woman's voice says from across the corridor. It's Anna - that's who it is. I open my mouth to say her name, but my throat stiffens and I can't speak.

The man sits at the foot of my bed. He puts his hands in the air. The classic "*I mean no harm*" signal. This is not Camp Overlord. This is somewhere I don't want to be. I guard myself against him.

"Hello, Jessica," he says, disarmingly. "I'm Jacob. And I'm going to get you out of here."

About the Author

Judd Vowell is a writer and musician who studied history and religion at Auburn University. He lives in Huntsville, Alabama, with his wife and son. *Overthrown* is his debut novel.

Made in the USA
Charleston, SC
07 July 2016